Dedalus Africa
General Editors: Jethro Soutar
Yovanka Perd _

EDO'S SOULS

STELLA GAITANO

EDO'S SOULS

translated by
Sawad Hussain

Dedalus

This book has been selected to receive financial assistance from English PEN's "PEN translates" programme, supported by Arts Council England. English PEN exists to promote literature and our understanding of it, to uphold writers' freedoms around the world, to campaign against the persecution and imprisonment of writers for stating their views, and to promote the friendly co-operation of writers and the exchange of ideas.

Published in the UK by Dedalus Limited
24-26, St Judith's Lane, Sawtry, Cambs, PE28 5XE
info@dedalusbooks.com
www.dedalusbooks.com

ISBN printed book 978 1 915568 13 7
ISBN ebook 978 1 915568 51 9

Dedalus is distributed in the USA & Canada by SCB Distributors
15608 South New Century Drive, Gardena, CA 90248
info@scbdistributors.com   www.scbdistributors.com

Dedalus is distributed in Australia by Peribo Pty Ltd
58, Beaumont Road, Mount Kuring-gai, N.S.W. 2080
info@peribo.com.au   www.peribo.com.au

First published in South Sudan in 2018
First published by Dedalus in 2023

Printed and bound in the UK by Clays Elcograf, S.p.A.
Typeset by Marie Lane

THE AUTHOR

Stella Gaitano was born in Khartoum in 1979 into a South Sudanese family. She studied English and Arabic at Khartoum University and trained as a pharmacist. When Sudan was partitioned, she moved to Juba, the capital of South Sudan in 2012. She has chosen to write in Arabic and has published two short story collections and the novel *Edo's Souls* in 2020. Her work has been on exhibit at the Museum of Modern Art (MoMA).

She currently lives with her family in Germany and her second novel in Arabic will be published shortly.

THE TRANSLATOR

Sawad Hussain is an award-winning Arabic-English literary translator. She has an MA in Arabic literature from the School of Oriental and African Studies.

She has translated two books for Dedalus: *Catalogue of a Private Life* by Najwa Bin Shatwan (2021) and *Edo's Souls* by Stella Gaitano (2023).

To the fertile worlds of abundance, wisdom and life;
from you I get my strength.

Women

*I was reborn. I persuaded myself to get up. My mother stretched
out her hand to pick me up, another woman dusted me off.
My daughter told me that women know the secret to being
born again. And so I rose from the dead and walked!*

Omer Alsaiem

1

Like any other living creature, Mama Lucy didn't know a thing about what fate had in store for her, having neither anticipated nor thought about this maternal generosity of hers that had struck her like a curse. All there was to it was this: her mother had given birth only to her, or rather, she was the sole survivor of ten siblings; the rest had all died before their first birthday. For many years, her mother had lived with the throbbing loss; renewed each year when a child would sprout in the way of an unwanted weed, only for death to come and steal each one away while they slumbered, without their health waning or their freshness wilting. When she buried them, they looked blissfully asleep, their graves warm for days, their cries ringing in her ears; their bodies had been warm, limbs supple even, but their hearts had stopped beating altogether.

After one of these sudden deaths, Lucy's mother had

kept the small body for several days, locking herself in by bolting the door and securing it further with a dried tree stump. Without telling anyone, without wailing like she had every time before, she barricaded herself in with the small corpse and decided to make a desperate bid to challenge death. She squeezed milk from her swollen breast into the dead baby's mouth; maybe that would revive him, maybe she had just been too quick to bury all his siblings. It couldn't have been further from the truth. The baby's body ballooned, its colour changed and started to ooze a foul smell, a smell that wafted out of the tightly shut room's cracks, causing people to bang on her door. "Edo! Maria! Open up if you're still alive!" her panicked neighbours called out.

When she finally opened the door, she stared at them with hollow eyes, her mouth dry like that of a corpse, her inflamed breasts engorged. The milk had dried on the loose housedress she was wearing, shrivelled up like a forgotten flayed animal skin.

She collapsed, sobbing at the doorstep, her friends edging closer until the stench smacked their nostrils. There was the small corpse, milk drooling from its tiny gaping mouth. They rushed to wrap the baby in a shroud and toss it in a grave next to the other small graves, which were scattered in the land in front of her home. With bereaved eyes she surveyed the scene from her doorstep, suspended between joining them and secluding herself inside.

When Edo's friends had paid their final respects to her child, laid to rest among its small brothers and sisters that had died before dissipating into nothingness, her gaze caressed the small graves that took up a fair amount of the unfenced dirt yard surrounding her gutiyyah, the mud dwelling she called home. Patches of the earth around her straw-topped hut were level with the ground but, in some places, it protruded like fat men's bellies. She looked out at her land, not as a mother ruminating the loss of a child whose waking she'd been awaiting for days, but as a farmer would, counting the handsome stalks that were thick with grain, only to be despoiled by mischievous monkeys.

The revolting smell remained for years, plastered to the mud walls and tucked in the crevices of the room, like bad breath from infected gums; though Edo couldn't smell it, everyone else avoided passing by her home.

Even when Lucy came into her life, Edo treated her as one would a foreign guest who would soon depart; so certain was she of her child's approaching death, that she would follow in her siblings' footsteps and leave her mother to lap up sorrow once more. And so Edo denied Lucy any motherly affection, in the same way that an animal ostracises one of its young for some unknown reason. As for Edo, she was protecting her heart from clinging to Lucy, from being broken by her sudden death. Edo kicked her daughter out of her sphere, neglecting to breastfeed her, which led to her friend Esai weaning Lucy at the same time as her son. When the baby girl's cries filled the village, Edo's friends Rebecca-Ilaygha and Marta-Esai convinced her to do what she must as a mother; that the past was no fault of this child; that it wasn't right for Lucy to bear Edo's fury towards fate.

An old woman advised Edo to give the baby girl an ugly name so that Death wouldn't touch her. She named her Eghino, the one who defecates a lot. This name stayed with the child, and the village people didn't call her by any other until the fair-skinned evangelists came in their white clothes to Edo's village to guide them to the Lord and His salvation. They were renamed with names of the saints: there and then, Eghino was baptised Lucy.

Edo was among the first to embrace the new religion. She prayed regularly and was somewhat rigid, not because of the faith itself, but rather to know the way to God so she could go to Him, because she had a score to settle. Once her sadness had calcified into anger, she wanted to know: why did He feed them so freely to Death? Was God the one behind her pain and sorrow? She was determined to find out, so she remained on her path to the Lord and died a believer. A great prayer was spoken over her. Incense and a coffin were brought from the land of the whites; it was shiny with a glass window, through which her face, framed by a nun's habit, could be seen. She was clean and peaceful, as if she would break out into a smile at any moment at being the first person in the village to be buried in a coffin. People were usually buried in the clothes they died in, or naked in a not-deep-enough hole, meaning that a lot of the time, they were dug out by hyenas or other wild animals that wandered the night.

Edo had been a woman known for her silences, the perpetual sadness etched on her face. Tall, slender, with no time for chit-chat. Scars like distant stars danced across her belly and cheeks, and the teeth of her lower jaw had been pulled out. Hers was the first generation that had refused to have the outer ring of the ear scalloped, with small arches cut out comparable to the edges of an embroidered sheet. The women of her generation were satisfied with the ritual scarring

12

on their cheeks and the removal of some teeth during their adolescent years. Having a golden tooth was a fad that swept through all the communities. She and her friends had a golden incisor implanted, only to be branded as shameless, 'fallen' women — a glittering smile meant you were on the hunt for a man, your tooth flashing in the dead of night, a glowing ember visible from the furthest distances.

Edo kept her mouth shut most of the time, fearful that, if she opened it, secrets would come tumbling out, as smoke did from the mouths of elderly women who puffed the ghalyoon. Everyone knew she was good, and pitiful, even wrong in the head at times, but she would never reveal her secret world to anyone, even her closest friends, Rebecca-Ilaygha and Marta-Esai. They knew she had rebellious and outlandish ideas, that if voiced, would stun the community. Edo feared chatter because, in a village as small as this one, if someone even passed wind in his home, you'd find the children giggling about it while swimming at the head of the river. Her comments on the everyday were biting. She was against much of what the men had imposed. For instance, she was against a murderer's sister being offered up as compensation to the victim's family, for them to do whatever they wanted with her. Usually, they'd treat her like a servant: making her plant, harvest, cook, fetch water from the river and bear many children; punishing her for a sin she hadn't committed. Her neighbour's daughter had suffered such that she hanged herself from the ceiling to put an end to her torture, while her brother the murderer carried on with his life as normal.

Edo believed that men wouldn't hesitate to kill as long as the punishment wouldn't personally affect them. The murderer was among the walking dead that the victim's family would lie in wait for. So either he had to be handed over, or they had to be compensated with livestock so that the young girls could be left alone.

But everyone dismissed her and considered her touched in the head because of her perpetual sadness and the fury at God that crested in her chest. But after a long time had passed, the tribal chiefs adopted her view, and reconciliation meant the killer's family paying compensation in the form of livestock. It went on like this until the government appeared, pushing the chiefs to the sidelines, dedicating itself to all the issues that had been carrying on for years: violent disputes, contentious marriages, rifts between families... prisons were created and killers were promptly executed in front of a crowd. And so, the spirit of tolerance went up in smoke. Murders swelled, revenge was swiftly meted out and more people got away with it. Fearful of being assaulted, confessions were no longer given, but buried deep instead.

* * *

At dawn one day, Edo stopped by Rebecca-Ilaygha's because they had arranged to gather firewood together. Rebecca was a short, full woman: a tree stump with luminescent ebony skin and an infectious laugh reliably accompanied by tears. Edo found her drying sprouting maize, its honey-coloured water dripping onto the dirt yard now hard with compacted layers of silt and manure. Ilaygha forced her six children to kneel and lap up the maize-infused water, the way livestock do from puddles. Meanwhile, she moistened her broom with the same liquid and used it to beat their bottoms, convinced it was the cure for wetting themselves, having tried every herb and root under the sun to no avail.

Edo arrived at an astonishing idea — she advised Rebecca to fasten toads round their waists. The creatures' racket would keep the children awake and they'd have no choice but to go outside to relieve themselves. Rebecca cackled and told Edo she was out of her mind but in the end, smacked with despair, she tried it. She caught six toads from the swamp and wound them round the children's middles amidst their screams, with Edo's help as the orchestrator. Rebecca sent them to bed, shuddering from having such creatures stuck to them, even though she couldn't sleep, what with the toads croaking and her children crying, until daybreak approached and silence settled in the room. Exhausted, the little ones fell asleep and the toads fell silent, squashed under the worn-out bodies, their tongues hanging out and excrement oozing.

In the morning the reed mat was dry and the dirt floor was no longer decorated in moist designs. Rebecca removed the flattened toads from the children's waists before sending them to pass water, their bladders full to bursting. Some developed rashes all over from the toads' poisonous secretions and scratched for days and days, and from that point forward they never wet themselves again.

The other mothers copied what Rebecca-Ilaygha had done and soon it became what everyone did, but no one knew it had been Edo's idea all along. Rebecca never revealed as much to anyone and it was one of the many reasons why their friendship was so strong. She then became the wet nurse to Edo's only daughter.

Edo's other friend Marta-Esai was the most battered woman in the village; everyone was accustomed to her wailing and she to the beatings — her bones warped due to fractures she had neglected to set straight, her body a map of cicatrices and her features always hard to make out through the bruises. She was a statuesque, fleshy woman, as solid as an ancient citadel, while her husband was an entire metre shorter than her, the vile drunkard that he was. They never had any children and so Marta, crippled with guilt, bore the beatings, claiming that she deserved them. Edo had stopped by after one of those nights where Marta had been howling and weeping, her husband having abused her with the foulest of words, painting her infertile and a lesbian, her arse as barren as they come. Her friend was crumpled on the reed mat, a diseased rhino, ribs probably cracked, spitting blood. Furious with what had become of her neighbour, Edo scoffed, 'You just can't get enough, can you? Don't you know how powerful you are? You're just lying there like a rhino caught in some trap, rolling around in the mud. Look at yourself, how can you let that rat play around with you like this? Breaking your bones and giving you new bruises every day?'

'What am I supposed to do?'

Edo picked up the thick cane that Marta's husband had lashed her with; her eyes travelled up and down the length of it — a customer appraising the quality of a product. 'Beat him,' she determined.

'Beat him?' Marta bit her lip. 'Can a woman even beat a man? No, no, it'd be far too disgraceful and I'd be the talk of the village.'

'Are you safe from their tongues now? People are going

to always talk, why not change what they're talking about and make it more thrilling? More shocking?'

'But he'd kill me!'

'You're already dead. A man like that will claim that you're no longer of use to him and slit your throat like you're some diseased goat. He thinks he's wasted his cows and sheep on a marriage that didn't do what it's supposed to.'

Marta grew tense to the point she started coughing and spat out a sticky red clot of blood.

Edo calmly placed the cane down, letting it point toward the lump of bodily matter knitted with threads of blood. 'In any case, it's up to you.' She gazed out of the door, her eyes glowing as the sun's rays began to cast their shadows. 'People's tongues were made to wag. They must be going on and on about how you let a small frog like him play with you this way, a man whose feathers have all been plucked out. And how maybe, his third leg doesn't even have what it takes to give you a child in the first place.' Trying to keep a straight face she added, 'Stupid woman.' Then she slipped away, soundless as a snake.

Marta started to stare at the red sticky lump and her crooked bones. She gritted her teeth. She grabbed the cane, its thickness filling her palm, reduced her eyes to slits and inhaled deeply. She held it behind her weary body, her pulse racing, her chest swiftly rising and falling. Hot air escaped from deep within and the muscles in her face and body twitched; thick grains of sweat pooled on top of her nose and forehead, then slowly slid down like raindrops.

That evening her husband stamped into their home and started raising hell with her, insulting her, complaining about all the cattle he had lost in paying her dowry. He threatened to kill her, slice her up, and feed her to the flying and crawling critters, all the while kicking her in the stomach. She rose up before him, a tree breaking forth from the depths of the earth, and stood in the middle of the room, in the exact stance she would use when chopping wood with her axe, her legs firmly spread apart, the cane heavy in her palms. She crashed down upon him with all her pent-up frustration, beating, beating, beating him — with every blow she whacked him so fiercely that his mother, his family, even his ancestors, felt it. Panting, her insults fell into rhythm with her blows.

Thwack-you son of a —
Thwack-you dirty —

When he broke out into a womanly wail, she dragged him outside to the dirt yard for everyone to see, and with a practised grunt, she lifted him up on her shoulders, and dumped him on the hard earth, again and again. She then beat him with the cane as one threshes maize, until he lost consciousness, at which point she sat on top of him heaving sigh after sigh like a wild animal.

Some of the men tried to approach and free her husband from her grip but she pointed the cane at them, her breaths staccato, 'Come any closer and you're dead. Where were you when he was beating me every night? Was it a dead animal skin he was beating? If any of you have an itch you need scratched, come here.' The ring of onlookers dispersed, rolling back as rings of water do when you toss a pebble into a lake.

Breathing heavily as an agitated bull would, Marta spewed

bloody mucus out at great distances. She had stretched out and expanded till she resembled her gutiyyah in size, her eyes as wide as they would go.

Her two friends Edo and Rebecca drew close to her, each of them grabbing an arm. Grinning so widely in the darkness that her golden tooth flashed, Edo whispered, 'Nicely done.'

'Get up you madwoman,' Ilaygha said. 'You'll kill him.'

Marta removed herself from him, electrified, and then crouched with her back against the round wall of her home, cane in hand, while people flocked to revive her husband, welts visible on his skin.

In the morning he was broken, a wet mouse, looking at Marta with unbelieving eyes, as if seeing her for the first time: how she towered over him, her broad pumpkin-leaf-ears flapping. She sent him a thousand messages by tossing the stick he would beat her with into the fire that flared up between a trio of large rocks. The hot reddish-orange tongues started to lap over the bottom of the bubbling pot — she was preparing him a hot drink of fermented millet dough that was given to sick people and new mothers to soothe wounds.

He kept stealing glances at her, but each time his gaze would quickly flicker to the floor, defeated, afraid to meet her eyes. She kept her eyes on the cane and its smoke rising towards the overcast sky; filled with an indescribable joy, eager to meet Edo and for them to collapse in laughter.

When she finally met Edo, Marta greeted her coldly in the yard to prevent anyone from finding out that she had been the grand conductor all along. The moment they set foot inside Marta's home, they couldn't control their cackling and coughing. Marta narrated the details of how she beat her husband, while they happily slurped down some merisa. Ilaygha joined them, and brought with her a large gourd of more brewed merisa: clouds of foam with large, dark dancing bubbles at the surface. Marta picked up the gourd and blew away the bubbles that popped without a sound, and started to drink, and drink, and drink until — to the amazement of her two friends — she set down the empty gourd, a foam white moustache sliding down the corners of her mouth, and burped so loudly the roof nearly blew off. They erupted in raucous laughter. 'I feel so strong,' Marta, now drunk, shared. 'Like I could fight a bull, like I've been born again and now I want to beat up every man in this godforsaken village.' She then, with sadness, added that her only weakness was not being a mother. Edo rose and filled the gourd again. 'Sleep with another man,' she stated plainly.

Her friends screamed at the same time, 'Edo! What?'

'It's like I said, try it and we'll cover your tracks.' She winked at Ilaygha. ' You've got so many admirers from way back who probably still want a taste. A little taste won't hurt anyone — it's just for you to see who the problem really is. The rhino or the mouse.' Conspiratorially, they all crowed with delight.

Less than a year later, Marta gave birth to twin boys, so identical that she'd spend all day nursing only one of them, thinking that she had switched to nurse the other. Once she realised what she was doing, she tied a red string round one's wrist and a blue string round the other's. Ecstatic, her husband sacrificed livestock to celebrate the birth of his sons. Then a year on came another baby. And so her husband's jugular veins strained as he bragged at the men's get-togethers, raising his voice in song, shaking his spear at the sky, feeling that he had got his dignity back after that accursed night where his wife lost it and beat him to death, only to — with a little ad-hoc first-aid from the villagers — come back to life like Jesus.

People grew merry with him and forgot all about how they'd once taunted him for being the only man in the village to ever get beaten up by a woman. He celebrated his twins' birth for days, oblivious to the secret harboured by his wife and her friends. Marta kept on bringing forth strong children, great in number, without her friends knowing their real fathers or playing any part in the clandestine couplings. It was Marta's little secret that kept her husband by her side and made him treat her with respect. But one day he announced to the men that he wanted to remarry because Marta had grown old and couldn't bear the labour pains of twins anymore. Barely a year had passed with his new wife when he started to beat her, proclaiming her infertile, and claiming he had lost all his money to this barren plot of land. But then Marta sat beside her and whispered in her ear. Two moons later his new wife's belly grew round and their husband fell silent at home whilst boasting once more at the men's sit-downs of his many offspring that would farm the land, tend to the livestock; of his family stretching out forever and ever.

Using her devious intelligence, Edo initiated many secret matters without anyone being the wiser — to them, she was nothing more than a hapless woman whose soul had been consumed by grief, and owing to straitened circumstances, her mind lost. Before she died, she took a bath, wore her white Sunday dress and sent Lucy to call Marta and Rebecca over. She told them that her daughter was ready for marriage, and that Lucy's blood had come, and that she didn't want anyone standing in her way, and if they did, her friends were to say this was Edo's will and to tell Lucy's husband to look after her as a hen does an egg. Otherwise, she would rain her wrath upon him. Then she whacked her daughter's belly right where her womb was, and clawed at the lump of flesh just below her belly button with a full fist, then chanted as if casting a spell, 'Let any being inside of you meant to be shaped like a baby be so, and if God is here then He knows how I have followed his path. I'll forgive Him if He makes you bear all your siblings who died. Let no child of yours ever die, and may you never feel the pain of motherhood; may you bring forth enough children to fill the entire Earth, let there be so many you'll be shooing them away like flies. May you live to be a mother and that alone, and die from the ruckus they'll raise.'

She then straightened her dress and made the sign of the cross, folding her arms over her chest, then closed her eyes and let out a sigh of relief, a joyous sound as if addressing someone calling her from the Other Side, a sound that said, 'Hold on, I'm coming, you madman!'

Just like that, as simple as can be, sat beside her two slack-jawed friends who thought she was having another hallucinatory episode — although this time she'd stopped breathing — the smile in the corner of her mouth froze, and her golden tooth glinted, like a distant star.

She died just as her warm children had, in full health — whoever saw her body thought she was merely asleep. She hadn't complained of any aches or pains, as if death was a decision she had made firmly by herself. Lucy knew that her mother understood the way of the Lord but could be lured elsewhere if the madman reached out to her.

Edo's curse, the curse of her name Eghino and of motherhood, haunted Lucy. Behind closed doors, people would burst out in peals of laughter and, out in the open, children would heckle her and put their hands to their bums when she passed, while the youth would pinch their noses from the stench supposedly wafting off her. Sometimes her nostrils would flare and at other times her eyes would grow wet, but it was all useless — she was powerless to change her name because it was a matter of life and death. She would have preferred death, but took pity on her mother from the grief that would probably drive Edo over the edge, so she stayed as Eghino until the missionaries arrived. She believed in them just as her mother had, although for completely different reasons. Eghino wanted a name, a better one that wouldn't remind people of the toilet, that wouldn't disgust them or make them snigger, while her mother's intention had been to know the Lord's path so she could take revenge on Him when she died. They'd never miss a Sunday service, or a chance to tell people about the Lord's love and reverently draw a cross before every meal.

Even though her mother had given her this loathsome name so that Death would overlook her, she still came close to it on occasion. Once, she had crawled out in the middle of the main road when an enormous herd of cattle with their fearsome horns were returning to their pens. The herd carried on without stopping and Eghino was caught in the middle, rolling around like a palmyra palm fruit amongst the hard hooves. Once they had finally passed by, there she lay, sucking her thumb, choking on dust and the stench of manure rising around her like fumes.

Another time, Edo found her upside down in a large pitcher of water, feet in the air and the rest of her body submerged. Her mother pulled Eghino out by her tiny feet, her chest thick with water, eyes bulging, belly about to burst. Edo shook her daughter like someone would the jaws of an animal sunk into their wrist. Eghino crashed to the ground and water spurted out from all her orifices, a punctured balloon. Once all the water had come out of her, she got up. 'I'm so thirsty,' she announced.

In this way, Death continued to duel with her mother even after the child's first year, making Edo's heart tumble down to the Seventh Circle of Hell, only to then bring her later joy by letting her sole child survive certain death. Edo grew weary from these battles; each time, her heart nearly stopped altogether. She finally decided that perpetual sadness was better than the temporary happiness as she was never sure how long it would last. She turned a blind eye to her daughter and treated her as if she wasn't there, preferring the asperity of her sorrow. Eghino was dead to her.

Lucy was an orphan: no one knew her father. Following the curse of her dead siblings, her grandfather returned the dowry cows to his son-in-law so that he could divorce Lucy's mother and go find another wife to bear him children who would live longer. Broken, Edo lived alone, raging when her husband abandoned her and returned his dowry to his livestock pen.

At least he had got some compensation; all Edo got was isolation and being branded 'unhinged' for the pains of repeated childbirths, as well as anxiety over her children's lives and frightening predictions of their deaths — she would turn them over in their cribs and wake them up from their deep sleep, always believing them dead. Death alone would relieve her of this persistent worry, of being unable to unburden herself to anyone.

She used to feed a madman who came to her every day — a sort of sacrifice to shoo away the wings of death from her children — who then became the only person she'd speak to, without him ever uttering a single word. He'd eat her food and disappear to wander the streets of the village, children sneering, adults hurling abuse. In his honour the concise village dictionary of pejoratives that was bottom-driven had expanded; now likening someone to him was one of the worst entries in there, worse than those about your mother's arse.

Behind the fence is where he stood, begging for food in the evening as he always did. When she walked slowly to the room to bring him some, he fell in step behind her and lingered, breathing heavily and quickly. He was silent but everything in him was roaring. Like a long stick, his member stood up pointing to the darkness between her legs, and he had a particular glow about him that made everything in him visible, even the stubble on his face and short hairs on his body; he looked at her with unbridled desire and bottled up pain — a lusty billy goat. He scratched his thick hair, then scratched at his manhood that was resisting him, running away from his fingers, filthy nails at the tips. Her heart fluttered unexpectedly and he let out a low growl. She swallowed her saliva with difficulty; it was as if something warm within her was commanding her to lie down and open every single pore without holding back, for him to enter her.

As with other creatures, at such times, smell is the only

language. He circled round her sniffing like a dog in heat, while she tried to outswim the tidal wave of his rotting smell and focus on the fresh scents they both were secreting, scents that the sun had yet to spoil, scents with meanings difficult for language to unfold, akin to flowers coloured with the desire to be fertilised. Colour is a language and smell is a language. A soundless language that ushers its eternal nature to the soul of beings; cold sweat is a language, unbridled smells of desire are a language — a language of unity shared with a being whose voice she had never heard, but whose movements she now understood, as naked as he was. He wanted her and now she, too, wanted his thrusts— she lay down, stretching out like a plain of wet grass, welcoming creatures of the Earth to graze. She reached out to the flame of the lantern and pincered its burning soul with her two fingers, sinking the room into darkness, but he was somehow glowing and she could see him as if he were moonlight slinking in through an opening, like a being from the spirit world or perhaps like one fresh out of water softly incandescent.

He rammed into her, crushing her over and over until she was swimming in slick albumen stickiness, craving him more and more in each moment. He was quiet throughout save for his ragged breathing like a wounded calf, and his childish sob in her embrace when the water of life came out thick and warm. Beneath his heaviness, she was struck silent, yet weeping, a scream stuck between her heart and her throat like an under-chewed piece of meat, making her breathing tattered. At times she felt they were in the air like flies atop one another, and at others, she felt they were plunged into the depths of the Earth at a dizzying speed. She clung to him and pressed him to her, having grown as wide as a hurricane to engulf him whole. Sapped, she wished he would get off her, but he kept on, the two of them soaring to new heights to then crash to the ground, and she, a crater able to envelop a man to her depths without any trouble and birth him anew. She felt a great joy for the first time and sensed that Death was standing helpless nearby, hands tied before two people in a battle with life to the death. She felt him expand within her like a prickly root with all its tentacles, holding fast to her as she clung to him, the way soil does to a tree.

She couldn't recall how long they kept on in this cycle of life and death, but at some point, he was overcome with serenity, all his energy in the waves of liquid that shot out of him. He started to withdraw from her as a soul does a body, ever so slowly, a withdrawal unlike death but more like a new birth, slow and sweet, quietly surrendering to an eternal rest; he slipped out little by little as if he was afraid of some piece of him being left behind. The firm member that had faced her with such boldness was now soft like an intestine, weary, curled inside a thick skin, like a small animal ready to doze.

He left and sat outside squatting, waiting for his food, returning to the beginning with absolute ease as if nothing had happened, as if no time had passed, like he had entered a dream and left a few seconds after. When she took too long and didn't come with the food, he left her house silently, cutting through the village streets in the darkness, hearing her muffled vomiting in the distance.

He never came back after that. The encounter left her curled up on the ground for two days, retching from his stench, never to see him stand in front of her home naked again, muttering, begging for food — he disappeared from existence. She'd learned of his whereabouts from the rumour mill, which told of how he had drowned in the river, his body swept away behind the village to the end of things, and some said that he had gone back to that very spot in the forest where no one had set foot and morphed into an invisible being, as happened to the many who had disappeared behind the dense grassy hills — one of the village's convincing, convenient endings to whirlpools of gossip.

Her village was like any other small village, everything bordered, its dimensions clearly demarcated, extending out to nothing. Only the forest was allowed to reach out and everything else had to be set apart; even the sun would rise from behind the forest and sleep behind the mountain, and the rains, too, would pour down from the sky and gather in the river to wind down: everything that disappeared, disappeared behind the mountain. The mountain was their border and what was beyond it was unknown and difficult to explain, leaving them naturally disposed to defining everything apropos of it. Vagueness grated them, and so events weren't left floating without endings.

The madman left and she grew pregnant with Eghino, who would eventually become Lucy. No one asked where the girl came from; perhaps she was a memento from Edo's husband, placed in her womb after he had left her for another woman who wasn't cursed or didn't have Death stationed at her door waiting to kidnap her children.

This was just one of the many endings the village came up with to silence the gossipy chatter that did no one any good, but after their encounter that one night where she had drowned in his virility, she knew in her heart of hearts that the girl was his.

The story goes that one day he lost his way in the forest and eventually reached where no human had gone before, where no living creature could be killed, a place of invisible beings. Often the beings would call out to people by name, their voices echoing throughout the forest, but everyone had been warned not to turn back or answer such calls, whatever the reason. Do so and you'd be lost forever, spinning round and round in a vicious cycle, starting in one place and ending up in the same spot no matter which direction you went in, growing smaller and smaller, until eventually being lost to the wind, becoming one of the invisible beings. It's said the man was given the name Aulayo after he had been found. The voice sounded like it belonged to one of his friends. He'd been wandering for days. Following his disappearance, the banging of drums stirred the village alert and, for an entire day, the strongmen armed themselves with spears and arrows, and ventured into the forest to look for him. When they finally tracked him down, he, wild-eyed, never talked of the unseen beings who called people by name. But he did speak to himself without using sound; he made gestures in the air and smiled to himself at times. Edo had her own theory that he had gone to the ancestors and heard such terrifying tales, both from time past and yet to come, that he was left devoid of words, though the ancestors still spoke to him from time to time.

She wanted to get to the bottom of it all, to get to know on her own terms; that's why she drew close to him. She fed him so that he might reveal why all her children had died and what fate held in store for her. He remained silent right up till he disappeared, leaving her with a foetus in her womb. Going forth, when someone wanted to travel to their village, it was referred to as 'the madman's village' and has been that way ever since.

After her mother had gently pushed her out, Lucy was brought up by the villagers, and to protect herself from sorrow Edo withdrew into herself. Ilaygha nursed her as an acknowledgement of the secret favour between friends. Lucy was taught how to walk by the other children who played in the street, and she would drift off wherever sleep took hold of her. Edo never missed her, preparing herself so that, if Lucy did in fact die, she wouldn't grieve for her. At the height of her mother's negligence, Lucy became the centre of attention in the village. Everyone would call out after her, want to play with her, give her their best clothes, food and all their love. She wanted for nothing, and never had to go hungry or roam round naked like some of the other children, who only wore clothes on special occasions, and she never cried.

As a teenager, she would help all the village women — mothers to her — fetch water from the river and would fill their buckets and pitchers, cook for them and keep some of their children company till they returned from the farms or from gathering wood. Her back was always carrying children, though she didn't know their names or those of their mothers. She was like a tree or a stake that people would tie their animals to while they took care of other business. Using an enavi, mothers would tie their children to Lucy's back, the cords from each corner of the khaki fabric meeting at her chest in a tight knot that Lucy would toy with throughout the day. Lucy's enavi was known as 'the incubator': children would cry, urinate, defecate and sleep on her back until their mothers came and washed the filth off both Lucy and the child, before dressing Lucy in a fresh outfit. In every home, she had clothes to wear and a place to lay her head at night. She never had to worry about finding somewhere to bathe or eat. Her mother would tell herself that she must have inherited this from her father.

Despite hating its meaning, Eghino transformed her name into the most beautiful thing one could ever wish to be called. Hungry for the blessings of her name, women gave it to their daughters, even those older than Eghino, so they'd be just like her: obedient, active, patient, never complaining, and fresh-of-face, too. The name spread so much that the girls could be mistaken for attentive students in a school when someone called out Eghino — in one loud voice the entire village would respond affirmatively, 'Yooooong'. The birds, startled, would scatter from their nests atop trees and thatched roofs. Other times, thinking that the call must be for another Eghino, none of the girls responded. The only solution was to affix the mother's name after Eghino to tell the girls apart, leaving only the original Eghino, who had no mother's name attached.

After the man whose sanity was in question deserted Eghino's mother, she didn't leave her room, plagued by dizziness and nausea. She endured terrible days of pregnancy, cravings and every kind of agony possible. The madman had infected Edo with his malady of neglect: she neglected herself, her home, failing to attend to the black mud floor of her room. Humidity and insects ate away from the inside at the walls that still bore the faint patterns of moulding fingers. Several cracks appeared, allowing light and lizards to slip through as well. A tiny corpse's stench, caught in-between the mud layers, started to thicken the air once more.

Sometimes she would sit at her doorstep until the sun went down in the evenings and retrace her steps back inside, as if she was luring someone to follow her, and to fly with her in the spaces of love and pleasure, death, and giving birth to life. She wasn't right in the head herself, but she loved madness — to be precise, his silent madness that had captured her heart, her mind, her soul. He who had drowned into oblivion.

Her friends would take turns to come and visit her every now and then, and would declare that Edo's grief had come back. A mother grieves for even one lost child for her entire life — how gruelling, then, it must be for the mother who'd lost multiple children with names of their own. It's always that much crueller when the child dies after being named — the mother's heart clings to them for all time.

Edo no longer spoke or shared mischievous schemes with Marta-Esai and Rebecca-Ilaygha; both of them believed that she had truly gone off the deep end and that they'd best leave her alone in her own world, as such people preferred solitude and were unwelcoming of intrusions from pesky, chaotic, right-minded individuals. Rebecca and Marta contented themselves with cleaning her room and providing her with food and water. They soon grew preoccupied though with their own affairs and simply kept an eye on Edo from a distance.

Edo, too, kept an eye on everyone through the cracks in her wall, watching and surrounding her daughter with a halo of protection from afar, waving away the people clamouring over her; their love and preoccupation with her was almost a celebration in itself. She thought deeply about her daughter's actions, cursed just like her father, and secretly was joyful because she had given birth to him once more, to be fawned over — just in a different way. She was bargaining with Death, for Him not to come any closer. But perhaps she had been the one to attract Death to her children after all, her desperate maternal love a spell that had brought their end.

She remained in seclusion while the grasses in her courtyard grew mercilessly, blocking the door and hiding her room from view, drowning the small graves in green. Now and again one of her neighbours would have the goodwill to trim it all back so that no mosquitoes, snakes, hyenas or creeping creatures would wander in.

Then one day, through the cracks, she heard shouting and howling, and spied someone being dragged along the ground, passing before her one eye that was watching everything. Eghino had fallen from a tree. Edo's eye twitched like an enraged madman, and she started talking to an apparition of her conjuring: *Didn't we agree that you'd leave her alone?* Her enemy, Death, had become a sort of friend that she cajoled and scolded in whispers.

She flung open the door and shot out like an arrow, following her heart that had already jumped out ahead, rolling furiously in the direction of the accident. She raced there, with the speed of a professional runner, her body gangly like a sickly papaya tree. Edo found Eghino lying there, her limbs twisted in all directions, her face turned toward the sunset, grunting like a bull.

In a flash, she gathered her wits, and became suddenly aware of every little thing; just as misfortunes can make minds go, they can bring them back, too. She ordered the crowd to stand away, and the people respected her as Eghino's mother

— it was only right that she should be the closest at such a time. Edo then crouched over her and called out for the first time, 'My dear girl... Eghino', in a voice laced with all the tenderness of a motherhood damaged by loss upon loss, fearful of Death's unfulfilled vow. She was challenging Death itself, even though she believed herself accustomed to loss by now. Straight to Eghino's heart, she whispered, 'When I touch you somewhere and ask if it hurts, just blink once if it does.' That was how she started to gingerly adjust her daughter's position. Eghino blinked furiously though, certain of her mother's cautious touches. Edo then finished rearranging her daughter's limbs to their natural position, as everyone deserves to die in a dignified manner. Her hands and legs were fractured, her neck twisted, her face full of bruises and cuts from the branches, and she was missing two upper teeth. The crowd carried her to Edo's hut on a makeshift stretcher of crisscrossing branches, like an animal that had just been hunted, and Edo then threw them all out.

Struck with an abrupt vigour and presence of mind, Edo began kneading black mud and moulding it round her daughter's broken hand and leg. She adjusted Eghino's head slightly and stuck mud around her neck as well as the rest of her body, setting her in place like the walls themselves so only her eyes moved. With the leftover mud, Edo patted the walls of her room from the inside, sealing cracks through which the smell of Death wafted, stopping any lizards from scuttling in, too. She pulled out the rags she had stuffed in the hole in the wall, allowing sunshine to filter through. Down at the river, she washed the remnants of mud off herself, transforming into someone worthy of nursing a sick child.

Leaving Eghino like that to dry out completely for a few days meant pain and stiffness for her daughter in the mud's embrace. Patiently, as only a mother would, she watched her daughter heal. At night, Edo slept next to her as if keeping vigil at a grave, embracing her and telling her old tales: the story of a sultan vanished into thin air, who flew away with his wife on his back after the village had caught him slitting his children's throats to eat their livers. The story of the cunning rabbit, Unyeh, who played tricks on everyone, suggesting that they get rid of their mothers, kill them in fact, while he hid his own mother away at the top of a high dalaib tree, fetching her food and water in secret. That was, until everyone found out and the other rabbits secretly got rid of Unyeh's mother. He searched for her, but to no avail. At the council of the elders, while they warmed themselves by the burning branches spewing thick smoke, full of sorrow, he started to cry. *Ehee, ehee, ehee*. What's wrong, Unyeh? they asked him. He pretended that smoke had gone in his eyes. *Ehee, ehee, ehee*. They all exchanged smirks — they'd finally had their revenge! Unyeh had got a taste of his own medicine.

A few days on, Eghino started speaking to her mother, kindling a sudden camaraderie — she shared the story of how she fell and the two giggled while they ate their turtle and fish broth. Edo knew her daughter had started to heal, and that the pain was departing from her: laughter is a sign of wounds closing up, and later, all that would be left were scars and the enjoyment of telling the tale.

With each day, their laughter grew louder and louder, and when Eghino began to feel an intense itch on different parts of her body, Edo broke the mud mould. White ants had built their nests on her, laying thousands of tiny shiny eggs, and had started to store their grains.

Edo propped Eghino up as she began to walk again, and from that day on they were joined at the hip, until the missionaries came to baptise her and changed her name from Eghino to Lucy. With that, every girl who had thoughtlessly answered to the name Eghino would only respond to Lucy. But Edo refused to change her name, telling the priest, 'You know, I was named after my great-grandmother, and I'm scared the name will be lost. I don't have any sons, and if my family name disappears as well, my family will be wiped out forever — surely God himself wouldn't be pleased, would He?'

But one very humid and rainy night, she justified herself to her daughter. 'I'm just worried that God won't know who I am when I meet him, and then I won't be able to ask about my children that He fed to Death.' But in the end, she accepted having her Christian name pegged to her original name, becoming Maria-Edo. From then on everyone kept their old names pegged to the end of their new names, like a needle and thread. All the names reflected a duality, Marta-Esai, Rebecca-Ilaygha, but not Lucy-Eghino. In her case, there was only one name: Lucy. Later, families dropped the name Eghino after its owner left the village with her husband for the big city, while the name Lucy stayed on as sacred. But still, when the grandmothers asked any of the girls their names, and 'Lucy' came as the reply, they would say, 'Bring me some water, would you, Eghino?'

2

When her mother died and was placed in that shining wooden box with her glittering smile nearly leaping out through the glass window, Edo's two closest friends sat next to the body and shooed away flies from the coffin's exceptionally clean exterior as salty tears streaked their cheeks. The priest said a solemn prayer, fitting for a woman like Edo who was a devoted follower of the religion's tenets — she hardly ever set foot outside the church building, which she cleaned herself. She was devoted in her prayers, and rattled a hollowed-out gourd in time to the beat of the hymns, her soul sometimes soaring whilst her eyes were closed as she rocked back and forth declaring, 'Amen, amen, amen!' All this without the priest knowing her true intentions, a little secret she only shared with her daughter.

During the funeral service, a young man approached Lucy. Like a ripe piece of fruit, her body had filled out, skin lustrous as polished ebony: undoubtedly she was a beautiful woman. Once close enough, he knelt and whispered, 'Marry me?'

She glanced at him briefly through her tears. His face didn't look familiar — he wasn't one of her many brothers in the village. Having been raised in so many different households meant everyone was her brother, and so she couldn't run away with any of them. Unlike the rest of her peers, she didn't have a boyfriend because they all thought of her as a sister; no romantic attentions were ever cast her way. But this was different. He hadn't been brought up in the village, so he must have come from far away. Well-dressed, clean, fierce eyes, artfully carved lips, thick coiffed hair, a shirt with a large collar the hue of the dark smoky thickets drifting up above.

Without a word, she squeezed his hand and pulled him outside of the church towards her hut, with the heavens about to burst open. Once inside, she stripped and they explored each other's bodies until sunlight seeped through the hole in the hut's wall, announcing sunset. When she went to open the door, she found it barricaded with a large branch from a thorny tree, an accepted sign that those inside were no longer of this world. Her mother's grave — now in the dirt yard before the hut, in between the smaller graves of Lucy's siblings — was a mound of dirt atop the buried coffin, like a hill that had fallen asleep mid-step. There was no one else in sight; the bereaved were at the square dancing at the funeral that was fitting for a woman like her mother. She heard the drums beating, the sad songs that glorified death, yet at the same time reprimanded it for stealing loved ones away, dirges that emphasised the insignificance of man. The young man's arms wrapped round Lucy's waist from behind, and they both cried together silently.

'My friends, they put this thorny branch here so that no one would come in here wailing,' he said.

She wrapped a tanned hide around her waist, and rubbed herself from head to toe with ash from the cold hearth. Removing the thorny branch from the entrance, she spoke roughly, 'There's no need to bar this door — it's hardly the end of my family line.' She went on more tenderly, 'I'm still here and you are too, of course. Together we'll create, and make all of those in the graves breathe again.'

Like a stone from a slingshot, her protruding breasts covered by a delicate layer of ash, she shot into the middle of the square, snatching up the solemn death song being sung:

> *Youuu, youu youu ayyyy*
> *iroghoyeh yo yooooo*

With spears nearly twice their height, the men swiftly circled round the drums like a whirlpool, an intimidating forest of spears that pointed every so often aslant in the air, creating a dome that blocked out the sky. Lucy was inside the circle, the men's rumbling voices enveloping her, the women's heartrending cries breaking through; she was spinning between rumblings and nostalgia. Breathless, she saw her mother in the crowd, wearing her coffin and smiling through the glass panel, waving at her. Lucy's eyes strayed from Edo, and she retched, but she kept on dancing and dancing.

> Round
> and
> round.

As she jumped up and down, her breasts bounced, pointing straight ahead, perfectly round and firm. With her elbows folded inwards at her ribcage and her hands curled like a bird ready to take flight, she would jump, but her feet stayed firmly stuck to the ground, her soles crawling to a rhythm that would make every member of the group howl in their own way, to free themselves from grief, for the severity of what death had brought upon her in life, every leap of that death dance was in honour of Edo, until she rejoiced in it and accepted it peacefully. Lucy was shedding tears that refused to cease, remembering her mother's voice, her features, her secret opinions about everything; singing the special song that had belonged only to her beloved mother since birth.

All the village folk took part in the funeral, which lasted for three nights. The final night turned into a sort of celebration where everyone felt a lightness of spirit, having banished their grief through vigorous movement and rhythmical beats.

The indigo skies poured down for long hours, the tears of those mourning washed with the ash and soil that caked their bodies. Cold seeped into their bones but everyone felt that the earth was exhaling a warmth that spread little by little, like a mirage. The entire village slept in the square, while Lucy and her newfound companion Marco were in a private dance behind the door barricaded with the thorny branch. Everyone dreamt of Maria-Edo wearing her coffin, waving, only to then disappear into a disc of the sun that had opened up like a hole in the sky, a hole that started to cough out child after child, each of them floating down to earth like soft baby-bird feathers.

At dawn, the grave was moist and cold, allowing its dirt

surface to be swiftly smoothed down. As Edo's closest surviving relative, Lucy's head was shaved by an old grandmother. Soon enough Marco arrived and respectfully sat to have his head shaved too, in commiseration with Lucy. A queue of girls, who went by Lucy-Eghino as her name-sisters, formed and many a grandmother sat shaving the heads of those in line till midday. Hair floated in every direction for several days until the villagers began to find tufts swimming in their food and drink, and when it got too much, the young men swept up all the hair and burnt it next to a nearby bush, filling the air with something like burnt feathers. The funeral, as with weddings, ended with a feast.

The priest arrived and the villagers built an enormous cross on the grave with burnt red clay bricks, sealing it with cement, on which was written, with a dried tree branch, the inscription:

Maria-Edo
Beloved Holy Mother

The grave of Maria-Edo the saint became a village landmark on which children would play, sheep would frolic and women would spread out their sprouting maize alongside other vegetables that required drying. Sometimes, on moonlit nights, teenage boys and girls would sit there flirting, agreeing to run away with one another, the common way for couples in the village to announce their engagement, and get married afterwards.

Three moons had passed since Edo's demise. The village had found out that during the funeral Lucy had run away and slept with Marco, thereby announcing their engagement, whilst Edo's body had lain still warm as if asleep in her coffin on the table in the sanctuary towards the front of the church. Out of deep love for her, the village turned a blind eye to Lucy's timing, though they secretly envied Marco for singlehandedly comforting her on that fateful night. Many of them knew that Lucy had her moments of eccentricity, which were at times quite pronounced, granting her an unusual sort of freedom that prevented society from questioning her actions or criticising her at all.

Little by little, her belly swelled. As she was everyone's daughter, Marco asked the whole village for her hand. Given Rebecca was one of her mothers, he gifted her two goats as gratitude for nursing Lucy, and gave a goat to every other woman because they had all looked after and raised her.

Marco hadn't spent much time in the village — he, too, was alone, an orphan now. His father had enrolled him in a school far away from the village, distancing Marco from any danger as much as he could. Fearful of the treachery of the river and that of the forest, his father had been relieved to have Marco under a teacher's supervision. His son progressed steadily in his studies until he made his way to the big city to keep learning, only coming back to the village on days off and during the Christmas holidays. Marco inherited a large number of livestock and farmland plots but he had ambitions other than burying his prime years in the village, which would involve spending his life tilling the land and shouldering the worries of how to breed animals, or taking part in wars against governments eerily similar in their stupidity. Nor did he have any political drive to lead a pitiful population who knew no better to their death. The military didn't suit him because he was a gentle, faint-hearted fellow, who would cry aloud, his heart pounding at the slightest hardship. This was all aside from him being an only child, charged with preserving the family name.

He knew of the far-off news stirring beyond the mountain, and after the rumours really started to fly, he grew aware that a war would break out in the not-too-distant future. A rumour precedes every war until it ends in a bloodbath. Young men started to disappear, having been conscripted against their will in preparation for a rebellion; there was an atmosphere of suspicion and self-preservation. With apprehension in the air, rumours bred like fungus. Times of war were alike, infecting individuals like a disease — everyone could feel it without having anything in their power to stop it.

Simply put, Marco would rather retreat, aspiring to an ordinary life with no heroism. Living in peace and quiet, siring many children to inherit all the farmland and cattle that he had lost count of. In Marco's absence from the village — and after his father had died from a stray bullet shot by a drunk soldier boasting about his military service, declaring how anyone who didn't wear the khaki uniform was a she-male — his father's family took charge of his wealth. Marco found out that everyone in his family tree was an only child, tracing back to his grandfather's grandfather. They were all only children, which kept his family on the precipice of extinction; nothing could be allowed to happen to the sons before marrying, so their homes were always fenced off with thorns.

Lucy and Marco had similar inclinations, so he told her of his intention to leave the village without coming back any time soon. She agreed and they decided to depart, treating the matter as a mission that must be accomplished, no less important than the civil wars of alleged dignity and righting past wrongs.

The village folk agreed to the marriage and couldn't have been happier; from every direction Lucy's many mothers came with jewellery, adorning her with enough for thirty brides. Little coloured suksuk beads, threads hidden vein-like in their hollows, caressed her skin, entangling her like a fish caught in a net, while delicate round copper ornaments orbited through her ears, nose and lips, beside feathers of strange birds, gleaming hides, and ivory bracelets. Despite the delicateness of the jewellery upon her, she felt its heaviness, so much so that she struggled to breathe and move her limbs, as if shackled. This weight and paralysis took her back to when her mother had covered her in mud to heal her fractures. She felt a sudden yearning to undress behind the thorned branch in Marco's presence.

Today she would be yoked to him forevermore. She secretly counted him among the few decisive, bold men that only lucky women enjoyed: a man who surprised her by asking her to marry him before the church sanctuary and in sight of her mother's corpse. Marco chose Lucy because she was peculiar and took life by the reins; even death had failed several times to snatch her, as she revealed to him later. Though they had been inside the gutiyyah hut, he might as well have made love to her on the edge of a grave about to be sealed forever. Neither of them heard the dirt being shovelled, the wailing, the priest's prayers, or the mournful choral hymns that led the dead woman to her final resting place.

Livestock was slaughtered and banquets were held for days. Dancing, people were drunk on joy while a baby crawled in Lucy's depths, and that was how the first signs of Maria-Edo's wishes came to pass: that everything inside of her daughter would bear fruit.

Melancholy engulfed the village. Bullets tore back and forth through the dome of the sky in the darkest of nights, and back again, whistling in the air, for a distance, their spark eventually burning out, like stray stars. People started to seek sanctuary in their villages, carrying the news of the dead, fires, the dried blood of victims on the surviving villagers' clothes, unable to bury any of those lost.

The government sent soldiers and enforced an evening curfew, and the regime also started to apprehend young men, claiming they were the eyes for the rebels, passing on information to the rebel leaders and supplying them with provisions. These young men were tortured to the point of death, whilst the rebels captured other young men saying they were government spies revealing rebel secrets. Rebels had their own methods: cutting off their captives' ears before forcing them to chew and swallow them, and then ordering them to return to their villages as a message to anyone who even flirted with the idea of standing with the Northern Arabs.

Fear is chaos that can't be outrun; solace is only found by striking darkness into the inner beings of others.

The drums had quietened and people no longer celebrated anything; even funerals were terribly sombre. With the inexpressible sadness trapped inside, their bodies no longer jumped, sweated, sang energetically or danced to release their heaviness; the people were no longer able to forget their dead.

The women would wake up at dawn and sit round the graves in each of their unfenced dirt yards, reliving their loss and weeping as if their loved ones had died that very morning: their gravel-filled voices sung heart-breaking songs that extolled death and filled the mornings with gloom. Everything was performed with caution: farming, cattle breeding, hunting, gossiping, laughing, burying the dead — all of it was done with great discretion. People fled their villages without knowing where they were going, leaving their homes empty, and the streets bereft of rambunctious children; most young men either became collaborators voluntarily, paid informers or young soldiers, fighting and killing each other to survive. Others settled old scores under the mantle of war — once apprehended by soldiers they'd be forced to join the military. Neutrality was reserved only for women and children. The noose tightened further each day for the likes of Marco, who had other ambitions; he finally thought of fleeing on a cargo truck to the big city, amidst an atmosphere charged with bullets and fraught with death.

For several months while Lucy was anticipating her newborn, Marco waited for the truck carrying goods to arrive and, finally, it showed up. It was the only vehicle that had entered the village, laden with soap, salt and vibrant, multicoloured fabrics. An event in itself, children would crowd around the massive metal animal, running awed fingers over its body, touching its wheels, poking at its unblinking large glass eyes. When the driver honked the horn, the little ones laughed so hard imagining that the truck had passed wind that they wet themselves. When the engine growled, they scurried behind their mothers.

Lucy was as happy as could be and, at dawn, she commenced her farewells to the village, receiving blessings from her mothers, who sprinkled water over her, blew into her ears, and spat on her head, all to ward off the evil eye. Rebecca-Ilaygha and Marta-Esai communicated Edo's will to Marco, that if he harmed Lucy in any way, she'd come back and hack off his member. This little addition at the end of the will was the doing of Marta, who was now known as the husband-beater. One by one, tree by tree, Lucy said goodbye to the village. She stroked her mother's smooth, very large, cross-shaped grave, and rushed off with her husband to jump into the belly of the truck. They set off alongside others to Juba for a new life, leaving behind a village at the fringes of the ongoing war.

The truck sped along as fast as was possible in the forest; bursting greenness, towering goddesses, spreading shade, with creatures moving inside them and among their branches, lying in wait for passers-by. The truck was in an abyss of darkness, surrounded by swamps, and it trampled grasses underfoot, trudging along, not in the least bothered by the harsh terrain nor the creatures and armed men lying in wait. The driver anxiously put his foot down on the accelerator to make up for lost time, until one of the back tyres came loose and rolled off into the mud, nearly causing the truck to tip over. Miraculously, the driver was able to lean it against a hefty tree trunk. Pandemonium erupted: passengers' voices tore through the tree branches to the skies above, startling birds in their nests.

Everyone alighted from the truck while the driver attempted to repair the damage. Growing worried, he and his assistant started to work even faster before night fell, as the road was unsafe, even more so in wartime. The passengers lost hope once the repairs dragged on; the driver and his helper were coated in black oil and despair, and darkness started to swiftly crawl and envelop them.

After ruling out the presence of snakes, some of the passengers climbed trees in the hope of sleeping, whilst others swept away dry fallen leaves and lay down on the ground, quiescent. Lucy made her way behind the bushes to relieve herself, and Marco followed soon after to check on her. He drew close to her and lay her down on the grasses; her sounds stirring and throaty, a stone's throw away from her excrement. While he hovered over her, she soared higher, over the forest, poised in a place beyond their worries and fears. Then they both heard a commotion: gunshots and screaming. Marco placed his hand over Lucy's mouth and remained stuck to her on the ground until it had quietened down completely. He crawled cautiously, hardly making a sound, pushing the long grasses out of the way. With difficulty, in the dark, he saw that everyone had been killed and their belongings stolen; all that was left behind was a baby barely a year old, crying hard, trying to draw milk from his dead mother's breast. Marco whispered to Lucy that they should stay where they were, in silence, till dawn.

'Who's the war even against? Were they Arab?'

Marco gestured at her to keep quiet.

'But they speak just like us, I knew some of those words.'

He insistently put his finger to his lips.

The baby's crying concerned Lucy, so she got up and — as if in a trance — made her way over to him. Completely disregarding Marco's choked warnings, she hopped over the corpses, her feet finally landing in a pool of warm blood. She unfolded the dead mother's arms from her child and, with her palm, closed the dead woman's eyes, which were staring blankly at the darkness. Lucy picked up the baby and hurried back to the hiding place, despite Marco's objecting glare. 'What were you thinking? What will we do when his crying gives us away?' Then more firmly, he said, 'Put him back!'

She wrapped the child round her back and tucked his tiny hands under her armpits. 'No, Marco. He's just an innocent child.' She kneeled down and hid her body in the long grass, rocking the baby and humming to him. So skilled at calming children was she that the baby slipped into quietude, and slowly into a deep sleep, sighing now and again.

At the first sliver of dawn, they made their way through the forest, taking a route parallel to the dirt trail so they wouldn't lose their way. They had been walking for many hours, the baby letting out a thin squall all the while, hungry as it was. Lucy fed him an entire papaya after picking out its sticky black seeds, and then secured him on her back once more, where he drifted off to sleep again for the rest of the journey. Eventually, at night, they reached the city, where Marco's relatives welcomed them, and they spent the entire night recounting the tale of the killings and how they walked all that way through the forest.

On the morning of the second day, Lucy saw Marco and one of his relatives listening keenly to a man's voice coming out of a black box, which had something very thin jutting upwards out of it, pointing straight into the sky: it was her first time seeing a radio. News broadcasts shared the danger on the roads to the villages, about the people slaughtered along the way by unidentified individuals, with no indication of whether there had been any survivors. Marco's relative advised him to keep quiet so that they wouldn't face questioning by the authorities.

According to the news in the village, which showed a preference for gossip and drew neat conclusions to everything so that nothing was left hanging, all the passengers were killed, even Marco and Lucy. The villagers, who no longer publicly announced funerals, grieved for them in silence. They had placed all the possessions of the deceased exactly in the middle of each respective gutiyyah, and assigned each object to their acquaintances and friends. They then dragged a thorny branch outside the family home after erecting a memorial in place of a grave. Afterwards, the village grew preoccupied with the war, which was marching towards them like a tornado, warning them of misfortune and pure chaos.

3

Lucy stared at everything with the naked and natural curiosity that villagers were known for; she had always thought there wasn't much life beyond the mountain, which she'd believed was where the world ended.

Trapped right in the middle between squat mountains, Juba was a small city. Very little was familiar here. The houses, scattered here and there, were similar to the ones in her village, with round straw roofs pointing upwards. Other houses looked different, with no straw at all, each of them clearly fenced off to separate them from the next one. So many people, and serious too; unlike her village counterparts, these city-dwellers didn't raise their voices when conversing, and spoke multiple languages, while she only spoke the tongue of her mothers back home. Every day they had new clothes, while she would get a new outfit only once a year at Christmas. Everything here was outside the realms of her knowledge: was this what had been beyond the village all along?

In the mornings, a short, sturdy girl would arrive carrying a large plastic cup full of tea and a plate with sliced boiled pumpkin layered with peanut butter. Lucy supposed to herself, 'So, people here drink this brown stuff then, instead of having a full meal at the break of dawn.' Lucy was used to having a stale gruel of yesterday's leftovers as soon as she got up.

They slept in beds like the one she had seen in one of her many mothers' rooms, whose husband had brought it for her after one of his trips beyond the village. Many of the neighbours had elbowed their way into his house to get their fill of the bed, staring at and touching it. Now, here she was spending the night on one of them, even though she nearly fell off several times during the night, which prompted Marco to push her bed up against the wall and his in the other direction in case she and the baby rolled off.

The sun rose from the opposite direction to the village. She had thought this city was their final destination, but Marco had soon bought more supplies, food and clothes for her and the child, clothes more like what everyone else was wearing — eye-catching and fresh-smelling.

He came to her saying they were going to ride the river to the biggest city in the North, and that they'd reach there in a couple of days. It'd be a harsh journey but, in the end, they'd set down their roots in a place where everything was available in abundance. Even money could be found flung on the streets for them to pick up and buy whatever their hearts desired. They'd live the good life, far from the popping sounds of gunfire, and could focus on growing their family. He said this final part and winked, rubbing her belly, which had started to protrude.

She fell silent. Weighed down by disappointment, she concluded that arguing wouldn't make any difference, because here, even just a few hours from her village, she felt it was useless to speak. Even here she'd been struck by the strangeness of everything — the people, their homes, their possessions, the steaming brown drink with pumpkin on the side — what would it be like further afield?

The next morning, in a car with no roof, Marco's relative dropped them off at the riverbank, where there was an alarming creature the size of a house floating on the water. She heard them calling it babur, an enormous river vessel travelling in the direction of the river current, transporting people northwards. Lucy climbed aboard with the child she had rescued. She concentrated her line of vision on Marco, a fixed spot, to save her from being entirely lost. Little by little, she started to look around her: at people jabbering away, and goods of all kinds. There was fruit that had been snatched off the branch before harvest time, still green like leaves: bananas, mangos, and pineapples that would ripen along the way. Mahogany, teak and ebony planks were stacked up on the sides, and there were ostrich feathers and eggs, crocodile skins, smoked meats and dried fish fashioned into thick, long hanging ropes.

This was the first time Lucy had travelled on the river, right in the middle of it, without touching the water. To her, everything was spinning endlessly, and she was overcome by acute fatigue and vomiting. She tied a rag tightly round her head, hoping it would ease her symptoms.

Days passed as they floated down the river; soft waves

like a sleeper's breath rocked the boat, making it rise and fall rhythmically. The flow of the river carried them forward and the land with its trees receded into the horizon.

Like young girls playing hide-and-seek, the towering trees hid themselves and stacked up on top of each other in the boat's wake. Other trees started to come into view, running towards the horizon, where the end of the world was. After several days, long slender grasses took over the view, clouds grew thinner, and a pale mist, easily pierced by sunrays, appeared. They found themselves surrounded by short, somewhat lean, tame trees.

Lucy was in a new era of motherhood; she used all her experience as a babysitter in her village on the small child whose mother had been killed, betrayed by bullets in the dark in the forest long ago. She would ply him with whatever food was available; what mattered the most though, was that he didn't cry or get on Marco's nerves, as her husband's eyes would widen whenever he heard the child making a fuss.

One day, a number of the children were struck by a frightening diarrhoea, and Lucy's foundling child was one of them. He stained the small bedsheet swatches and her clothes with a greenish-yellow liquid; no sooner had she cleaned one than the next held more loose faeces. She scooped up water from the river and washed him with it, whilst also tying the sheets round a stick and dunking them to allow the river current to clean them. Some of the other women tried to help her stop the baby's diarrhoea, but it was near impossible. His eyes sank into their sockets and he started to cry soundlessly, without tears — big eyes staring into emptiness, unblinking; his small dry mouth open, releasing a feeble sound like a kitten's miaow.

Anxiety gnawed at her and she didn't sleep for two days. Though utterly exhausted, she kept fighting the drowsiness, whether standing up, or sitting down, or in any other position. She finally surrendered and slept deeply as children do. In her sleep, a dream led her to the forest where they had been peppered by gunfire from every direction. She tried as hard as she could to prise the baby from his dead mother's vice-like embrace, but to no avail. She tugged in one direction and the mother's corpse pulled the child in the other, till the child was torn in two and his hot insides slopped out onto her feet, steam rising from the intestines.

Heart racing and hands clammy, Lucy woke up, searching for the baby everywhere, as one does a lost shoe in the middle of a packed suitcase. She finally came across him, dry as firewood, flies crawling all over, his eyes and mouth wide open doors. His spirit had departed and hadn't shut the doors upon leaving. Lucy's shoulders quaked and her vision blurred. Marco tried to close the child's mouth but it would just keep slowly opening, a wallet stuffed with too many notes.

The river was at its highest and the boat didn't stop. They were unsure of how to bury the child. An older passenger remarked, 'There's no land nearby. If you just leave the body as it is, it will decompose and no one will be able to stand it. People are loved when they're alive, but when they die, they become something scary because, to put it simply, they now belong to another world, a distant and strange one, and we fear the unknown. That's why even if it's just a baby barely a year old, the sight of dead bodies terrifies us. You've got to toss him in the river. We often bury the dead in water.' Lucy was far away, her sorrow tearing her apart as she remembered her terrible dream where she went up against the dead mother. She could still feel his hot insides on her feet.

Marco wrapped the small body in a bedsheet, its mouth still gaping open like a fish's. The river bid it farewell slowly; the body kept floating even far in the distance, bobbing like a bottle cork. Little by little the body then began to sink, before disappearing out of sight.

For days, Lucy grieved, neither eating nor drinking, her vomiting returning. She remembered her mother, and how she had buried her young. She told Marco, 'If our children's destiny is the same as my mother's, then there's no point in us running away.' Then she shared her disturbing dream.

Marco grabbed her by the shoulders and looked deeply into her eyes. 'Nothing like that will happen to our children. Remember that this baby wasn't even ours. You were just trying to save him, but it seems his mother needed him more.'

She sighed heavily, letting her head drop onto his chest, and gave her eyes free rein to roam over the vast wilderness.

4

Khartoum was a large city, difficult to comprehend: it was congested, with people yelling in the bus stations and the marketplaces, their shapes peculiar compared to the people she was familiar with. These people all spoke one language, seemingly that of their mothers. Some of them looked like the people in her village, while others had long, sleek hair like that of sheep, with skin not of a deep brown; some of them didn't have any colour to speak of, like slabs of raw flesh stripped of their skin. A few of them looked like the priests who'd buried Maria-Edo. The people here were full of mirth and good-spirited… until they weren't, growing angry just as easily, sweat dripping off them.

The perfectly blue sky, naked without its clouds, looked just like her village's during the rainless months. The sun was brazen, beating down with a bravery she hadn't encountered before, the trees few and far between. Smells and unfamiliar colours whose names she didn't know. She did recognise, though, the smell of grilled meat on the fire and hungered for it. Marco brought Lucy a plate and she wolfed it down whilst looking around her to store away everything for later: there were incredible goods she didn't know the first thing about, colourless people, and there she was without a language to speak to them in. Being in this city made her feel like she didn't know the names of so many things. She wished she could tell them all to shut up for just a moment.

'This is Khartoum at its best,' Marco finally said. 'The big city.'

'Who are they?' she asked.

'They're Arabs,' he said, cautiously.

Lucy rocked on her heels in place. 'Why have you brought us here, Marco? I want to go back to the village. Are you sure that these people are Arabs? I had pictured them differently.'

'What were you expecting?'

'I don't know, maybe ogres lying in wait to kill people and then eat them.'

Marco snorted so loud, heads turned towards them. Lucy buried her face in his shoulder so she wouldn't have to meet their gaze.

A friend of Marco's, called Peter, received them both. He had studied with Marco and then come to the big city with a trader, in search of his father who had been imprisoned in one of the northern cities. Peter's father had been accused of playing a role in the rebellion during the departure of the British colonisers, in which several northern teachers and merchants were slaughtered. Most of his father's friends had been executed, but news came to Peter that his father was still holed up, under lock and key, serving a life sentence in some prison. And so, Peter set out to track his father down, never to return to the South again, except to carry out his military service as a junior officer.

She set off with them in a small car the colour of a fully-ripe mango — a taxi, they called it — to some place far away. After cutting through many streets, and passing over straight, black roads, which gleamed like a river frozen solid under the moonlight, they finally arrived to a small welcome party at Peter's house, crowded with friends, relatives and students.

No straw houses here. The homes were clearly demarcated by unhearing walls and exceptionally straight streets. 'Why do they keep themselves locked up like this?' Lucy asked, gesturing at the boundary walls.

'They're not locked up. It's just a way of showing that every person owns his piece of land, that every family has their designated area.'

She nodded, not understanding the entirety of what he'd said, but she went on. 'In the village, we don't need all these walls — in the village, everything belongs to all of us. No one cares about fences or house numbers. You might only have one room and it's enough; the entire village is big enough for everyone, and there is nothing to make anyone feel anxious. My mother buried her children wherever she wanted, as long as no one else was already using that spot.'

Marco smiled in agreement.

When they got inside Peter's house, Lucy blinked rapidly at her surroundings and talked to herself. There were lamps fixed on the walls of each room like small illuminating moons, and there were larger-than-life windows that opened out onto the hosh — even when she stepped outside into the large uncovered sitting area, Lucy felt suffocated by the harsh lighting. The yard was completely flat with no protrusions or bumps; no graves here. It seemed like no one ever died here.

She asked Marco how to get to the river as she needed to bathe, and he pressed his fist against his lips. 'No one bathes in the river here, there's water in every house.' He then guided her to the bathroom, where he turned on the shower and water spilled forth like sudden rain. Alone, she stood under it and couldn't catch her breath, drowning standing up. She sought refuge by stepping towards the shower wall, sticking to it, while she cupped her hands together to catch the water little by little and wash away the map of soap and filth drawn on her body. When she was done, she stepped into the water once more to wake herself up. It must be a dream — was she really in the big city? She held her breath for so long that the being inside her kicked.

Her first night in Khartoum, she didn't sleep well. Marco and his friends chatted late into the evening, clinking glass against glass, bottle against bottle, eating grilled meats and roaring with laughter. Later on, they were no longer sitting upright but reclining on their seats, mellowed by alcohol, languorous with ideas. In the end, they fell asleep where they sat.

Lucy tossed to her right. She tossed to her left. The bed creaked, and she was smothered by a yearning for home. Her village, and everyone in it: her mothers, Edo's grave… thick tears ran into the pillow while her mind thrashed, just as the city night did. Sounds came from every direction: music, loud voices and dogs barking, which meant that everyone must be a stranger here. Mumbling voices in the streets despite the curtain of night being drawn. She remembered her village, and how dogs only barked if hyenas drew close to uncover fresh graves in the yards.

She heard the dawn call to prayer and figured it must be the same man from her village — at last, a familiar sound! — the voice had the same rise and fall to it, after all. The call to prayer came before the church bells rang or the rooster crowed. She remembered well that the appearance of the mosque and the army Majrus trucks had been the first signs that the government had been interested in their village. The government built a breathtaking mosque, its minaret stretching to the sky, making it the second house of God to be established in the village. And so God had two houses; the new one held soldiers and some men who had deemed it better to leave the church. They changed their names for a second time, but used Maria-Edo's approach and kept their names tagged onto one another, fearful of being lost. She remembered how Marta-Esai's husband embraced the new religion and changed his name to Mohammed-Tito; he no longer beat women, left his drinking behind and came back one day with his manhood bleeding, because the new religion required him to not approach women whenever he wanted and to devote himself to prayer. According to Lucy's mother, the man who announced the call to prayer cut his member with a knife and slaughtered some sheep. After all this, people started saying that the Arabs 'don't want us to get pregnant and have more children, they want to stamp us out, so they can come and occupy our villages, our farms, get rich off our livestock'. Despite such far-reaching talk, Mohammed-Tito still plunged into the religion with complete and utter faith. Whenever he'd walk by, people would wink at one another and whisper that they'd made a hole down there for him like the one women had, that now his women were the ones riding him, because at least *they* still had something protruding somewhat outwards.

One night after his wounds had healed, he tried to get close to his new wife, but she rebuked him. 'What are you planning to do with your penis cut off like that? We're one and the same now, maybe we both should marry a real man!' She said all this looking down at the state of his manhood, her lips curled in displeasure as if she had bitten into something sour.

Mohammed-Tito felt his mouth go dry. 'Who told you my penis had been cut off?'

She crossed her arms, her feet astride. 'The whole village knows that the Arabs cut off your penis so that you'll always belong to them and that your behind has been stamped, too.'

'What?' He said, pressing his fingertips hard against his temples.

With her hands on her hips now, she hurled a forceful stream of hot air at him. What an insult he had brought upon the both of them. 'It's the truth Tito, and the whole village knows it.'

'The whole village?' he glowered.

'Yes; the men, the women and even the children. Some men in the saqifa even winked at me, telling me they were available if I ever missed "it" while pointing to their privates! Then they all laughed. How you've shamed us.'

Mohammed-Tito didn't sleep that night; he was boiling within, impatiently waiting for dawn.

In the morning, he went to the village square, dragging the

large communal drum. He started beating it as one would when a weighty announcement was about to be made. Everyone in the village turned towards the noise, wondering in a panic if one of his wives had died. When he had made sure they all were there — men, women, and children — they started to chuckle and whispers slipped out of their mouths. What else could he do but undo his trousers and face them all with his fullness underneath, waggling it at them like an index finger, clean, smooth, and erect — a banana brought from verdant, fertile Anzara.

'How do you like this, then?' he growled. The women ran back to their huts in fits of laughter and the grandmothers declared that he would bring misfortune to their homes with this blatant public nakedness. The men stayed behind with Mohammed-Tito and persuaded him to put his trousers back on, and they all then started to whisper amongst themselves in the saqifa. He related how simple it was really, just the removal of a flap of skin, and such a thing helped him be more virile, never growing tired or flaccid. There was no longer any burning when he urinated, and that neverending itch had finally been laid to rest and, most of all, he added with a wink, his shoulders back, 'My wives can't get enough of me.' And so some of the men went in secret to get their manhood snipped as well, but they didn't change their religion or their names.

Lucy woke up after the call to prayer rang out and started cleaning the house, now in a mess after the men had stayed up late: she washed the plates, the cutlery, the pots and pans, scrubbing them with sun-seared sand to make them shine; she set things in order, washed the men's shirts, which were thrown everywhere, and hung them on the line to dry. Then she waited and observed the lady of the house, plump to a degree she wasn't accustomed to, as she slept. Lucy then approached the woman and gently shook her awake.

'What is it?' she snapped.

Lucy cleared her throat. 'The sun's nearly up, aren't we going to fetch water from the river?'

'Again with the river? There's no river or firewood over here, everything is either in or near the house. You're in the city now, go on back to sleep. You were wandering around all night in the hosh — take care that a thief doesn't bash your head in.'

Lucy returned to her bed and curled into herself, her shoulders tight. Homesickness washed over her once more, painfully this time, and everything within her insistently asked: *What is this place?* Tears rolled silently down her cheeks.

The sun rose from the completely opposite direction again. If she had been back home, it would have been as if it were rising from the mountains, which was where it usually set. Beyond her village, it was all topsy-turvy: the sun, the people, everything else.

The people here only woke up when the sunrays started to whip them, and most of them then crawled back into their rooms from the hosh, the paved central yard in the middle of the compound, to keep sleeping, which convinced her that she was in a senseless city where the sun rose from the wrong direction and the people must be ill for sleeping till noon with no shame or work to do. But deep down, she thought that they must have every right to do so if there really was money just flung out on the streets as Marco had described. Even the river came right up to their houses, the water clean. *The food over here must prepare itself too*, she mused.

Finally, the lady of the house, Peter's wife, woke up and found the house spotless: even the places where her broom couldn't reach had been cleaned of filth and unnecessary accumulations; the hosh felt wider than before, the pots and pans shining and well-stacked, free from any grease, with the clothes on the line starting to stiffen. She looked at Lucy in wonder, trying to fight a smile of admiration that nearly skipped off her lips. 'When did you do all this?'

Lucy spat out a sizeable hunk of bitter saliva from chewing and picking her teeth with a damp twig she had broken off one of the scrawny neem tree branches in front of the house. 'It's all since that poor man started saying Allahu Akbar.' She paused. 'As if there was anyone to even hear him.'

Amused, Peter's wife snorted and stretched out her hand, 'I'm Theresa, and you?'

'Eghino. I mean, Lucy! My name's Lucy.'

'Thank you for doing all this housework. But you shouldn't have, you're our guest.'

'A woman is only a guest in her grave,' Lucy replied. 'That's what my mother used to say.'

'Today's the weekend, so we usually all sleep in. But on weekdays we wake up with the azan because Peter has to leave early for work. You know how things are for officers in the army!'

Lucy didn't follow much, so she didn't respond. They both walked slowly to the kitchen where Theresa lit a fire inside a round iron stove — it was raised from the ground, and laid on top were crisscrossing rows of thin metal, creating square gaps through which the ash fell. They called it a kanoun.

She started to learn the names of other things in the kitchen and grasped how to prepare some foods and drinks in the way of the city dwellers. She discovered there was an art to preparing food in different ways to give different tastes. She thought of her village and concluded that the only difference between them and their cattle, when it came to their meals, was that the villagers would add salt and wild earthy herbs to their vegetables in the cooking pot, and a hunk of animal fat. During hunting season they'd always eat meat, but if one of the cattle died from illness, oh the misery that would follow!

Theresa didn't withhold any information related to housework, and a few months later, Theresa no longer did anything at home. She'd sleep the entire day: after getting up at dawn to help her husband get ready for work, she'd then go back to sleep once more and only wake up when the time came for Peter to come back home. Only then would she ask Lucy to go inside, bathe and rest. At this stage of her pregnancy, Lucy would wheeze like a dog about to die of heatstroke, her belly pushing outwards, her feet swollen.

Marco had started leaving early with his friend Peter to look for work, but without much luck. He'd come back, disappointment etched on his face, calculating the days before the arrival of his firstborn, still without any steady work or one measly coin in hand.

Peter was a rare friend, supportive in every sense of the word. An officer in the army, his financial situation was comfortable, but that didn't stop Marco's embarrassment. And so Marco started to search for work, no matter what it was, on his own, until he came across a building under construction, and went to the foreman to ask for a job. The next step was to take off his clothes and stand in his underwear and a coloured singlet, a bucket in his hand to transport dirt, bricks and gravel to the top of the building. Despite how strenuous the work was, he felt satisfied because a lot of the workers were sons of the South, which made it all the easier for him to fit in.

He'd come back to the house covered in thick dust, with sores on his shoulders from weighty loads, his hands rough and countless grains of sand nested in his bushy hair.

One day, Lucy was removing a chunk of clay stuck to his earlobe. She tilted her head. 'It seems like finding money in the city takes some real digging!'

All he could do was laugh heartily. He then installed himself on the edge of the bed and gently pulled her onto his lap like a child. 'I know that I lied to you about finding money in the streets — I was just trying to convince you to come here.'

'I knew you were lying, but I chose to believe you so we could be together.'

Marco's lips turned upwards and he placed his hand on her belly. 'And how's the little one?'

'Won't stop kicking.'

She then got up, collected his dirty clothes and left the room. He noticed that she had grown taller. *She's still growing like a fresh plant!*

And truly, Lucy was still a girl both in age and at heart. Once she'd finished her housework and Theresa had slipped into her long nap, she would sneak out onto the street with Theresa's three daughters and the neighbour's girls, making for a scrawny neem tree whose shade barely covered them. She'd play bayt bayt with them: teaching them how to make furniture and animals from mud, and how to collect leftover vegetables and fruit peels to throw together a 'meal' using empty cans as the pots, and lighting embers under them to prepare food for the dolls that she had sewn together from coloured pieces of fabric and stuffed with cotton wool and worn-out rags. The children would come to her with fabric scraps that the old tailor at the end of the street had thrown away, and she would fashion hair for the dolls. Lucy and the girls had no common language between them — she'd speak in her own, and they'd talk back in Arabic. Once she'd picked up a few words, she'd throw them out into the air unanchored by sentences, like a child fishing for words from the mouths of others. Sometimes she'd tag on a complete sentence in her language, and at other times gestures and giggles were enough when they were unable to get their points across. She might as well have been a child learning to speak, picking up a new language — Arabic — from them. They, too, came to learn a measure of her language.

It once so happened that Theresa caught her jumping rope with the other girls, even though Lucy's belly was as round as could be. Theresa scolded her and forced her back inside. 'What are you thinking? Do you want your child to pop out on the street? And you're a married woman now, have you forgotten? Playing with children...' She went on and on. Lucy cut herself off from the girls for an extended period, during which Theresa didn't speak to her much. Theresa was completely preoccupied with sleeping and visiting her girlfriends, leaving Lucy to weather the heavy feeling of homesickness alone. Soon enough though, the girls lured her out without Theresa knowing to play under the tree once more.

Lucy kept on sneaking away to play during the hottest part of the day, when the men would be at work, the women enjoying their afternoon naps, or gossiping at get-togethers at one of their homes. One day, they were to gather at Theresa's, and many things had to be put in order before their arrival. Once they'd arrived, Lucy circled round them, attending to their every whim, despite her looming delivery. Pleased with her dedication, one of Theresa's friends commented, 'Your housegirl is so attentive! She really knows what she's doing.'

Theresa's cheeks grew hot and she was about to correct her friend, but then stopped herself as she quite liked the idea. With her eyes on Lucy in the kitchen, who was absorbed with washing the dishes, she said, 'Yes, I'm very lucky.'

And with that, the entire neighbourhood started to shower praises on Theresa's experienced, active housegirl who never grumbled.

One morning, a neighbour came to ask Theresa to send Lucy over to her house because she had a lot of work to be done. She'd make sure to pay her well. No sooner had Theresa collected the money than she instructed, 'Lucy, go over to my friend's house please — she needs help. She's ill, actually. I'll do everything over here today, just go on and help her out.'

Lucy agreed and made her way over, doing a lot of work once she'd arrived. After a few days, the same thing happened with another of Theresa's friends, and so on and so forth. Theresa would secretly pocket the money while Lucy took every opportunity during these excursions to learn more about her surroundings. It went on like this for a long time until Marco happened to come across his wife stepping out of an unknown house, pouring out dirty water into the street. She was walking as if in a trance, and had grown so much that the dress he had bought her when they were back in the South had ridden up, exposing her thighs. Her belly might as well have been a large, ripe pumpkin. Nostrils flared, he called out to her. 'Lucy! What are you doing here?'

'Helping out one of Theresa's friends. She asked me to,' she replied, innocently.

He grabbed her by the hand and dragged her back to Peter's house. Once inside, he faced Theresa. He pounded his fist on the nearest surface. 'Can you explain why Lucy is helping your friend?'

Theresa squirmed, and stammered, 'We... we all help each other out from time to time. I just wanted L... Lucy to get to know some of my friends. That's all!'

He turned his head to his wife and threw her a reprimanding look as a father would.

'How many times has this happened?'

Lucy's eyes smarted with emotion. 'Nearly every day.'

His glare then fell on Theresa, and before he could say anything else, the neighbour, whose house Lucy had been at, burst in. 'Theresa, where's your housegirl? Just because I already paid you for her doesn't mean she can just leave without finishing her work! There are still wet clothes in the basin.'

Marco's mouth slackened. 'Housegirl? Housegirl, Theresa?' The world started spinning and he began to shake. Hot tears sprung to his eyes. Lucy, her cheeks still wet, begged him to calm down — it was difficult to see a man cry. Sapped, Marco fell to his knees, and clinging to Lucy's legs, begged her for forgiveness. The tears running down his face mixed with thick mucus and dripped onto her swollen feet. First, he addressed her as Lucy, and next, he called her Edo, pleading for her pardon. Theresa stood still, her arms wrapped around her middle, not knowing what to do next. Lucy and Marco bawled like children.

Marco stood up and pulled Lucy to him. 'Get your things together, everything. There's no place for us here.' He shook as he said these words through clenched teeth. Lucy was completely at sea. This was all just a bad dream, and any moment now he would wake her up.

Theresa started to apologise, her own eyes welling. Her neighbour swiftly left once she discovered how tangled the situation was. Theresa knelt at Marco's feet, but he was on fire, sweat from his brow making its way to his tear-stained cheeks, and bellowed at Lucy to hurry up. Lucy felt the room closing in on her. She couldn't help but pity Theresa, while Marco paid no attention to her pleading as she knelt at his feet. Finally, through choked words, he spoke to her, 'Have you no heart? This girl is an orphan, a poor thing. How could you exploit her like this? How dare you. If you wanted money, you could have asked me instead of sending her to serve Arabs. *Arabs*, Theresa. Never in my life have I been so insulted, and here I was thinking that you were treating her as a sister.'

At that moment, Peter strode in, a fearsome shadow in his military uniform. It seemed that he had heard everything. In what he said next, he was extremely slow and resolute. 'Theresa, go back to your parents' house.'

'Peter, please,' Marco intervened. 'We don't want to be the reason your marriage falls apart. Lucy and I are the ones who should go.'

'You heard what I said, Theresa. Get up and get out of here. Don't come back.'

Sobbing, Theresa stood up and started to collect her things. She rounded up her three daughters. 'Only you. Just how you came here. The girls aren't going with you.'

The atmosphere was charged. Marco tried to get Peter to change his mind, but his friend stated coldly, 'If you still want to stay friends, then stop talking *now*. Lucy, put your things back where they were.'

Theresa left, and Lucy had never seen a more humiliated creature. As for the girls, they held tight to Lucy's dress, wailing when their father ordered them to get away from their mother.

Marco and Lucy cried openly while the little ones fidgeted amidst their wordless weeping.

This was a serious injury not just for them but for the entire family. Lucy remembered her mother, who had cautioned her against squandering her dignity. All of a sudden, she was back there on that day when Maria-Edo had thrashed her and forbade her from crying; Lucy had shuddered like a rain-soaked sparrow. It was the first time she had faced her mother's wrath — Edo had beaten her as if she was intent on killing her.

It had been back when Edo would follow Lucy's every move through the cracks in the walls of her hut. A girl of a similar age picked a fight because the boy her heart was set on was wooing Lucy. She subjected Lucy to a stream of invective: she was a fatherless piece of trash with a lunatic for a mother, who wandered from house to house sleeping with every boy she saw, and would end up as wide and deep as a pitcher of merisa. Then she called Lucy, Eghino, and spat on her feet. All that while, Lucy stood frozen, unsure of how to respond. She didn't have the snappy comebacks or rude vocabulary necessary to respond to such words flung in her face like that. All of a sudden she heard her mother's voice, usually so quiet, loud and shrill as she shouted, 'Eghino, come here now!'

Lucy went over and Edo opened the door ever so slowly. She squeezed Lucy's wrist and began to beat her with abandon, and when Lucy tried to scream, Edo picked her daughter up by the skin of her stomach, her eyes protuberant. 'Hoossssssh — not a sound.'

Lucy swallowed her saliva, her tears and her voice.

'Look at me.'

It was difficult for any person to look into the eyes of a woman far from sane, even if she was their mother. 'Don't you ever let anyone insult you, you hear? How can you let that idiot girl treat you like that? Standing still like a pile of shit.'

Lucy had been oblivious to the fact that her mother had been watching her until Edo pointed to the cracks and revealed, 'I saw everything.'

Pain flashed under her belly, and her feet kicked at the air like someone hanging from a branch. 'Mama, please let me go, please.'

'If you're going to throw away your dignity and allow just anyone to insult you like that, you'd be better off like your siblings. Understood?'

Lucy nodded violently, hoping that the torture would end. At last, her mother released her.

Looking out at the girl who had insulted Lucy, Edo ordered,

'Go now. I want to hear that bitch begging for mercy, and if you kill her you'll be clearing the village of trash anyway.'

Lucy set off after the girl and rained blows upon her, leaving no spot on her face unscathed by her nails. Edo heard the girl's cries for help and rushed to free her from Lucy's clutches, while Lucy heaved like an agitated buffalo. She created some distance between them and apologised to the girl's mother, who had also arrived on the scene. 'What's all this? Girls these days, I tell you!' Edo exclaimed and then shoved Lucy inside the hut, slamming the door behind her.

Edo lifted Lucy on her back like a newborn, and started singing a song that she had composed for her while she had been isolated in her dark hut. Edo danced and twirled with Lucy on her back, lifting up her own feet now and again, in the way a bull does before it charges.

You're my only girl, my special girl, my only girl,
There's nobody but you who lingers
The others I had were just bubbles
Popped by Death's long fingers.
They disappeared, never found —
Disappeared without a sound.
But you, my love, will remain a delight,
So beautiful and intangible in the morning light
Just like the dalaib palm fruit high above.
Death's fed up because it's you he'll love
He'll have to try hard to get you, my girl,
Edo's daughter, gem above all others — my strong,
tough pearl.

74

Edo rocked Lucy till she fell asleep on her back and let out a small sigh. Edo then laid her down to sleep on the reed mat, before lying down next to her, gently picking out the dead skin from under Lucy's fingernails — the skin of the girl Lucy had so ferociously attacked.

5

Lucy, her homesickness torrential, pulled the young girls to their mother's room and started singing Maria-Edo's song to them. She cried along with them until sleep overcame the children. She, too, soon fell asleep, seen off by Peter's words to Marco, 'Theresa's a bad woman. You two weren't even the reason I threw her out. For so long there have been so many reasons, but I've been patient. Today, when she dared to humiliate my dearest friend's wife in this way, I thought enough was enough.'

So this is the city, Lucy told herself the next morning. The men still beat their women, but just differently, and the women are lazy, avoid doing the housework, are afraid of motherhood, obsessed with money, jewellery and buying pots and pans.

The rest of the day was tinged with a film of melancholy; that evening, Lucy hugged the girls once more and fell asleep, while Marco and Peter readied themselves for a long night.

In the middle of the night, Marco carried Lucy back to their bed. She was almost folded into herself and Marco slotted himself in behind her, placing his palm on her taut globe of a belly, trying to fit his body into the spaces left by her on the bed. Bitter remorse coursed through him and he whispered in her ear, 'Forgive me, Lucy, forgive me, Edo.' He started to sob once more until sleep overtook him and he drifted off, exhausted.

As for Peter, he flopped down in the middle of his three girls and put his arms round the youngest. He stayed awake and waited for the sun to rise before making his way into the kitchen. It was the first time Lucy had ever slept in. By the time Lucy woke up, her face and feet were swollen, and he had already prepared tea for everyone. An uncomfortable, acidic taste lingered in her mouth. Upon seeing Peter, she felt lightheaded. She went back and shook Marco awake, 'This isn't right!'

'What?' he said sluggishly.

She gestured to the kitchen. 'Is he a she-man?'

Marco clicked his tongue and stifled his laughter. 'Please get those village ideas out of your head, Lucy, otherwise all you'll see are men you think are women.'

In her village, a she-man was a man who went to where food was prepared — a women-only area — and this was her only explanation for why Peter would be in the kitchen making tea.

She tugged at her lips, unconvinced, and didn't take a single sip of Peter's tea, avoiding his eyes the whole time.

The girls were happy with Lucy. They grew more lively

playing with her: she sewed dolls stuffed with cotton wool for them and braided the girls' hair into cornrows, the endings as straight as nails. She carried out her duties for Marco and Peter at the same time. That was when Marco noticed her talent for cooking. 'Wow, you're really good. Where did you learn how to do all this?'

'From Theresa and her neighbours.'

She saw his forehead crumple and his eyes fall to the ground, as if he was swallowing an insult.

'Won't you have a word with Peter about Theresa coming back?'

'Peter doesn't want to get into all that again.'

'I feel like I'm the reason she got kicked out.'

'Maybe you were just the straw that broke the camel's back. Peter did say he had plenty of other reasons. Leave it and give Peter time. What's more important, Lucy, is that you don't hide things from me. Don't leave me in the dark again like that, please.'

She cast her eyes downwards and nodded slowly.

Marco still worked on building sites — Peter had yet to find him another suitable job, hard as he had tried, speaking to numerous friends and contacts. But Marco was happy where he was and got used to the drudgery, while his muscles no longer felt like they were going to split apart and, on top of it all, he was learning something new.

Lucy felt her labour pains but she didn't know what they were and so ignored them. She cleaned the house, cooked, and gave the girls their baths. She then started to pace around the house until Marco finally came home, and as soon as he saw her, she started to cry. 'My belly hurts a lot. I feel like I need to poo but then nothing comes out. And then I just keep peeing on myself.'

Marco grew very worried, but aware of what was going on, was exhilarated at the same time. He scooped her up from the ground and placed her on the bed. Sweating profusely, he said, 'Lucy, I think the baby's coming.'

He kept pacing in and out of the house until Peter arrived. They swiftly got into Peter's car and rushed to the hospital downtown, having left the girls with a neighbour. Lucy was perplexed. She had never seen a woman about to give birth leave the house. *Maybe they don't think well of women giving birth at home*, she told herself.

The hospital was teeming with people, the hallways loud with moaning. She was sent to the delivery room, where women were yelling and biting down on pillows, and the cries of newborns abounded. She kept to herself, unmoving, and took in the scandal of it all — how could a woman scream during birth? Where she was from, it was a shameful thing to do — the pain of childbirth was part of the feminine mystique that should never be revealed. How could these city women call themselves women?

She stayed where she was while Marco and Peter went to buy some essentials. Her labour was long and the midwives in the room started to worry about this silent young girl, who looked so weak, but persevered until one of them decided to bring a specialist doctor to inspect her. When she saw the man enter the room, she grew terribly afraid and shook her head violently. 'Marco! Marco!' she shouted.

The doctor and the midwife tried to calm her down. Once she had quietened down, he examined her by inserting his fingers inside. Her eyes clouded over and she went back to the day when there had been a disastrous birth in the village, and the child had refused to come out of newly-wed Imura's belly, for whom it'd been her first pregnancy. The entirety of both her family and that of her husband's came to sprinkle blessed water on her, but it was all of no use. An old woman decided that a man must come and trample on Imura's belly to apply some pressure. The strongest of the men soon showed up and stood on her stomach with both feet; all the child could do was shoot out like a missile, alongside other unidentifiable objects. Everyone rejoiced at the child's arrival, but Imura kept on bleeding out until her tongue turned blue, her eyes turned completely milky and she died, pale as animal fat.

Lucy trembled in the presence of the towering doctor. He left the room to call Marco over and tell him that because his wife was so young a caesarean would be necessary. But Marco staunchly refused, saying that Lucy just needed more time. He knew she was young, but she was also ready for motherhood and everything it meant, both the highs and the lows.

While the doctor was talking with Marco and Peter, Lucy appeared at the door of the delivery room in a hospital sheet, tied like a laweh as the grandmothers did in her village: a knot resembling a rose on her left shoulder, with her arms exposed, and the rest draped over her body. Marco had never before seen her so weak, and yet so mature — the pain had made her age years in a matter of hours. Marco and Peter strode swiftly towards her. She saw the alarm in their eyes. When they were close enough, she whispered, trying to breathe through the atrocious pain, 'Theresa. You've got to bring Theresa. She must still be angry. And my baby is stuck. Please, bring her here.'

'But Lucy...' Peter protested.

'Just go,' she interrupted. She took a few short breaths. 'All this anger has got to stop. I can't go on like this. Help me. I'm going to die at this rate.' Marco grew even more anxious and started to dab at his wet cheeks. He took Lucy back into the room. When he returned to the corridor, Peter was nowhere to be found. Heavy, dark hours passed as Lucy grew weaker and weaker. The doctor was alarmed by the fact that she hadn't screamed once, so he decided to take her to the operating theatre immediately. On the way there, Theresa appeared with Peter and approached Lucy. Crying and swearing upon her daughters, she spluttered, 'I don't have anything against you, Lucy, I need to ask you for forgiveness and apologise for all I've done. Forgive me, Marco, forgive me, Peter.' Then she fell to her knees, sobbing bitterly.

'Bring some water,' Lucy told Marco. 'All of you should spit in it, and then sprinkle me with it, just like we do back home. We're in the city, but there are still so many things that tie us back to our ancestors and our village. I need your blessings, all of you. Evil, curses and black magic don't stop in cities, they can catch us wherever we go.' Marco did as requested and finished sprinkling the water under the watchful eye of the doctor, who was anxiously taking in all of these rituals whilst counting every minute that passed. Finally, Lucy made it to the operating theatre, and behind her features contorted in pain, everyone noticed her ease — she had got what she wanted and what happened next didn't mean a thing to her.

Inside the operating room, the lights blinded Lucy and then her mind went blank. Only hours later did Maria-

Edo's voice call out to her, telling Lucy to get up and offer her granddaughter her breast. When Lucy's eyes fluttered open momentarily, she spotted the massive doctor who she'd thought was going to trample her belly with his feet. He roused her with some soft taps to her cheeks, and once she'd opened her eyes fully, she saw a baby girl screaming insistently in her arms, and everyone beaming at her: the doctor, Marco, Peter and Theresa. Letting out a long ringing trilling that tore through the sky, Theresa started to distribute sweets to all present.

Lucy was wearing new clothes with a giant red rose print, and her daughter was wrapped up in a white blanket, like a face peeking out from the clouds.

The best thing was that the family were all together once again, and Theresa was noticeably different. Everyone was happy: Peter, Marco, the daughters. The neighbours brought Lucy hot drinks and Theresa treated her like a real sister this time round, assuaging any feelings of guilt.

Lucy knew that Theresa had gone through some difficult times, because the worst thing for any mother is to be kept from her children — that's what she thought while she pulled Maria-Edo, her little girl, closer to her breast, which was gushing out milk, and splattered her little face with white milky drops; Maria-Edo sucked greedily, her eyes closed. Lucy became a mother with plenty of milk, her breasts swollen, leaking in rivulets whenever she heard her daughter scream. Lucy felt fully mature, that she'd been born again, and she sensed motherhood coursing through her bones; the only thing that irked her was the smell of her milk, redolent of chicken entrails, soaking her clothes.

Theresa tried to lessen the raw smell with incense or strong perfumes that the market women had made, but it just caused Maria-Edo to sneeze and break out in a rash. Theresa tried washing Lucy's clothes with fragrant soap, but it was no use, so she then gave Lucy a sort of sling made of two rags to stop the milk flowing out, but it just left Lucy in pain, her breasts like rocks. She would then yelp when Maria-Edo started to suck, and so she and Theresa agreed to leave things as they were. Lucy didn't want to go against the natural way of things; it would always be a sign of bad things to come, as her mother used to say.

During these times when her breasts would produce more than her daughter needed, Lucy would get a basin that she would lean over and let her milk thread its way down like streams until it stopped on its own. She'd then ask Theresa's eldest daughter to water the scrawny tree outside in front of the house with her surplus milk. They all got used to the smell of chicken entrails.

Lucy would rock her baby to sleep with a song that she had composed:

> *I see my daughter, I see my mother,*
> *I see my sister, Edo, Edo*
> *I'm no longer a waif, I feel so safe*
> *I'm not alone, not going solo.*
> *Listen to your father calling, Edo*
> *Listen to his lament*
> *He's too tired and he's too busy*
> *To build you a home*
> *So here I am, mother, my shining light*

I'm bringing my brothers and sisters out of the night
Please forgive the Lord — he's been good to me
He's given me you again, beautiful baby.

She would repeat the song so often that everyone in the house learnt it, and even Theresa's daughters would rock their dolls to sleep with it. Lucy would talk to her daughter in the language of her mothers in the village, and tell her stories of a faraway village swimming in greenery, a place where death, like life, was a cause for celebration for those who danced, their cheeks clothed in tears borne of an eternal parting from beloved ones.

6

The way Lucy was shooting up reminded me of a climbing plant. Even after our third child, she kept getting taller until she was nearly my height. She took all the changes happening to her body in her stride, as if they were as normal and temporary as could be, like any other being growing and reaching its eventual desired perfection: she grew heavier without growing flabby, and her hair shot skywards — the shape of a leafy tree — never drooping to her shoulders. Her skin remained soft and dark, her hair unruly night-black and coarse. Every two weeks, she would try to tame her hair with a comb, her wide eyes guarded by thick eyebrows, her short lashes curled in a come-hither stance, her laughter like pearls lighting up my world.

Lucy's eyes never lost that glint of surprise and keenness that marked villagers visiting the city. She still spoke loudly as if addressing someone two fields over. She was an overgrown forest; sure, a paved road had been laid through it, but her innocent playfulness and mystique were as ripe as ever, and so we let her be. She wore city clothes and ate city food — actually, she was really good at making all kinds of food and treated our children as tenderly and patiently as any city woman would, just like Theresa did, but she was still as loud as ever, always saying what was on her mind, still taken aback even by things she had seen before.

Whenever her belly emptied, she would fall pregnant again, giving birth to three children in two and a half years, with just a few months in-between. What's strange is that she never seemed in pain — she'd just give birth to them as if relieving herself from a heavy meal, always with her head held high. The odd smell of her milk became just another member of the household.

At that time, I still hadn't been able to hold down a job, jumping from building worker to conductor in the big yellow Abu Rajila buses; sometimes I worked as a cleaner or server in one of the bars in the large souk. Peter still put a roof over our heads, and we lived in his home, becoming a real family, one with strong ties, especially after that whole episode between Theresa and Lucy that made us all cry like children.

What happened reordered both us and our lives in an astonishing way, and we all just felt so grateful: Theresa had been transformed into a kind woman, tender in fact, and she liked the new her just as much as we all did. She really was wonderful, a true sister to us both. Lucy was in her own orbit of pregnancy and breastfeeding. Before any child could turn one year old, the cycle would start again. No one could believe it when her stomach announced yet another child on the horizon. Sometimes I got the feeling she was somehow impregnating herself, like a primordial lifeform, as if she were stuck in eternal motherhood, always rocking the newborns to sleep with fresh songs she had come up with for each child, wiping their bottoms, lapping up their leftovers with love. The scrawny tree outside that Lucy had named Anim kept sucking up her surplus milk. Anim's trunk swelled.

Peter's house was a large guesthouse of sorts: family, friends, acquaintances, university students and those who had come to Khartoum in need of medical treatment all came to stay for as long as they liked, before departing, leaving us fixed in place, no different from the walls, rooms or the large hosh in the middle of the house.

Peter never grumbled or got frustrated with it all; he was open-hearted like a father, happy to make everyone else feel safe and content. That's what he'd always say during our heart-to-hearts, far away from the chatter of guests and the noise of the women and children, especially when he sensed that I felt less than him — without a steady job I couldn't move my family into our own home; meanwhile, Lucy had overrun their home with our children.

'Marco,' he'd say, 'you're only looking at this from a financial perspective. You've got to know that with you around, I'm at ease. A man needs another man next to him, and you, yes, you're the one I've chosen. As fate would have it, we're both alone in this world, without family, so you're my brother and that's all I want. Even if we didn't come from the same womb, this whole world is one large womb, and all of us in it are family.'

I tried to convince him otherwise. 'But Peter, some things have to be said: this family is only going to get bigger and then it will be even harder to stay on top of things. I know you're understanding, but—'

He cut me off. 'Let's cross that bridge when we come to it.' He reassured me, 'If you're still worried about it, I'll keep on helping you look for a job.'

He was always so resolute and decisive, without a second thought, like any soldier used to giving orders and taking decisions at short notice. When he stretched, reaching out his arms and legs, yawning in a forced manner, it was very clear the conversation was over. I sat uncomfortably in my silence. Peter tried to treat us differently from his subordinate soldiers, making it seem like he wasn't imposing any ideas or opinions on us, but in the end, he always got what he wanted.

He liked everything to have its place and time, even chaos itself; he wanted it to have order, even though his life seemed to be characterised by confusion, with the ups and downs of the temporary house guests coming and going, and his lasting friendships increasing in number each day, especially among his military officer peers, as well as some of the soldiers, and a few women. But he always had his own space, an isolated room where no one else was allowed in; Theresa only went in to tidy up. We called it the Control Room, never knowing what was inside, until the day some military men stormed in to search for evidence that Peter was a spy for the Southern rebels.

It was a truly unusual room: everything in it pointed to a different stage of Peter's life and its upheavals, the history of a person laid out in the small possessions he'd collected with the utmost care. Now, Theresa spent most of her time in that room, waiting for her husband to come back wearing his smart military uniform, sharp-edged after being meticulously ironed by her, an officer's wife, practised at preparing everything with precision and order: washing laundry perfectly; hanging shirts on the line by their collars in such a way that they wouldn't wrinkle; ironing with such focus that no crease would appear, creating razor-sharp lines with the iron; shining shoes with sharp-smelling polish until she could see her face in them; attaching the medals to the pocket and collar; and finishing with the shoulder lapels studded with stars and two overlapping swords; all this in addition to waking up before the rooster crowed to prepare the hot water for his bath in wintertime. She was so rigorously trained that she grew to know in all senses of the word what being well-groomed meant to a serious and unstintingly loyal soldier, committed to the military way of life.

Sometimes, when we'd had one too many beers or too much wine, Peter would become fragile and delicate, tears springing to his eyes without warning. He would become like a child, taking off his military uniform and seizing the opportunity to be vulnerable, to feel, allowing himself to be supported by others and held in their arms. I was the only one lucky enough to know this child hidden behind his hard shell. So many times, he'd pull me along for the adventure of going back to his childhood, memories crashing over us like waves: how he'd grown up without a father, how his mother had left him in the care of a trader who would then take him on his travels into the unknown, how Peter had never stopped searching for his father who sat rotting in some far-off prison.

In those moments Peter would ask himself, 'What kind of mother does that? How could she?'

'We don't know why, Peter, but she probably had a good reason.'

'Maybe,' he would reply, slurping at the dregs of his drink.

I knew this topic was painful for him, and the conversation, after having covered so much ground, would abruptly halt there, the way a vehicle does with a sudden puncture, right at the peak of an arched bridge.

One time, trying to cheer him up, I suggested, 'So many mothers give their children up in far more cruel and dangerous ways, because they believe they're giving them a better future, like Moses' mother who left her baby on the river.'

'Well, my mother's no saint.' He exchanged a knowing look with me. 'And I'm no prophet.'

'All mothers are saints, to some degree, but most of them are unlucky — since God stopped sending prophets, they have to give birth to ordinary humans.'

'I suppose God didn't really have anything left to say,' Peter mused.

'I disagree, God speaks to us every day, one way or another. There are unofficial prophets that God speaks through, but they're not your typical worn-out sandal-wearing, ragged type, living through hardship, seen as pariahs for their noble values by their societies, which then crush them and spit them out without mercy. These unofficial prophets are probably like you and me, men who commit sins wilfully and feel sorry the next day.

'People these days aren't simpleminded, they're not tempted by the idea of heaven or threatened by the flames of hell — what they really need is an alternative prophet. A musician — Bob Marley, for example — would actually be perfect. His songs speak to the heart and the soul. Someone God hasn't necessarily sent in his name, but still an individual who is set apart, with the world's attention on all that they do. But sadly, most of the time, because musicians have so much power and influence, their lives go down a dark path.'

'Be careful, Marco. That kind of talk can get you stoned or your head lopped off.'

We laughed so hard our eyes streamed; we just kept singing along to Bob Marley's voice flowing from the stereo next to Peter. He got up and started swaying back and forth, swinging his imaginary locks. I just danced sitting down and slow-clapped along, worried that I'd had too many drinks and would probably fall flat on the floor, or that my head would crash into the furniture.

Peter had been raised by a well-off trader who used to work in the South, and he remembered when his mother had brought him to that trader as a young boy, nearly a teenager really, in the afternoons after school, to learn a new skill and contribute to his upkeep. Apparently, his mother had been a beautiful woman, with dark brown skin and an eye-catching figure. His father had been arrested along with others and deported, dumped in prisons in the North. It all began with a soldier breaking the rules by dancing naked in front of his northern commander, something which was widely accepted in his village. Southerners grew angry that those people, the Northerners, had forced them to change their ways. Peter's father was accused of having been involved in the massacre of northern civilians: traders and teachers stationed in the South.

Other rumours of Northerners mistreating their southern neighbours gained momentum, embittering people and fuelling them to fight back against the miserable conditions in their distant villages.

Peter's father was imprisoned, leaving a kicking fruit in Peter's mother's belly. She waited for him for several years, and during that time she was branded with many inaccurate names — no one knew anymore whether she was a wife, widow or divorced. Until the trader started to woo her, she had been shrivelling up like a once-tasty mango, neglected and decaying, her spirit and body eaten away from the inside. And so she and this trader formed a relationship that didn't last under those circumstances; their relationship was described as an unnatural demonic plant that grew only between executioner and victim, where the North Sudanese were seen as slave traders, murderers and exploiters of wealth, inheriting the mantle of the British and continuing their enslavement of Southerners while all the time belittling them. Society just wasn't ready for any confusing relationships that might lessen their feelings of hatred and chagrin towards a people who had historically been their enemies. And so Peter's mother was endlessly harassed, branded a whore who slept with Arabs and was thrown out of her village, never to be allowed to return.

At the time, and in complete secret, Peter's mother had entrusted her only son to Abdelsalaam the trader and expressed her wish that he would help her son find his father, who'd been discarded in some prison in a city by the sea — that's what she had heard anyway. She'd also heard that his father was serving out his sentence by hacking away at salt formations on the shores of the Red Sea. Abdelsalaam, fearing for his own safety and that someone might betray him, had had enough of the South, when his own beloved disappeared under mysterious circumstances, and he ended his trading and brought Peter with him to the North. His mind still held the memory of the massacre ignited by the southern soldiers. Peter was an intelligent young boy, and Abdelsalaam treated him as his son, as if he were his right hand, trusting Peter with his money, his home and his four daughters.

At the threshold of manhood, Peter joined the army and was one of the most exceptional officers who had graduated from the Military Academy. Honours decorated his uniform and he had his picture taken with the president; it was this very photo that Theresa consoled herself with during the whole time Peter went missing.

One day, we had been eating our lunch in silence, when Peter asked me to meet a friend of his to talk about getting a stable job for me. I was so elated that I lost my appetite. We stepped out, cutting across streets, giving way to a car here and there, and crossed a metal bridge to the other side. A little bit further on, we stopped in front of one of the city's fanciest multistorey hotels, and when I raised my head, the name Zanobia, written in an elegant font and illuminated by lights pointing in various directions, stared down at me from the third floor. The jasmine bushes and countless flower pots that lined the entrance had clearly received the utmost care, watered regularly and pruned as necessary. Once inside, there was an enormous swimming pool that had stolen its blueness from the sky above, with small clouds floating here and there.

We found a place to sit in a peaceful saqifa, the open-air structure bringing a sense of calmness to our inner selves.

There were a few White customers here and there, as well as other patrons lounging poolside ready to slip in for a swim, and lovers in far-off corners about to exchange a kiss.

Peter's friend took hold of us warmly in greeting; he was of average height, his posture was upright like every officer, his skin almost yellow, wide eyes of a strange colour framed by swollen eyelids, large nose positioned above a mouth made of thick lips, hair coarse and close-cut. All reminders of the bloody battlefields that several dynasties had tread: Africans, Arabs and Turks.

He shook our hands roughly, though his palms were as soft as a painter's. A cloud of cologne hung in the air. He was clad in a white jalabiya, with an embroidered shawl flung over one shoulder.

He brought out a golden Benson cigarette packet, pulled one out with his full lips, then held out the packet to us, two cigarettes peeping out from tight rows. We thanked him for his generosity. He spoke about the hotel and how he was a partner of one of the Greek investors who helped the hotel find its footing. Peter's friend made sure to maintain a high quality of service and to keep pace with customers' appetites for everything new and fashionable.

Puffing the smoke from his cigarette, he turned to me and asked about my qualifications — how good was my English? Then shortly after, a man with sun-kissed skin swooped down on us, his whiteness now a glowing brass. He was small and playful, wearing shorts that revealed his knees like a schoolboy, with a palm frond hat shading his face that made him look more like a fisherman than an investor. Peter's friend spoke. 'This is my partner Gerges Simon, the Greek who just can't wait to be African. He's hoping if he stays out in the sun long enough, he'll turn black.'

I chuckled, and then in a matter of minutes my future was secured. 'The work needs someone with good English; a people person. A smile is key,' Gerges began. 'I hope you'll be able to fill Jon's shoes. The lad packed his bags and went back to Greece. Family needed him. His old man got diagnosed with Alzheimer's and was just stuck in the past, you know. Wouldn't have needed anyone otherwise. Looks like luck's on your side, Marco.' And with that, he got up and ordered a waiter to bring us the finest wine in the hotel, 'To toast the new employee,' he added, smiling tightly without revealing his teeth.

The next day, I began work as the concierge at the Zanobia Hotel, a grand stone building on El-Gamhuriya Avenue. My desk faced a small statue of a bare-chested Zeus on his throne as he watched everyone with a stony stare, a sceptre in one hand and a fluttering angel about to place a wreath on his head in the other. El-Gamhuriya Avenue was one of Khartoum's liveliest streets, with distinguished long-standing buildings, like the King Farouq mosque, lining either side, in addition to high-end stores; a street that oozed elegance and sophistication, its trendsetters obsessed with British fashion houses, Parisian perfumes and sumptuous Italian footwear. Every day I arrived at this avenue that never slept. The Zanobia was known for its food: dolmas, rice-stuffed grape leaf rolls seasoned with herbs; a spicy sausage dish called loukaniko; moussaka; and who could forget their desserts, served during parties for the Greek community and for other guests every weekend!

My task was to record guest information and keep their

keys on the board with all the room numbers written on it. It hung behind me at the reception desk. I was in constant contact with the room service desk to ensure complete comfort for the guests: tourists; businessmen; and adventurers who spent most of their time wandering the city, visiting the most important landmarks, snapping photos as mementos of the Al-Muqrin shore where the Blue Nile ran down from the Ethiopian highlands and the White Nile flowed from Lake Victoria, meeting to unite as one powerful river, one of the longest and the sweetest-tasting in the world, the mighty Nile.

On that day, the day I started my new job, I felt a rush of joy and tears in my eyes. I didn't know how to thank Peter for all this. He sensed me fighting back the tears and looked at me as a stern father would — no man does this in front of foreigners, is what his face said.

I took out a pineapple-coloured handkerchief recently embroidered by Lucy, its edges carved out into small waves of the same size, on each corner a red rose whose petals had started to fall, which swam in the deep yellow of the handkerchief. Drying my tears, I stayed up until midnight drinking too much Scotch. I got drunk to the melodies of George McCrae, warbling *Rock your Baby*. Some attractive girls danced with each other, their hairdos reaching for the ceiling, wearing sleeveless short dresses, their captivating legs and fleshy, firm arms making us truly believe in the God who created such beauty. An older White woman swayed with me, clinging to my shirt collar, searching for my mouth so she could brush it with her lips, between which were her dentures. Beautiful teeth undoubtedly, but dead. Peter gracefully saved me from her by muttering, 'Someone is waiting for him at home for that, you cradle-snatcher. You're lucky she's not here or she'd poke your eyes out.'

As we left, it felt like the whole world was celebrating with me. Sounds of music, mostly jazz, coming from different establishments, two drunk men weaving about as the wine started to play with their minds, lovers whispering, obscene laughter from prostitutes in the company of wealthy men, cinemagoers just having watched John Travolta's *Saturday Night Fever* at the Coliseum theatre, employees, couples and families, the notes of Abba songs still ringing in their ears, all spreading out under the starlit sky, with its shadowy clusters like clouds floating high and cheerful.

Khartoum was calm with its clean, wide streets. The city spread out its arms to embrace me. The whole way home, I never got tired of thanking Peter and started crying again. 'You're my brother,' I said. 'You're really my brother. Did you know that? We're family, Peter.' Noisily, I blew my nose into the soft handkerchief, my tears coming hot and fast. I just kept repeating, 'You're my brother, you're my brother,' until Peter cut me off, irritated.

'Marco, enough. You've had too much to drink.'

My voice was faint by this point. 'Alright, alright. I'll shut up, but only because you're my brother. But if you asked me to jump off from this bridge into the river below, I'd do it. I'll owe you for the rest of my life. Thank you, my brother. Don't ever forget we're family. You're all I have.'

We made our way over the bridge, which looked like the rib of a giant that had died a thousand years ago and laid down to rest on the banks of the Blue Nile.

Once we were back and had made our way through the

front door to the hosh, we found everyone sleeping, except for Lucy. Our baby was shrieking, unable to sleep. Singing and rocking him had been of no use. The baby kept crying even when she carried him on her back. She gave the child her breast but he refused to feed. Lucy started to cry as well. She then remembered how she used to improvise when taking care of other people's children back home in the village. To make him laugh, she smiled widely at our son and played with him, blowing raspberries with her lips, opening her eyes as wide as they would go. But it didn't work. He kept screaming. Theresa came to sing to him as well, but it didn't help — they both were past exhausted. Theresa observed that our son's temperature was slightly high, but said it was nothing to worry about. When we walked further into the house, into the rooms themselves, Theresa came with us to escape the child's screams and to go back to sleep. 'Would you both like dinner?' she asked, her eyes heavy.

'No, thanks. You should sleep,' Peter responded, making his way to his room.

'What's wrong?' I asked Lucy.

'I don't know,' she responded tearfully. 'He's been at it for hours.'

Peter retraced his steps. 'We can take him to the doctor.'

'You've got to rest, Peter,' I countered. 'It doesn't seem that bad — I'll have a go.' I hugged both Lucy and my son and started singing a Bob Marley song. Bob, whom I'd proclaimed a prophet earlier that day. Whilst rubbing the baby's back with my hand and my cheek against the top of his head, I caught a whiff of something foul. My arm, on which his bottom was balanced, went from warm to hot. I chuckled. 'Seems like whatever was bothering him has come out.'

He calmed down and started sucking in gasps of air one after the other, interrupting his shrieking. Lucy sat there completely worn out, practically half-asleep, when I shared the news of my job. I told her how we were indebted to Peter and his family for the rest of our lives, and how I hoped she truly understood what I was saying. We both cried tears of joy, the air heavy with the strong smell our son had pushed out.

I gently placed him down in the cot and opened the window to let in the fresh breeze. The light from the full moon poured in and lit up Lucy's naked lower half. I drank in the image of her. My beautiful wife: a celestial body. She came apart in my hands like a seed that breaks through the earth to announce its existence and take part in soaking up the sun's rays with other living creatures. In moments like this, she was completely ready to make love as usual.

'But you're so tired, Lucy.'

'Since when has that stopped me?' She winked in the darkness. 'Come on then.'

The next thing I knew, she was glowing in my arms like an amber rosary. She lit up the room with a light that wasn't light, but instead an extension of shadows glittering in the darkness, like a being that had swallowed a lantern, which could have just been her lover's fantasy, the intoxication of wine playing with his mind. She grew full of life and gave off a fragrance reminding me of trees, the waves of scent that come one after another on an autumn day. An orchestra of fragrance from lives to come, forcefully announcing their hidden existence in a time and space beyond our bodies, our blood, our beating hearts. Soul-dwelling creatures for whom Lucy stood as a gateway to pass into the world. Each time, I got lost in the details of this wild girl who grew each day like a forgotten forest, her flavour getting stronger with each stage of maturity. I hunt for her in the various timings of her peaks. Her body speaks to me from the depths. She manoeuvres me through her wet, dangerously deep curves. I am like a child chasing a butterfly, not knowing where I'll end up: in a swamp haunted by spirits. Like a knight and his horse, we rise up and descend together crazily — our limbs scattered in the spaces between our souls. We catch our breaths in the long moments of drowning, making death as beautiful as a wish about to come true.

We cried and laughed in whispers so that we wouldn't wake the children, and then started once more, lasting till daybreak. I was certain that Lucy had now conceived our fourth child that night. This was what it was like being married to fertility.

It was a different kind of morning. My head was heavy from drinking too much, but my soul was light, like it had sprouted feathers. Deep down, I was excited as I'd never been before — all thanks to Peter, of course. He kept acting as though he hadn't done a thing. He asked after our son, but Lucy assured him he was well and had slept through the night — after I had sung him a song in a language she found strange — and that the pressure in his stomach had been released.

Somewhat relieved, Peter nodded and turned towards me, 'Well, haven't you scrubbed up nicely! Are you ready to get to work? I can drop you off on the way.' I was in my best clothes: a white shirt with blue horizontal stripes, tucked into black trousers fitted at the waist and flared in the legs, concealing my shiny shoes. I topped it all off with a light brown belt the same colour as my shoes; it had an enormous iron buckle the shape of two dragons breathing fire mid-combat.

Lucy had worn her hair as a large black globe, and had put on some strong perfume.

Peter and I made our way to the door. Theresa's, Lucy's and the children's eyes all glittered. They looked exactly how I felt.

In the evening, we clustered round the dinner table. I was the only chatty one, going on about my new job, while the rest pounced on the three large, hot, fried fish: the white tender flesh, split into two large pieces, was like an ancient prophet's sandals. They chewed away, savouring their fish from the Nile, and gave me looks now and again, encouraging me to go on.

Lucy was happily feeding the children the fish; she had made sure there were no bones in it. Theresa, on the other hand, ate silently and cradled my son in her lap.

Peter spoke. 'Tomorrow, we should stop by the school and enrol the children for this year. What do you think?'

Pausing mid-swallow, I managed to get out, 'Great idea.'

Lucy's eyeballs nearly popped out at me, two steps behind as usual. I nodded, letting her know that I'd explain things to her afterwards. As soon as we were alone, her voice broke with emotion. 'Where are you taking my children?'

'To school, Lucy. They've got to learn.'

Straightening the beds out for us to sleep on, she grumbled, 'Is that really necessary? I never went, and I turned out fine.'

'Times have changed, Lucy. We've got to prepare our children for the society they'll live in. A society that doesn't treat illiterate people kindly. They'll end up poor and will be humiliated over and over again. Do you want our children to end up like that?'

She forcefully shook her head, and then added, giving in, 'Where is this school?'

'We'll find a suitable one. I'll take care of it.' We lay down on the beds.

'Will I see them again?'

I clamped my lips together. 'They'll just go for a couple of hours each day and then come back home. It's not that complicated.'

'Will they be taught by someone like my old *cheachar*? She'd beat the children till their noses bled, and shove them out of the school with one tight slap.'

'Like your old teacher? I doubt it.'

She sighed, unconvinced. My clipped answers, which weren't one hundred percent confident, didn't help. Instead, I was focused on my penis which was growing firm against her thigh. I started to caress her but she gently pushed me away and turned to face the wall instead. I embraced her from behind and tried to pacify her, but it seemed she stayed wide awake till daybreak.

At the breakfast table, I winked at Peter as I drank my tea and let him know that Lucy hadn't slept, having worked herself up into a state. Peter contemplated the steam rising from his cup as if there was someone down at the bottom having a smoke.

'She's really attached to them, isn't she? She's even worried Theresa is competing with her for their affection. What a keen motherly instinct she has!'

I felt the spectre of Peter's mother pass before his eyes as they stared at a single point on the ground. His mouth

102

was pinched.

Peter called out to Lucy. When she arrived, she stood at a distance like we were criminals. She tried to shrink away from our eyes, which were fixed on her. 'Your children won't be gone for long each day,' Peter started. 'They'll be back before you can even miss them. They'll be at the school that belongs to the church. The one we pray in every Sunday and on Christmas.'

Lucy tugged at her collar, her tone defensive. 'I swear on the one who created thunder, if a single hair on their heads is hurt, I'll beat everyone in my path — the nuns themselves won't be spared.'

I pressed my fist against my lips. 'Don't worry. They'll be fine.'

'Another thing,' she said, showing that it was inevitable she would relent after we'd stuck our noses in the matter, 'I don't want them becoming priests or one of those pathetic nuns, refusing marriage and pregnancy, burning with desire their whole lives, without being able to do anything about it. Even God himself doesn't like this foolishness; humans were created to make more humans. Every human has got to do what he was created for.'

'I'm with you, Lucy.' Peter chuckled. 'I promise that won't happen.'

Lucy, stooped over as if she had suddenly grown old, retraced her steps back to the verandah, and sat as usual on the wide bed, where she spent most of her time with the children, playing with them, feeding them and falling asleep between them after they had tired her out with their neverending demands and mischief. Lucy drew the kids — Rebecca and

Jena, Theresa's girls, and Maria and John, our older children closer to her — and hugged them for a long time and, for the first time, it seemed that she felt they had grown up. Theresa got them dressed in fresh-smelling clothes and shiny shoes, with socks that stretched up past their knees. 'Oh, you're looking so smart!' Lucy said, with tears in her eyes. 'I'll miss you all so much.'

Lucy fetched some water from the zeer clay pot and poured some into her mouth. She then spat over all the school-going children three times while she recited some tribal verses to combat any witchcraft against them, and then made the sign of the cross above their small heads whilst reciting The Lord's Prayer in her mother tongue. The children were standing with droplets of water on their faces that she had just sprayed, glistening like the petals of flowers that open up in the early hours in a film of morning dew.

When we came back with the children at the end of the day, we found Lucy slumped against the tree by the front door, her eyelids swollen, exhausted from not having eaten or drank anything since the morning. She even neglected our baby, who Theresa ended up taking care of while Lucy waited for the children to come back from school.

Lucy began to anxiously ask them if they had been harmed, whilst looking for any signs of bruising under their shirts and long milky-white socks, so she could charge to their school and exact revenge, but her search turned up nothing. When the children started chitter-chattering about their first day at school, each speaking over the others, she felt reassured that they'd had a good day.

She didn't get used to their affinity for school until two

weeks later, during which period she didn't speak to Peter or me, thinking we were hard-hearted for sending them away. Slowly, she began repeating the alphabet and numbers after the children, as well as the songs they brought home, suffusing her being with a new kind of happiness that finally allowed her to forgive us.

Lucy had had an appalling experience at her first and what actually ended up being her last day at school. She told me it had been traumatic because she had been slapped by her haughty teacher, whose hand was as rough and hard as a farmer's foot. Her teacher had always kept books tucked under her arm, strutting around like the queen of the universe. The kind of person, as they say back home, who wouldn't pass up the chance to crap on your head. She could even read the Bible and never let anybody forget the fact. Although, according to Lucy, she read it in such a stern way that it made the word of God into a stone difficult to swallow and digest; if we weren't such strong believers, Lucy told me, then we would have given up on God by now. Whichever verse this teacher would read, God hadn't intended it that way. 'Can you believe that she slapped me with all her might because I couldn't say the word *cheachar* in English? She said the word was shattered glass in my mouth. On that first day, I said it as quickly as I could to get rid of it, and the whole class burst into laughter, which is when she whacked me so hard that I couldn't hear anything for two days. After that, a green-yellowish liquid started to leak from my ear for a couple of weeks. By some miracle, I was healed after Mama Ilaygha poured the melted fat from a snake that she found coiled up under one of those giant merisa pots, in my ear. That slap sent me outside of the school walls, never to come back, and I never regretted it. And whenever I'd come across that evil woman who twisted the neck of God's words when reading the Bible, I'd spit the word that she slapped me for in her face, challenging her, until everyone else started calling her *cheachar*, too.

'If learning one single word made me deaf, I don't doubt that I would have ended up dead if I'd kept on going to that school to learn all the herds of ants that swarmed in the bellies of those books.'

And so that's why Lucy was in a panic when we packed the children off to that torture chamber, or so she called it.

Not wanting to disappoint Peter, I gave my work all the attention I could. His friend wouldn't regret employing me. I quickly fell in step with my colleagues, and established some decent friendships that made Gerges Simon compliment me and invite me over for a glass of bright red Cypriot sherry at the end of the day.

At the end of each week, I'd come home with arms full of food from the hotel, food prepared with secret mixtures that gave diners the satisfying feeling that it was the tastiest thing they would ever eat. The children really enjoyed the strange desserts and fruits, while Peter and I, of course, enjoyed the fine drinks, spending the long nights hanging out and letting off steam.

I felt such a sense of relief that I could now contribute towards the household expenses. This job had brought me stability and confidence — how demeaning it is to have to depend on others.

We threw ourselves into our new lives — I, at least, saw it that way, but I sometimes felt that Lucy's relentless nostalgia kept pulling her back to the village. She'd remember her mother and cry, or miss every tree and stone, as well as her other mothers and childhood friends. Theresa told me that on such days, Lucy would sing in such a homesick voice, bringing tears to even Theresa's eyes, prompting her to take her own walk down memory lane.

Nostalgia is the fuel of the heart. Nostalgia may be blanketed by the ashes of busyness, but it will never burn out. How easily a smell or a kind of weather or a person's face can suck us into the depths of memory, striking us at that very moment with joy or sadness, making us anticipate the coming of something joyful or disastrous, our hearts beating in a different way altogether.

Lucy isn't afraid of nostalgia in the least — she flows with it till the end, digging into its depths with the resolve of a hundred ants, creating a web of tunnels in which she hides her most intimate secrets, like a food store that can sustain her through the foreignness of any time or place.

The autumn season here in Khartoum keeps her awake, tormenting her. She returns to the village all at once; autumn is different here, significantly shorter — lacking, from her point of view. Raindrops usually fall lightly in Khartoum, without booming thunder, but that doesn't stop the rain from taking her back down South. She does as she likes down there and all we see is a faint smile that lets us know she is well.

Winter here is a harsh season, and Lucy feels that it repeatedly reminds her that she is in a land that isn't her own, a land so dry and naked, not like the cold in the village that comes after a season of heavy rain.

One time after we had shared an intimate night, she

announced, 'My mother's here!'

I panicked. 'What?'

'Keep it down — you'll scare her off.'

I gawked at the darkened room, and then squinted, trying to locate Maria-Edo's ghost in the pitch black.

'She helps me out with the children,' Lucy went on. 'Plays with them sometimes.'

I took a sharp breath.

'She doesn't speak, but I understand her. I think I'm the only one who sees her. The children did, too, when they were nursing. But now that they're older, they don't see her.'

I swallowed loudly. 'Is she here… right n-now?'

Lucy giggled. 'She just went through the wall. She doesn't want to see her son-in-law's cheeks while he's mounting her only daughter.' Once we were done, she slapped me lightly on my behind and pinched me like she did with our younger children.

I let out a tense laughter and pulled the blanket over my naked body, before realising how naïve I'd been for believing her. 'You're joking right, Lucy?'

Her head jerked. 'Have I ever lied to you?'

'No,' I said into the darkness, my eyes as wide as they would go.

'Then go to sleep,' she said, straightening her pillow.

I didn't sleep until the call rang out for dawn prayers. At that point, I dozed off and dreamt of Maria-Edo threatening to cut off my manhood if I hurt her daughter, saying how she knew that I had made love to her daughter a stone's throw away from her grave. She gave me a menacing look and then melted into the wall. I woke up short of breath.

After this dream of mine, Theresa confirmed to me that Lucy sometimes talked to someone that only she could see; how she became more reassured than she had been, and didn't worry about leaving the children alone. 'Haven't you seen that she's started taking more of an interest in herself? Taking baths? One day Lucy actually told me, "My mother keeps an eye on them."'

Maybe this is what explained the feeling I got when I held her because Lucy wasn't just Lucy on her own, she was a soul inhabited by a tribe of other souls: her mother, her dead siblings. An astonishing mix of innocence and wisdom that would shoot out like machine gun bullets. Her mothers in the village were full of life, dedicating their existence to their families and their tribe. Lucy was every tree she had ever climbed, every blade of grass that had ever bent under her bare feet; she was the thunder, rain and wind, the threads of sunshine when the clouds cleared; she was the fragrance of the soil and the fields while they waved, laden with grain. I sometimes feel that she's just too much for an ordinary man, that she's too much for one man, that her feminine waterfall might almost drown me. I'm just someone who has run away with her from the darkness of war and thrown her into the gloom of being away from home. Alienation and nostalgia make her shatter into many Lucys, their presence slowly fading away. For people like Lucy, the simple act of removing them from their home environment is an unforgivable sin. Her entire being belongs to her land and its people. Often, she travels far away, following the tunnels of her nostalgia into the depths of the villages that remain behind in the world just beyond those mountains. She only returns after the end of the short autumn in Khartoum, with its silent rains unaccompanied by the clamour of thunder or flashes of lightning. Silent rains without any roar, no water overflowing from the roof for weeks to become a hotbed for frogs and mosquitoes.

When Lucy comes back from her journey down memory lane and connects back to reality, she's more lively, radiant, like freshly watered grass. When she comes back to the house the home is joyful again, everyone laughs at her observations; she treats us to stories that are still soaked in the fragrance of the last autumn.

7

Little by little, the smell of Lucy's milk faded from the house until it disappeared altogether — or maybe we had just got too used to it. It took me back to those stuffy summer evenings by the sea when we lived near one of the ports; Peter's peripatetic way of life meant we would move from one state to the next, his mandatory military service taking us to all sorts of places. The smell disappeared altogether — I don't know if Peter even noticed. Of course not — he isn't one to care about such domestic details. Lucy had started bathing several times a day. Though her anxiety for her children's safety had eased somewhat, she'd still cry out through the whoosh of the shower, 'Theresa, is the baby crying? Is he hungry? Theresa! Has he pooed?' I'd be so preoccupied with this until she quickly darted out, her dress only partly over her head by the time she'd reached the hosh, unconcerned that she was half-naked.

I even wondered if she no longer believed what she had told me one day, about how a child recognised their mother by her scent. A scent that makes them feel safe and reduces their tearful episodes. All of that made sense, but then she went as far as to say that this maternal scent affirms the mother's presence not only to the child, but to any evil spirits prowling around — those of dead dogs, wild donkeys or crushed insects. Spirits that roam searching for a body to inhabit, because even spirits have to face homelessness. On the face of it, it's quite straightforward for them to take over a baby's tender body, because the child's spirit is as delicate and fragile as a sparrow's egg, making it easy to push the soul out. She went on to say how she didn't want any of her children being possessed by snakes, or even by lambs, as they'd be too meek for their own good. 'Don't you see the wicked people around you? It's all their mothers' fault. The switch happened and their innocent human spirits were shoved out, left to wander while another made itself at home. It all happened in the blink of an eye while their mothers were enjoying their soapy water in the shower.'

What it came down to was that she didn't want her smell to upset Peter. I heard them talking about it, arguing really, under the tree out front. It ended with Peter holing himself up in the Control Room. I tried eavesdropping on him from one of the windows, to make sure he was okay. Whenever he decides to squirrel himself away in that room, it frightens me. When he turns in on himself, I can't help but think that one day he's going to succumb to the foolishness of shooting himself with a gun.

The only thing that made my fear slither down a hole was

when Marco turned up — he was the only person who dared knock on that door and force Peter to come outside.

Lucy didn't bother herself with anything other than looking after the children; even my own children were under her spell. Of course, anything that went on that didn't have to do with the children would naturally be disregarded by her.

She confined herself to a harsh kind of perpetual motherhood in honour of her mother who had suffered the deaths of so many of her young, and had lived a kind of amputated motherhood till her brain matter started to decay — dementia, some said. Lucy would constantly remember how her mother had entrusted her with the mission of having Edo's children that had been devoured by death.

She no longer cared about herself; the whole time, she was either nursing one child, soothing another, combing the hair of this one, following that one into the bathroom to make sure his shit actually hit the hole in the ground, preparing food for so and so, or pouring a drink for another one. Then came the long hours of bathing them in the basin: yelping from the roughness of the loofah on their backs, and their eyes burning from the soap.

Whenever I told her to rest or have a quick break, she'd always have a ready excuse: He'll fall off the bed, she'd cry, or those two will get into a fight when I'm in the bathroom.

We naturally divided up all of the duties. She was the mother of nana and kaka and nunu — bye-byes, poo-poo, and yum-yum — and I was the big mother who'd spend most of the time cleaning and in the kitchen. We were a perfect pair.

I've been dazzled by her ever since her first day in this house when she woke me and I found everything spick and span, while she stood chewing away on a bitter neem twig, spitting out giant globs of saliva now and again. She kept on doing all the house chores until I took things one step too far, and it all came crashing down. Peter still hasn't forgiven me to this day and never misses an opportunity to make me feel bad about it. Now Lucy? She's blocked the whole episode out from her mind and heart. She has the memory of a child, forgiving to the point where you start to pity her. Marco didn't seem to replay the event much, considering it a lapse in judgement that could happen to anyone — one that left both him and me forever changed.

I've taught Lucy and she's taught me, I've supported her and she's supported me. I can truly say that, thanks to Lucy, I've been born again. She wakes up early and does what needs to be done without relying on anyone else, without grumbling, even though she's so much younger. She bustles about, her mother's sayings rolling off her tongue, 'Patience is a woman, and it's easy for an impatient woman to wake up with a moustache and a penis.'

Lucy taught me to be patient with my large household, which requires the effort of more than one woman to keep it as tidy as Peter likes. To be patient with Peter, who is obsessed with cleanliness and having everything in its place, who requires his military uniform to always be ready, and his shoes shined. To be patient with the children's endless demands, to be patient with having to let my pleasures fall by the wayside and dedicate myself to homemaking, to be patient with the pains of pregnancy, nursing and childcare.

With the arrival of each child, Lucy was reborn, becoming more feminine, more mature, more beautiful, and more experienced. Having said this, she also grew more anxious for each child, her heart leaping out of her chest whenever one screamed or cried — which was, most of the time, for no reason at all.

She didn't see any difference between her children, mine or even the neighbours'. She would nurse whoever was of nursing age, play with them, spinning tales, knitting together songs and dolls, speaking with the children in the language of the forest.

One day, my middle daughter Jena was bitten by an ant, and she came to me crying. Lucy spent the whole day stamping on ants and pouring boiling water on their ant hills, shaking her fist at them. I can't forget when the children were attacked by the dog next door. The moment they started screaming, Lucy was out the door like a shot, a thick stick in hand. She whacked the dog one good hard blow on his head, making his eyes go still and his tongue loll out the side of his mouth — he died on the spot. In the evening, Lucy dragged the corpse away so that it wouldn't decompose in front of the house; the neighbours didn't say a word. Even the dog's owner — who Marco apologised to by bringing an adorable puppy for him the next day from some they'd had at the hotel — never said anything to Lucy. With each child, her motherly instinct to protect just grew stronger, instincts so fierce she would lash out and attack whoever came near them.

Sometimes I try to speak to her about taking control of her over-the-top fears because all children are at risk of harming themselves in one way or another. That's how they discover and learn new things, after all.

'I can't bear it,' Lucy said one time. 'A current shoots

down my spine whenever a child is hurt.' Then she added, 'Don't you feel it, too?'

I was sceptical. 'Sometimes. But don't you think you're taking this all a bit too far?'

Her maternal instinct was so acute that she might have ended up killing a person one day, not just a dog. But in the children's eyes, Lucy was their hero. The day after she killed the dog, her conscience was weighing on her. 'Poor dog, maybe he was just being playful? The children must have teased him first. All their shouting really wasn't necessary; I wouldn't have lost control otherwise. Maybe it was just all fun and games? Poor dog.'

I just smiled and said that's what I meant by taking things too far.

Impatiently, dusting her hands off, she snapped, 'I'll take it easy next time.'

That was her way of ending a conversation she didn't want to get deeper into. I knew that I had to stop at some point before it turned into me trying to throw her out of the house, not wanting her or her children anymore, that she embarrassed us in front of the neighbours; it would all end up with her sitting under the tree outside on top of her massive metal trunk with all her belongings inside.

A deadly pregnancy crept up on me like an incurable disease. I can't begin to imagine what I would have done without Lucy. The colour of the meat hanging on the drying line in the hosh was enough to make my insides spill out of my mouth. Agitated, I would moan at Peter and pick fights with him for nothing and anything; even his cologne was enough to get me riled up. Smells are the enemy of pregnant women;

our noses become that much more sensitive to every smell, as far-reaching as elephant trunks.

Stupid neighbours! The leftovers in their pots were starting to go off, making what my stomach had just about managed to keep down jump into my mouth — bitter and thick. Everything did, really: the children, shoe polish, Peter's cologne when he'd pull me close and pin me to his broad chest. I couldn't help but hate him now; he made me so nauseous.

I craved the scent of soil freshly sprayed with water from the gutter, and when I got within range of it, I'd dig into the moist soil with my fingers like a chicken with its dark veined feet, and then stuff a handful of the earth into my mouth secretly, no different from anaemic children.

I folded into myself, to a frightening degree, always blocking my nostrils with a rag to keep out the smells, which curdled my insides. It was an illness, not a pregnancy by any stretch. I neglected my hair and my skin became rough as fish scales. I couldn't stand a comb raking its way through my hair or any butter on my skin, only water. At times, I'd gnaw on the fruit of the neem tree, sticky and yellowish, which would fall to the ground in the wind at night; this gave me some sugar.

Lucy commented one day, anxiously, 'You're going to starve to death.' She then made me a drink of cornmeal dough, which had been fermented for several days. She stewed it, without adding any sugar, on a low fire until it thickened and pleaded with me, her eyes shining, to sip just a little so I'd regain some strength.

'I know the child is stubborn, but you shouldn't starve it to death, too,' she muttered. 'Nothing works for nausea like something sour. Here, have some. Drink.' She knelt down and patted me tenderly, reminding me of my family who lived in the southwest of the country. I sank down to the ground at the memory of them, my cheeks hot with tears. I was going to die, so far away from them, and so alone.

I was spoiled, the youngest daughter of a well-off father who worked in the educational field, married to several women and living in a large house adjoined to a farm thick with banana and papaya trees, and pineapples. All his daughters had arranged marriages, their husbands carefully chosen; men who would treat my father's daughters with respect the way he had treated his three wives — never raising a hand to them. We, his daughters, had never experienced heartbreak. My father didn't believe love came out of nowhere — he said that kind of love was just a fixation, no different from when something in the market catches our eye and we scramble to buy it, only to find out later that it's doesn't really suit us and would maybe look better on someone else. He would say that people are like clothes, some may be too tight, some too loose, or some just in bad taste. Rushing into things usually ends in regret. If people allow such a small muscle the size of a child's fist to direct their life, then wolves will roam in their lives freely: it's rare for such spouses to die happy. Which was why a life partner must be chosen carefully by someone experienced, and there was no one more experienced than my nearly sixty-year-old father, having spent his years contemplating the earth's creatures and teaching generation after generation.

My father would always say, 'As strange as it is that we can hate someone who we've never met, isn't it stranger that we can love someone who we know nothing about? We humans, at the end of the day, are like animals, puffing out our chests and fluffing our feathers, just as roosters do when trying to attract hens — but it'll only end in disappointment .'

My marriage to Peter was my father's choice, because he knew what men were really made of, and Peter was a real man. Peter had been wandering the earth for long enough searching for a father he knew nothing about, and yet he continued to respect and admire the man who had raised him until he had made his own way in the world.

The marriage happened without any of Peter's family present; he claimed to be an orphan. A group of soldiers and his brigade commander stood in as his family and shouldered the obligations of the wedding. We had a loud party that started with traditional dancing to drum beats and local musical instruments, and ended with a jazz concert interspersed with bullets shot towards the sky, celebrating our union.

My mother was the middle wife, a position that she cleverly managed, bang in the middle of the bullying of the first wife who insisted that nothing ever happen until she gave the go-ahead, and the selfishness of the spoiled last and youngest wife who always felt everyone was plotting against her, lusting after her position as the most recent addition, and the love she received from her husband, who would always relent to satisfy her every desire.

When I told all this to Lucy, she commented, 'Whenever a new woman arrives, the first wife slowly becomes the second husband for the younger women. She turns into a man with large breasts and a sour expression, giving orders and watching everyone closely, waiting for them to make the smallest mistake so that she can then have a go at them. All that's left is for her to have sex with them.' We cackled at that till our sides hurt.

On a more serious note, I chipped in, 'She may even feel like these women are a new and improved version of her. Any mistake she makes is corrected in them, and all her inadequacies and her vulnerabilities are laid bare.'

I grew up in the care of a father who never let me want for anything. I was raised by three mothers, each of them keeping out of the other's way, as if they were on a sinking ship.

Brothers and sisters, too many to count, and a father who could grab the reins of any unruly situation with just a look. He insisted on us being educated to middle-school level. I was the only one among my sisters to go to secondary school. How I wished I could join my father in his educational career but then Peter suddenly appeared, a young officer dispatched to carry out his military service in the city of Wau.

Lucy pulled me out of my sea of memories, wiped away my hot tears and wrapped her arms around me, pouring me the bitter al-medeeda, taking care not to spill the hot cornmeal drink. She only let me be once the steel bowl was empty of the thick fermented mixture. I started to sweat profusely and slipped into a deep sleep, which camouflaged my nausea, allowing Lucy's drink to settle at the bottom of my stomach, fuelling me with energy.

Marco appeared anxious, and sat on the edge of the bed, attempting to feed me a piece of guava. I pushed his hand away gently but was consoled by his tenderness. As for Peter, he was keeping his distance so that I wouldn't throw up. Marco told me later on that Peter had felt insulted, and how strange he thought this pregnancy of mine — had this all really been happening? Even so, Peter still made sure to ask Lucy and

Marco, and even the children, how I was doing each day.

One evening, I found myself inside a car, my head resting on Marco's shoulder, Peter speeding along, his hands tightly gripping the wheel as we made our way to the Swiss doctor's clinic. That day my fatigue was so severe that I lost consciousness. But when I came to, the smell of fuel flooded my nostrils. I started to retch even though nothing was coming out.

We came back in the middle of the night armed with pills and pinkish solutions. We found Lucy in the middle of the house weeping like a wounded dog while the children slept. She grabbed me, held me in her arms and led me to lie down in my bed. Peter approached, his cologne travelling to my depths. I made a signal with my fingers in the air, as weak as I was, for him to go. I sensed that he was hurt and confused. Utterly drained, my eyes welling, I managed to tell him, 'Your cologne. It turns my stomach.'

He left silently, and Marco approached. He reassured Lucy I'd be okay.

Peter sat on a chair at a distance, staring at me while he downed glass after glass of whisky.

The following day, I was feeling more at ease and had regained some sense of control. The smells still swirled round in the air, but they were somewhat fainter. I asked Lucy to make me a meal without onions, meat or oil. What else could she cook except for the leaves from a bean plant with water and salt? She also poured in a little bit of water infused with ashes. It was the tastiest meal I'd ever had in my life, with a sour, firm porridge made of red millet.

At the end of the day, Marco bought Peter new pyjamas

and said decisively, in an audible whisper, that he shouldn't put
any cologne on these clothes. Peter looked at him gratefully
and went into the bathroom. Later on, he told me that he had
rinsed himself thoroughly, and then used the non-fragranced
soap — the kind that we use to wash our clothes — and then
washed himself again, getting rid of any lingering scents.
He wore the new pyjamas, and for the first time in months,
I smiled at him and allowed him to come within reach. He
caressed my sunken cheeks, saying in a half-swallowed voice,
'I've been so worried about you.'

I managed to croak, 'Your son is trying to kill me.'

He held my hand in his warm ones and whispered, 'I'll
have a word with him as soon as he's out of there.'

He was more sensitive than I'd ever seen him, as
transparent as someone who'd just descended from heaven. I
searched for myself in his eyes and his heartbeats, and found
myself there, the most important woman in his life. I felt the
fortresses crumble in my chest, and my heart, standing there
unarmed, slowly began to dance. I fell in love with Peter after
having had three of his children. My father's words about what
love is came back to me.

Whispering to each other, Peter laughed at himself
because all this time it had only been his cologne keeping us
apart, even though it was the very same cologne that had once
underpinned our most intimate moments.

He grinned. 'Are you sure you're pregnant?'

I pulled at my lip and shrugged my shoulders. Of course,
I knew I was, but it was difficult to put into words how I knew.
It would be difficult for him to understand, and more than
words, it was a feeling: the revulsion that hits us during most

of our pregnancies as women, a revulsion that wells up inside, showing itself as nausea and vomiting, which are revered by the general public. We women don't understand how everything appetising suddenly becomes disgusting, with us all the while preferring a clot of dirt gnashed between our teeth to a table of grilled meats and mahashi. A meal of plant leaves stewed in water and salt with freshly pounded red asida, like Lucy made, is tastier than lamb, fowl or any stuffed vegetables.

How can a woman hate her husband and the father of her children, and wish that he'd disappear? That was how I felt. It may differ from woman to woman, but it's a strange condition that we all find ourselves in. This is the bare minimum that can be said when a stranger is growing in the deepest part of ourselves, a strange being we call a child to make the situation tolerable. A being who imposes its control over our body, mood and whims; it's not mere flesh and blood and bones, but a possessor of the power of dreams; strength over our evil and not-so-evil impulses; the power of thought and ambition; the strength of defeat and breakdown; the power of joy, hope, intention; the strength of love and hatred; the powerful desire to come out into the world and occupy a place among the living. This is the strength of humankind.

I swallowed the pills to keep the waves of nausea at bay, and only ate what Lucy prepared for me: dishes that were ordinarily made in a hurry in her village, in their houses and on the farms. Dishes she had seen her mothers throw together, harvesting whatever their hands happened to chance upon: leaves or flowers from pumpkin vines, cassava plants and cowpea stalks. Her mothers would stew them on the flames of dried leaves and branches; in the time it took for them to chase away birds from the stalks of grain outside, the food would be ready. A flame gone as quick as it came, barely enough to boil the contents of the pot. When the greens were slightly wilted, Lucy would drain the green liquid and it would be ready to eat. The mothers said it was a dish that made one healthy, because the leaves were still alive, full of nutrients, and when they were eaten in that way, the leaves gave their strength and vitality to the one consuming it, allowing them to face life with less hardship and hassle.

The meal that Lucy prepared not only gave me strength but also nourished my spirit. Food without any additives, just water and salt; nourishment that had no add-ons like oil, onions or spices, that never used any other methods of cooking to enhance the flavour. This was exactly what I needed for this pregnancy that had taken me prisoner in my own body, leaving me to find refuge inside myself, searching for a safe place just to be at peace. I settle behind the glass pane of my soul so that if anything rubs up against me, I won't be affected: no colognes, no creams, meat, smells — just isolation and indifference sit with me, a beautiful condition of complete surrender to the power that occupies my body, a power I'm not strong enough to fight.

Poor Lucy! Since I fell sick, she's had even more to do: looking after the children, cleaning, cooking, welcoming our neighbours with her warm smile when they come to visit me and share their experiences of cravings, arms heavy with warm drinks. All the while I hole myself up in the furthest room possible so that nothing will trigger another spell of vomiting.

Marco was so helpful, and he even got some time off from work by telling them his sister was very ill and that he had to be by her side at this time. He'd play with the children and try to hand-feed me, all too aware of my disdain for eating, my eyes squeezed shut. I was constantly battling against this spirit of retching nestled deep within me. It would appear at any time and wouldn't depart until something settled at the bottom of my stomach. Marco took it upon himself to get Peter's uniform ready and shine his shoes.

As for Peter, he stood unsure in the middle of all this, like a child who had suddenly lost his mother, confused and disoriented. It's no wonder since he was a man who had always been treated like a prince by the women around him. Before she disappeared, his mother had always done everything for him. His mother and her daughters took care of everything in the home. I'm just as guilty of coddling him — everything and anything was ready for him before he even asked. In the kitchen, he was only good for the most basic of duties like boiling grains or beans: a task only fit for soldiers in those gruelling training camps outside the city.

In the evenings, Peter would wear pyjamas with no cologne, after having spent a long time in the bathroom removing any persisting smells so that I wouldn't swat him away like a fly. We'd whisper to each other like infatuated lovers, those who had just bared themselves to one another, till I'd fall asleep in his arms like a child — that was all that I needed some days.

Despite the age gap between us, Lucy was my friend and hero. She was as experienced as a grandmother and called upon all of the lessons she had learnt in the village to save me. Lucy, who radiated life and unconditional love.

I never saw Lucy go through the exhaustion I suffered

in pregnancy; she was a one-of-a-kind woman, enduring an overwhelming motherhood without ever seeming overburdened. The pain that I was in didn't seem to touch her at all! Or so I thought.

Peter, Lucy and Marco... was it some kind of coincidence that they found themselves alone in this world, with fraying threads to the past and their families? They were like glass beads whose thread had come apart, and now they found themselves surrounding me, focused on me. I was so grateful.

Thanks to the Swiss doctor's pills, the nausea receded, and I started to get better with each passing day. I put the rag I'd use to block my nose to one side, but I still breathed in anxiously, fearful of some new smell that might ram into me. I walked the way one does on ground covered with broken glass.

My ribs hurt from how much I'd been vomiting, and I felt pricks on both sides of my back from how long I'd been lying down. But then I felt an ease wash over me, a sort of quenching of my thirst, as if a river had burst its banks within me, flooding my veins with life.

I breathed in the invigorating scent of soil and felt my mouth water. I hoisted myself up into a sitting position. The whole room was spinning. My breath was laboured. I almost gave in and flopped back down, but there was a pressing need to eat the soil that kept calling out to me so insistently. I put my feet on the floor and stood up, holding the bedpost for support. I turned my focus to the hosh; Marco was spraying the ground with the python olive-coloured hose. I set off, propping myself against the walls and the door. I managed to situate myself in Marco's eyeline, but he didn't move a muscle. He just smiled and kept on watering the ground, rolling up his trousers and releasing that fragrance that had kept me alive the past two months.

I was no different from a corpse who had just left their grave. The sun cast my shadow before me, hair that hadn't had a comb run through it or been touched by any wax, standing up on end like a tree unpruned. My body thin, resisting the dizziness I felt.

I squatted, resting my elbows on my thighs — like we do in the bathroom — and started to claw at the soil. Marco brought me a stool, which I sat on with some effort. I then continued digging and shovelling the brown matter into my mouth like a worm sucking up dirt, till I had had my fill. Some gravel got caught in my teeth. Marco poured some water in front of me so I could wash my hands and rinse my mouth. I smiled feebly, thanking him for being my accomplice. The next thing I felt was water rushing down my back, pouring over my head, till I couldn't breathe. Through the whoosh of the water, I heard Lucy and the children laughing, while Marco howled. My entire body started to throb while my arms flailed in the air trying to get Marco to stop. But he was unaware of how much I was struggling; the water kept pouring over me while he was doubled over, amused.

When Peter came back from work, I was in the middle of everyone. Out in the hosh we took shelter in the shadow stretching out from the house. The sun slowly set behind the neighbouring homes. The house was thick with an atmosphere of kindred bonds, helping my spirit and body to enter into a stage of recovery that would be free of pain. Fluttering around me, Lucy, Marco and the children reminded me of butterflies.

We chatted while we nibbled on assorted fruit that Marco had chopped up. We chewed slowly as the smell of humidity wove itself through the place. Peter's face, creased by a smile, said it all. Lucy pulled my hair back into three large braids in the shape of watermelon slices, after having soaked the strands in sesame oil, and combing my hair into such a shape because any other style hurt my tender scalp.

Marco was always closest to me: supportive, kind, unafraid to express how he felt. The young age of his wife and their number of children made him into a mother, too. His active role in caring for us and the children would exasperate Peter, making him feel as if all his efforts to mould Marco into a 'man's man' had failed. Marco didn't fight any outpouring of his feelings that would burst through any appearance of manliness that he tried his best to maintain around Peter. Instead, he would get lost in the ridiculous demands of the children, cleaning their runny noses, and now he was using his fingers to wipe away the oil that managed to snake its way to my forehead and earlobes from my scalp after Lucy had tried to tame my hair.

Despite the smile on his face, I picked up on a tension in Peter's movements. I put it down to the recent security breaches, failed military coups and the increasing number of loyalists to certain political parties that were now in the army. Restlessness and dissatisfaction hung thick in the air. The failed military coups by officers ended with a good number of them being executed by order of the military courts, both publicly and in secret.

The current regime called such people enemies of the state, collaborators. They, however, called themselves revolutionaries, those who would set the country on the right path, and claimed that the current regime was the one who allowed corruption to thrive, dragging the country into the gutter. Some of the political parties sought help from army officers sympathetic to their cause as a pretext for seizing power from the ruling regime. But each time, the army itself stepped in to quell these attempts, and so many of their officers died.

Every time, I believed that Peter would never return, or that he would one day get caught up in these highly-dangerous political conspiracies, especially as, like everyone else, he was embittered from losing his friends and colleagues, one after the other. Though he was open-minded and saw himself as a son of the nation as a whole, he was always pigeonholed as a Southerner, someone who must support the Southern rebellion.

It was always an awkward situation to be in: where did his true loyalties lie? With the soldiers playing a part in the coups against the government? With those trying to keep the nation united? Peter's commander, under pressure from his peers, lost confidence in him, and soon enough Peter was isolated from the larger group. He was no longer entrusted with any tasks, and many files were taken away from him. Peter felt that he was under close surveillance, but by whom? No one knew.

Peter was filled with a deep sadness whose roots dug further into him each time he lost a close friend from either side. He was interrogated by both sides, each wanting to know the extent of his involvement in the others' activities.

Now he trusted no one and had started to treat everyone with the same suspicion, treading as cautiously as a tiger. He'd always say, 'Sometimes not taking a side can be deadly, especially in such volatile situations, because you're in the crosshairs of both camps.'

It was difficult for him to admit his apprehension about everything. I often had a sudden feeling that he was preparing me for a drastic situation — being abducted and executed like one of his friends, for instance, or joining the forces in the forest and fighting against the central government.

He didn't wade too far into the details of our family life, afraid that I wouldn't be able to carry on without him when the day finally arrived. He was afraid this absence would leave me in an inescapable dark hole of sorrow, and that's exactly what ended up happening. His sister Jalaa came by, and they both walked swiftly into *that* room. He came out afterwards without saying so much as goodbye to anyone; he only looked deeply into Marco's eyes, who responded with the slightest nod. Peter was never to be seen again. He left me at sea. Worry, confusion and sadness became my houseguests, gnawing at me. So often Peter would say that they got paid for promising to die whenever the nation required it. That the nation required them to live in the moment, but at the same time live a self-denying existence, without getting too attached to any earthly thing, left to wait for the bullet that would end everything in the blink of an eye. He'd gone on about how they had been prepared to protect human life, to protect living creatures, the sky, the land, the mountains — all these before themselves. He was convinced that death lay in wait around every corner: whether in the form of an enemy or a friend simply cleaning the mouth of a gun.

His Control Room was the sanctum for a man who expected the worst, at a difficult time when the army had made clear that its sole mission was no longer protecting the nation, but that it was rather aspiring for something higher. The glitter of power started to enflame the ambitions of the many who had party affiliations, and so senior officers who could easily round up their subordinates fell under stifling national security surveillance, to the point at which their every breath was recorded.

When, on occasion, I was allowed to clean that room, my curiosity to learn more about my husband got the better of me, as closed-off as he was inside his impenetrable oyster shell of privacy. Though crammed with objects, the room was still very much organised. There were books piled up to the ceiling, coloured folders shoulder to shoulder on the shelf; a makeshift archive for newspapers, including *Al-Ayyam* and the left-wing *Al-Sahafa*, and others, in English, as well as secret partisan newspapers carefully hidden away; a writing desk with old notebooks on it and multicoloured pens; scraps of paper with symbols I couldn't make out; open letters with stamps still on the envelopes; a wooden chest with many old and recent photos sitting on it, individual ones and group ones with a cross drawn on each of their foreheads to indicate they had died, even if they had been Muslim; unique paintings and sculptures from his travels around Sudan; the Bible and the Quran rubbing right up against each other, like two old friends in endless conversation.

A red phone sat on a raised wooden platform above the ground by three slender legs. I fought the urge to turn the number dial. A case of Scottish whisky and one of imported cognac from South Africa, all you needed was a few glasses. He would keep it aside for the friends who were high-ranking officers, influential businessmen, musicians, foreigners and sports stars.

On one of the blue walls was a long, slim, hunting rifle, almost animal-like, slithering across the surface. Next to it, the head of a wildebeest with its great horns branching out, and on the wall opposite, a blown-up, black-and-white picture of Peter from when he graduated from the Military Academy as a lieutenant, shaking the hand of the President of the Republic.

Once Peter sensed that I had been rifling through his things, he banned me from going in there, even when I made the excuse that his room had to be cleaned.

Worry radiated from his eyes, and his mind was always preoccupied with something or the other. What was going to happen to our family? We were in a city that seemed calm enough on the surface, but a riptide was building momentum underneath — and we would drown in its undertow.

He called out to Marco, his well of secrets. Marco rose from the hosh and popped a slice of mango, having already nibbled off a bit, into Lucy's mouth. He took one of the children off his lap and made his way to Peter's Control Room. My mind buzzed with what was happening behind that heavy wooden door, but the clamour of Lucy and the children celebrating my coming back to life made the men fade away, and I waited apprehensively for what would come forth from their emergency meeting.

8

Baba Abdelsalaam always said that everyone needs at least one friend they can rely on — even if you're the one who has to provide him the foundation he needs. I feel the same way. Baba raised me with care, not because I was the son of the woman he loved — the woman who, by associating with, he put his own life in jeopardy — and neither was it because he saw me as the son he never had. What it all came down to was his way of applying the principle of cost and benefit, like any trader worth his salt. What use would it be if I had ended up miserable, a stray thread of the familial fabric he'd woven me into? Rather, he could feel completely at peace knowing he'd always have someone like me whom he could trust and depend on. Our bond ran deeper than blood.

Marco didn't know much about this maxim of Baba's. Abdelsalaam would always say, 'A man needs a good man next to him, even if you have to sculpt him with your own two hands.' He'd go on, talking about how from the beginning of time man has been the protector, so, naturally, there would be an army of enemies lying in wait for him: people, no different from animals, seeking revenge, then sickness and poverty, as well as vulnerability. He'd reiterate how having a man there by your side in these landslides of life was paramount. Even if you need to step back from life, your friend should be able to carry on what you started, as if a natural extension of yourself.

This was what I had once strongly resisted, because I wanted to be me, to be myself, not the extension of some other person just because I was indebted to him; to be honest, I was fed up. I would never be able to repay all that Baba Abdelsalaam had done for me — all my efforts were desperate and flimsy in comparison. In such moments of entrapment, one may rebel and search for freedom, going so far as to bite the hand of generosity outstretched to them. I know not everyone will do that, but I did. I had no intention of harming anyone, but people need to be themselves, they need to be free. You will not always be understood by everyone.

This is what those do-gooders can't understand when they are stabbed in the back by someone they did a good turn for. Not having to pay Baba back overwhelmed me, and in the end made me submit to his will — even if only for a while. No one's perfect, after all.

Abdelsalaam wanted me to be the next Abdelsalaam Mohammed Abdelsalaam, the renowned merchant whose funds never ran out — his carbon copy really, characterised by a deep preoccupation with all things monetary, collecting it and spending it. Owning everything there is to own: land, houses, cars, important business hubs, shops in every location possible. His family lived in comfort, cutting them off from the trials of the outside world; they essentially didn't know anything other than contentment and satisfaction. He had provided for them and built up his business all by himself because, to put it quite simply, he didn't trust anyone but me. I might as well have been his handmade creation; he fashioned me to be an extension of himself, as if through me he would be made immortal.

Business wasn't for me, even though I soaked up everything there was to know about it: learning that every number made a difference, that every single red-tinged coin was the seed for a forest of Sudanese pounds. I also learnt, though, that the slow crawl of wealth accumulation, the constant need for innovative thinking to get the biggest pile of notes possible — even if it meant risking everything you had saved — was not for me.

Abdelsalaam raised me not just as a son, but as a friend and an employee. A fixed salary and incentives meant that I didn't feel exploited. He'd say, 'You Southerners are just too sensitive when it comes to exploitation, so I'll stamp out any room for doubt.' I was meant to follow in his footsteps, but I left him in the lurch, or that's how he felt when I joined the Military Academy after finishing secondary school. I'd abandoned him when he needed me the most: he'd wanted me to be a guardian of his wealth and a general supervisor for all his business projects, deals and possessions scattered around the world in almost every place imaginable. I left him and joined the military. He thought I might as well commit suicide; quite simply put, he said, 'How can you accept a salary from someone who could get you killed at any moment?'

Marco is the friend I have chosen; he's intelligent and kind. I met him when working as a teenager for Abdelsalaam in the large market in our village surrounded by small mountains. Marco was from the generation just below me; when my other friends were preparing to cross the threshold of manhood after their voices had dropped a few octaves, he was still much younger than all of them; all the same, we became close. I chose him because he had a good heart, was extremely sure of himself, persistent and empathic when others were in pain. It's difficult for someone like that to hurt another person unless absolutely cornered.

That boy quite recently became a man, and I had to do some things so that we'd start thinking along the same lines, then I could rely on him entirely. I surprised him with some clothes. He could now get rid of his old ones that made him look more like a student than a father. Some of his outfits were too feminine, which was unusual for a man who had nearly half a dozen kids by now: two girls, and two boys who seemed more like twins than regular siblings because of how close together they were born, from that woman who popped them out like a hen does eggs.

In big things and in small, I depended on Marco. So much so, he became far closer to our wives and children, while I was the man who carried out the difficult jobs and took the hard decisions. I preferred to watch over everyone from a distance, keeping my personal space as a priority, of course.

I lent him some books, in the hope that our exchanges would be on more of an equal footing. We'd go together to jazz parties and nightclubs, watch football matches, each of us having left the education system in our own way — he by finding refuge in another life for the sake of building a family as he was the last standing heir, and I by escaping Mama Fawzia's looks after she caught me slipping out of my sister Tahiya's room. I'll never forget how my cheek stung.

I was stunned to discover that Tahiya was completely bound up down there, mutilated really, and so I couldn't take things further with her.

My desire for her transformed into pure pity, morphing everything into brotherly affection, and this is what Tahiya didn't understand. Instead, she slapped me and branded me a sissy boy on that stormy night thick with silent anger.

As for Lucy, my dear friend Marco's wife, honestly, her bumbling village ways made me keep my distance from her whenever I could. That breast-milk smell didn't help things at all. I preferred her as far away from me as possible. I'd find myself recoiling from any room she was in. Even though I had told Theresa a dozen times to get rid of that stink from our home, if a guest popped by, they'd still be struck by it. At first, I insisted to Theresa that Lucy shouldn't prepare any of my food, and then I asked for a separate zeer pot for my drinking water to be stored in. I just felt that her milk trickled into every possible place, making my stomach churn.

When it was time for me to come home from work, Theresa would go over the top with the incense, but it was no use. Once I nearly exploded at her when the wretched milk smell smacked me in the face by the tree next to the front door. I suspect Lucy had produced too much again that day and poured what wasn't necessary onto the tree roots as she was prone to do. In my experience, when talking with simpletons about something that they don't see as harmful, their mood grows so dark, the conversation could easily be taking place at a funeral.

The many times when Theresa tried to talk to Lucy about simple feminine matters, or when the children would quarrel with each other, it would always end with Lucy gathering up her things and waiting with her children out in the street, until Marco and I came home and patched things up.

I dreaded the exaggerated emotional response that simple-minded people are so good at displaying most of the time. But it's their only way of defending themselves; they don't have any justifications and the vast majority of their vocabulary usually consists of words that harm others. Their reactions were always heated and groundless.

I called out to Lucy in the voice I used with soldiers and petty officers back at the barracks. She started to tremble and one of her breasts jiggled up and down, peeking out of her short, pink sleeveless dress like a mischievous monkey. Behind her was the cry of a child whose milk supply had just been interrupted. She shook before me and swallowed her saliva visibly. I felt somewhat bad for her; was I really this intimidating? Certainly, it's expected that some people will be scared of you, that's how you can swiftly get what you want without any back-and-forth. But the sight of Lucy's raw motherhood left me disorientated. It made me rein in my sharp tone to a fraction of what it normally was. I faced her while gesturing to the tree. In a soft but firm manner, that told her I wouldn't accept any backtalk, 'Lucy, please, don't pour your milk here.'

She stared into space and the moment felt like an age.

Afraid that she may burst into tears, I almost took back my words. Instead, I suggested an alternative, something better for everyone, with a smile that barely found its way through my stony facial expression. Scarcely able to mask my disgust, I suggested, 'Can't you just pour it down the hole in the bathroom?'

Something like a moan escaped her mouth and she suddenly crossed her arms across her chest, as if she were protecting something dear to her. She lowered her gaze to my feet. I sensed maybe I had been too hard on her, but there was no going back now. I was ready to take any sort of outburst, even ready to placate her if necessary so that she wouldn't leave the house as she was forever threatening to do. I depended on Marco too much to let this get out of hand.

But she defended her milk in a way that made me pause. Her face grew animated. 'This tree here needs this milk more than those worms in the latrine. Can't you see how much it's grown?' I turned towards the tree she was gesturing at, thinking she was talking about some tree other than the one in front of the house, and was astonished. How had this tree grown so large to the point where it gave shade, yes, a good amount of shade, its leaves long and vibrantly green, blocking out the disc of the sun?

It was as if the tree had just grown before my very eyes; how had I not noticed all this time? I had preserved the gaunt image of it, hanging on for dear life. Dry branches and leaves few enough for any child to count. I hadn't noticed any of these changes, even though every day I'd passed under this tree to get into my car for work.

How had I held onto the old image of the tree but refused

the new, real one? My mouth sat agape, while I tried to gather my thoughts into some kind of rebuttal. Questions swarmed in my head until her voice tenderly brought me back, as if I were one of her children and she was teaching me how to walk. 'Can't you see?'

I stared at Lucy. She was taller, and had filled out, her black hair standing upright, pulled upwards by some unseen force, her skin a deep brown glazed with cooking oil, temptingly smooth, her pearl-like smile that could melt the hardest of hearts.

'Peter? Are you okay?'

'Put that back in,' I said, pointing to her breast that was hanging out, large droplets of milk leaking one after the other, drawing rivers of moisture on her dress. My finger hesitated mid-air, trembling, like the sword of a knight about to lose a battle, and I, the knight, wanted to return the sword to its sheath, announcing surrender.

She grabbed the chest pocket of her pink dress, which was torn around the side, on purpose it seemed, to make breastfeeding easier. She widened this hole by pulling it lightly away from her body to pop the breast back inside where it bounced into its companion, causing both to jiggle. I felt lightheaded.

Then I stammered, 'Y-Yes, I've seen the tree.'

'Are you still insisting that I pour the extra milk down the toilet?'

I cleared my throat. 'It's been proven to me that the tree would benefit more, and the worms of course already have something to digest.'

She chuckled and went back to her baby. I watched her

leave, her footfall light and quick. My eyes then fell on the tree, its branches waving to me in the wake of a light breeze.

I headed for my private study, holding my cap in both hands as if at a friend's funeral, contemplating this wild girl, as Marco called her. I kept asking myself, how could I have overlooked so much? I really had missed the forest for the trees.

I fell deep into thought that day, going over in my head every person I knew, every single thing, all at once. I started to contemplate everyone's outlines, trying to recognise them once more; my reliance on my old images of them was now questionable.

Even this wild girl had changed, conversing with a clarity of mind and intelligence that stopped me in my tracks. She didn't get into a huff and storm out, saving me from having to say placating words. When had I last overheard one of her silly fights with Theresa about the children or housework? How long had it been since I last saw her lingering under the tree, sitting on her green metal trunk crammed full of her belongings, with its shoddy flower and half-crescent designs in yellow and red, her children all around her, one nearly the same age as the other, accompanied by a decent number of pots and pails — how I hated that sight. It would cost me much of my powers of persuasion and cajoling; then she'd inevitably cry, and declare that she couldn't spend another day in this house. Eventually, she'd calm down and feel satisfied that she had managed to thwart us all.

I turned them over in my mind, one by one: simple, horrid-smelling Lucy; compliant Theresa, who kept trying to make amends for the sin she had committed against my friend over two years ago, and for which I do not — even for one day — let her feel that she has been forgiven. I've made her a slave to this misstep, exploiting her to the nth degree. When I come home late from a hot night with another woman, just so that she won't ask me where I've been, I somehow weave this dark incident where she exploited Lucy like a servant into our conversation. I relish humiliating her with this, making her more dedicated to serving me, less likely to nag me, no longer asking where or whom I've been with. And that's the whole point.

Marco I know like the back of my hand: I know the way he is now; he's my brother and my friend. So why does doubt gnaw at me in every place? Damn Lucy and her milk-guzzling tree. I don't know, maybe he's another one I'm wrong about. If I missed the tree changing in front of my own front door, a tree that may well blow over in a strong wind, how was I to keep an eye on the changes in the people around me? I picked up a group photo taken at Christmas two years ago: Marco and I were standing next to each other, Theresa, plump, was hugging her daughters and smiling without showing her teeth, whereas Lucy's eyes were popping out as if she were about to bolt, her stomach straining outwards with another baby on the way. The harsh lighting in the photo studio unnerved her. I coughed back a laugh whilst looking at her, like an animal stuck in a trap, awaiting an unknown fate.

The girls, my girls, I wondered how they were doing after I'd washed my hands of the nitty-gritty of the day-to-day. I'd supply the money for whatever was needed but would never raise a finger.

My eyes drifted to the wall and fell on the group picture of my cohort at the Military Academy. I rose and stepped closer. We were all wearing our stiff peaked hats, visors pointed to the front, organised in exceptionally straight lines, sitting still and upright like goods on a factory production line. All looking at the same point off in the distance, gazes filled with pride and readiness to make even bigger sacrifices.

I wonder how my year group are. Our slogan was: one heart, one army, one nation. That year group were my brothers, my family. Which paths did they follow after we were despatched to different regions of this nation, serving this soil, dying for it? Some were executed for their involvement in plotting a coup from within the military against the powers that be, and others left the army to join the revolutionary forces opposing the ruling regime. I was so close to them all, but as of late, I have distanced myself. Was I a coward? No, I just had a different opinion from theirs. For me, we military men are only good for battle, for war. Authoritarian is what the military is, and so it's easy for us to subject other groups of people to our orders. The military makes everyone into a tyrant, so how can a tyrant lead a nation full of civilians to safety? Civilians, who crave democracy and freedom, and for their opinion to be heard on everything? How can we, we who are used to taking and giving orders, enter into a back-and-forth with civilians about something that could easily be achieved with a simple order from the lowest-ranking soldier?

But this way of being made me lose everyone's trust; no one knew whether I was with them or against them. I preferred to keep my distance, feeling a stinging sadness when individuals from my cohort would disappear after failed coups. Shame would weigh me down when one of them joined the armed resistance made up of southern officers in the forests and I was sat here at home, letting my hesitancy lead me, despite my conviction that something had to be done. Deep down, I felt that I was a coward; yes, I must acknowledge this. The political situation right now isn't one I support, like most other people, but I just don't have what it takes to do anything about it.

I went back to thinking about Lucy, who unleashed in me all these questions about everyone I know, about everything. When she dragged me by the hand like a child, my surprise at realising that she had nursed a tree back to full health after having breastfed her children… why am I thinking about my own mother now? She who led me by the hand and handed me over to Abdelsalaam, only for her to disappear forever. Why hadn't I asked after her or searched for her all these years? All my searching and questions had been about a father I never knew, and still don't. Did I deliberately put my mother out of my mind and erase her from my memory? Was I angry at her? Even when some of my army postings landed me in my hometown down South, I insisted on remaining a mysterious figure. I didn't give anyone the chance to get to know anything about me other than my name. I would always say that I didn't know a thing about my origins; a stranger had raised me and that was all there was to it. I didn't dare search for her, she could easily have been a prostitute or the whore of some northern merchant, exactly what the village people branded her back then. In the end, she handed me over to her lover and left. Did they ever meet up again? Had he hidden her away somewhere? Wasn't that why he was so dedicated to raising me, because she must have been watching him from somewhere nearby?

I never once asked Baba Abdelsalaam about her. And what about his daughters? Whose names he kept repeating in my ear: they're your sisters, your sisters, my sisters: Jalaa, Nidal, Tahiya and Hayat. Then there was Fawzia, his kind wife, my stand-in mother. It's been so long since I last saw them after I decided to take leave of them and make my own way. Baba Abdelsalaam wasn't pleased at all. I wonder how he and all his riches are faring.

The last time I saw him was that final day when I accused him of not making any effort to find my father; that he just wanted me to stay under his thumb and serve him the rest of my days. He started to shake with anger when I said this and cut me off, 'Your father died in prison more than ten years ago!'

The news hit me like a thunderbolt. His voice was unsteady. 'I didn't want to tell you because I was worried how you'd take it. Maybe I made the wrong choice. It's your right to know what happened to your father, after all. Peter, you've never been a servant here, not even for a day. You've been a hard worker, persistent. You were the son I never had. You're free, free to do as you like, to go where you please. You don't have to play the victim so that you can leave. You're a man and it's your life. You know the bonds that tie us. Go on, my son.'

The muscles in my shoulders knotted. I had been too harsh. How could I have been so loyal to a father who wasn't even around, who I didn't even know, and deny all the good things about Baba, a man who had tried to protect me, give me a stable life, who made everyone else accept me as I was? My eyes grew wet, and I let the tears flow from my depths. Oh, how I cried. Crying isn't easy if you're not used to it.

Tear ducts dry up if they haven't been used much. How I envied the way Marco bared his soul so easily when he cried. I thought of Baba Abdelsalaam and how strong he was, full of vigour, his customary elegance, his carefully shaved face, his small, intelligent eyes. He never wore trousers, always a white jalabiya and a large abaya atop it, which would balloon up with air, giving him the appearance of being mid-flight. He would also wear a large starch-white turban, its folds like frothy soap foam, his shoes made of wild animal skins, whether tigers or snakes, his distinguished cane made of teak, and large rings on his fingers, the precious stones glinting in the light. His eyes set him apart, shining, full of the intelligence of a hunter. He was pleasant but abandoned all formalities when it came to matters of money.

He'd say, 'When a merchant is forced into debt, he should immediately shut up shop. Losses knock a merchant down, but he can always get back up again. Debt, on the other hand, just humiliates him.'

What a man. I think of him often. I was overcome by a sense of urgency to go and visit him. I'm such a hard-hearted man. Why am I like this?

I shifted in my seat, waiting for Marco to come back from work. Once we'd finished eating, I told him I needed him to accompany me on a visit to Baba Abdelsalaam. Marco knew little about my family because, for the most part, I never talked about them.

When we arrived, the house was as it had been, three floors and overlooking the Nile. White walls, inlaid with stones the colours of the layers of the ground — yellow, burnt orange, brown, black — a spacious garden with every kind of flower imaginable, all fenced in by royal palms, giving it the aura of a natural reserve. Other trees ranging in width and height, a fountain right in the middle guarded by a stone lion, artfully carved, his mouth open mid-roar and spurting water. The notes of mango, lemon and basil plants hung in the air.

We made our way through by following a pathway consisting of square tiles that led to the inside of the house, the spaces in between overgrown with green grass, making each tile an island surrounded by a green sea. Silence cocooned the place, and an anxiety mingled with fear came over me. The kind that overcomes a person who finds themselves standing once again before a place they were forced to leave, that had once meant everything to them. I was overwhelmed by the desire to apologise; homes, like people, miss us sometimes, too. I wanted every single thing to forgive me: the trees, the stones, those living inside the house. I felt my heart pound in my chest — what if they threw me out? *I think I better leave now.*

Marco gave a slow disbelieving shake of the head. 'This is a palace.' In a voice that came out with great difficulty, choked by the different emotions jostling for space, I said, 'I grew up here. This is my home.' Tears collected in my eyes, but I stopped them from falling. I don't know whether Marco noticed or not.

Pressing down on the red circular button, I heard a ring from behind the door. I pressed again and let my finger linger. I wanted to resolve things. Marco sucked in a quick breath as he took in the birdsong around him, the birds' wings flapping as they returned to their nests.

The door opened with a jerk and a man in his mid-thirties

was standing there, observing us. He had on a green tracksuit with white lines running down the sides, his face pockmarked. Small eyes like that of a mouse, his gaze uneasy. His skin was lighter than mine, more of a yellow tinge, his ears large like the feet of a small child. Somewhat pudgy, his paunch was visible. His eyebrows were thick but his hair was starting to thin in the middle; around the edges, it remained thick — freshly cut grass, I thought.

In a hollow voice, completely void of any welcome, he said, 'Yes?'

I remembered him now: Baba's nephew. 'You've grown, Ismail, seems like life has run you ragged.'

His eyes grew large. 'Peter? I don't believe it.'

He exaggerated his welcome to sweep our old enmity under the rug, but the warmth of his welcome didn't even begin to thaw the iceberg floating between us. Before he had a chance to welcome Marco, everyone had congregated at the door. Tears in eyes, and embraces the only language. Even Hayat, who had despised me for some time, flung herself into my arms crying. Mama Fawzia kissed my head, her braids as white as cotton, her face patterned with shulukh, decorative scars now inlaid with wrinkles. I anxiously asked after Baba Abdelsalaam; everyone fell silent. My heart plunged so far down I thought I might faint. I stared at them, awaiting the final words to a catastrophic chapter.

'Your Baba isn't well, Peter. Not well at all.'

I rushed inside. Yes, I knew every corner here, the grey terrazzo flooring, the milky tea walls, the ceiling crowned with shiny golden chandeliers, the many corridors — *this leads to the shower room and the toilet, this to the kitchen, and that to*

Baba Abdelsalaam's office containing his large library of rare volumes. I used to steal books from there for Jalaa, because the girls weren't allowed to read them. You'll never get married that way! You'll end up spinsters, Mama Fawzia would warn them.

These steps led to the second floor, the girls' bedrooms. Under this stairwell, we'd play hide and seek, and afterwards, Tahiya and I would stay hidden. Wild, unruly Tahiya, our bodies close together, inhaling each other's breath, her hand daringly wrapped around my manhood, my palms on her budding breasts till the flesh pushed through the spaces between my fingers as I squeezed giddily. And like this, we'd explore each other's hidden body parts till someone noticed we were missing.

Tahiya's room, where we'd had an aborted expedition, was next to the stairwell. She'd been bursting with a feverish desire back then, and would brush herself against me several times a day. We were burning for each other. She invited me back to her room one evening, I stole in and we tumbled into each other's embrace. I kissed her the way I had seen a hero do at the end of a film. She sobbed and whispered my name with a hungry lust, her chest rising and falling rapidly. I could barely keep myself together. She started to peel her clothes off, one piece at a time, and lay down on the bed. Her breasts were like domes pointing stubbornly to the ceiling, her long hair strewn on the pillow around her head like smoke, her brown skin reddening, her enormous eyes lined with eyelashes like thorns, each one standing completely independent of the others. I sat next to her and licked her protruding breast. She purred and I put my hand over her mouth so that no one would hear us. She bit down on my palm, and opened herself up, her long symmetrical legs moving away from each other, and that's when I caught sight of it: down there she was completely smooth, there was nothing, just an extension of her abdomen.

She was sealed shut. Taken back, I said, 'So this is what happened that horrible day?'

My question woke her from the dream, and she shuddered, terrified that she had revealed what no one should know. She quickly began to dress again, saying, 'You shouldn't have looked down there.'

'What were you expecting me to do? We can't do anything unless I rip you open. I just can't do it. I can't hurt you like that, Tahiya.'

Her features took on a grave expression and she flinched at my touch. Her eyes turned cold and hard. My question threw us back into the distant past, to that day of uprooting; young girls stained with henna, women wherever you turned, incense occupying every corner. A fleshy woman in white with broad shulukh etched into her face. No sooner had she put out her cigarette than she picked up her sharp instruments and ordered for the girls to be brought to her in the room one after another. The door shut, and then the screaming began. Sheer terror. Outside the room, I paced in circles.

Though I wish I hadn't, I stole a look through a hole in the wooden shutters. I caught sight of something red: blood oozing between the legs of one of the girls. The women had pinned down her legs, arms and head with great force. The fat one then flung a piece of flesh the width of an ear to one side and began stitching up the area, leaving an opening the size of a matchstick head. I later learnt this was for urine to trickle out of.

The soul-curdling screams were deafening. I sprinted to Baba Abdelsalaam's shop, arriving breathless. Between faltering gasps for air, I said, 'Hurry — some women are killing the girls! Tahiya...will... die.' I started to cry as I clawed at his jalabiya, which hung flat, empty of its usual buoyancy. But he didn't budge. He refused to move an inch. I then snatched his thick walking stick. I could use it to protect the girls, or at least draw upon some of the authority that a teak stick bestows on its bearer. I ran towards the house telling myself, 'I'll beat them. I'll beat them.' I was ready to butcher whoever had laid a finger on my sisters. I shot into the house but countless pairs of hands bore down on me and carried me away like a sack of salt. Under no circumstances was I to cause a scene.

Baba rebuked me, and for the first time, he beat me. He ordered me to sit. I immediately did as I was told. My head was swimming from the scenes of blood and wailing. Once my rasping breath had steadied, he took a seat next to me and placed his hand on my knee. I was wiping away my tears when he said, 'No one is going to die. This is a rite of passage for all girls — to secure a safe future for them. At the end of the day, it's a women's matter, so why stick your nose in?'

A safe future? What kind of safety? From whom?

More than the act of sex itself, it was curiosity that led us to explore each other's bodies. She had wanted to experiment with what was beyond that closed door, beyond the matchstick-sized hole.

'I'm really worried about you, Tahiya,' I had shared with her. 'Can you even pee? Does it hurt when...' Before I could finish, I felt a throbbing in my cheek. She threw me out. I found myself sneaking down the stairs. My worry and pity for the girls weighed me down like a millstone.

I was startled to find Mama Fawzia standing at the end of the stairs. Her eyes sliced through me. My feet froze on the final step; I was searching for any excuse to stop what she must be thinking right now. My throat had dried up completely. The words vanished and the air was sucked out of me. With great difficulty, I managed to stammer that I had delivered something one of the girls had requested. Without actually turning to look, I gestured meekly to the top of the stairs. Her fiery stare singed me, confirming that she didn't believe a word.

'I didn't do anything. I swear.'

'I'm not your mama,' she hissed. She pointed to the door. 'Get out.'

I knew something had been broken that couldn't be put back together.

* * *

That day of the circumcision, when I asked my father how all this violence ensured a safer future, he remained silent.

Was I included in this protection? Or did the girls go through all that pain *because of me?* That's when I experienced the reproach of my conscience — of course, it's about protection from people like me; look at what you nearly just did, you idiot, she's your sister!

Thank God there had been something to stop me, and at that very moment, I started to plan my departure. I couldn't bear looking at Tahiya, who hated me now, and Mama Fawzia, of course.

This one incident became my only reference point to explain everything thereafter. Everything that had once been ordinary was now out of the ordinary: because I was in the wrong, Baba Abdelsalaam's preoccupation with his business was now a deliberate way for him to distance himself. The way he pinched his lips and crossed his arms in front of his chest when I failed to do something right was proof that he knew something. I took his silence to mean he was plotting how to get rid of me.

My reality was now a living hell.

I remembered the room that led to Baba's. And there he was, so incredibly small, like a once solid ice cube now mostly melted. How can old age trample one to this degree? At first, he didn't recognise me. Why had I been erased from his memory? I bent down to kiss his forehead and take him in my arms, but he still looked at me like a stranger. He tried to speak but no words came out. His mouth was pulled to the left side; saliva was dribbling down, and both his arm and leg on that side were completely out of commission. *What happened to you, Baba?*

Everyone was watching me as Mama Fawzia pried me from him gently. Silence engulfed the room. I felt completely exposed, a great number of feelings toying with me. A coldness took over my bones, grinding them to dust. Without raising my eyes, I asked the girls, 'What happened?'

'Two years ago, he had a stroke, and everything broke down, even his speech. His memory flickers and then goes entirely. One day he recognises all of us, and the next we're all strangers,' explained Jalaa.

I looked at Baba Abdelsalaam, a hot tear travelling down my cheek. Mama Fawzia bent down to his ear and started speaking loudly into it. 'This is Peter, your son. He's come back. Don't you remember him?'

His eyes scanned the room and he furrowed his brow, asking where Peter was. Mama Fawzia gestured to me to come closer. He seemed to be of sound mind momentarily, his memory crystal clear.

He raised his right hand, which still had some life in it, and reached out towards me, bringing me into him feebly. He mumbled some words empty of any letters, but the meaning seemed to still be there — every facial expression carried a thousand questions, and every look embodied the genuine love between a father and son who'd once upon a time been companions, and every gesture spoke of a tender memory. It was a warm welcome; as far as his left ear would allow, he stretched his mouth into a smile.

The house was full of veritable joy: noisy conversations and laughter. Baba's radiant face put everyone at ease. Mama Fawzia complained how he hadn't eaten since the morning and had refused his bath.

'Dare challenge Mama Fawzia, do you now?' I chimed in. 'Let's see how you stand up to a soldier,' I said, playfully.

'Nidal, get the bath ready, and make sure the water's warm. Jalaa, make the best soup that you can. Tahiya...'

In some corner of my mind, I was still chewing over our shared memories. After a moment, with half a smile, I said, 'Tahiya, please raise the blinds and open the windows. And you, my little Hayat, bring something clean and comfortable for Baba to wear. Mama Fawzia, please burn the most delicious

154

incense you have.' Collective laughter greeted my string of orders. A sense of vitality and liveliness ran through the house, fondly reminding us of familiar days that had passed by.

The entire time, Ismail had been absorbed in conversation with Marco. I was preoccupied with Baba and his daughters. When I stepped back from my family, I noticed Marco looked stricken, as if Ismail had poisoned him.

It was only later on that I learnt Ismail had married Tahiya, and had been put in charge of everything. And that the stroke my father suffered had been brought on by Ismail's mismanagement of a crucial deal. Baba had been forced to sell many of his possessions to stave off prison, and then one day he fainted at the shop and had to be carried home.

The girls had changed so much. Jalaa the eldest, unlucky in looks, education and connections, but now different altogether. Still less attractive than her sisters, but she had the allure of a strong, mature woman. She had embraced the idea of feminism and started to call for women's rights in both the big and the small. I came to know that she had continued her studies and become a renowned lawyer, refusing marriage. She had once shared with me that during one of her conference trips, she had undergone an operation to treat the mutilation of what lay between her legs, to return everything to its natural state, instead of a match-sized hole. Her gumption impressed me.

Nidal was easy-going, a captivating beauty who had been the well of our secrets, a true friend to all, loving and wise. She was the only one who responded rationally when things hit the fan. She married a pilot and has three children.

And then Tahiya, who was wild, and radical at times. Yet

now she sits before me, something in her broken. Her eyes remain on the ground and she doesn't engage with the others, except with a faint smile. She doesn't do anything without running it by Ismail first. I pitied her. What had happened to force such a transformation from an ambitious, intelligent teenager, arrogant in her freedom, to a being shackled by invisible bonds?

Jalaa used to read books in secret while Tahiya would do so in broad daylight, right before Mama Fawzia and Baba Abdelsalaam's eyes. She was stubborn and rebellious in a brazen way that harmed others at times. Where did that fearless teenager go to? The one who groped my body in the dark hiding places of our childhood was now a faint shadow of herself.

Hayat was our youngest, I remember how I'd play with her: I'd be a horse, sometimes a car. Sometimes I would be her child, and she'd hug my head the whole time, pulling at the skin of her chest to nurse me. I pretended to cry like a baby and then slept in her little welcoming lap. One time, I had been a dog barking for an entire day, chasing away imaginary thieves, sitting at different people's feet, while she sat on a comfortable chair, patting my back. I spoilt her like a daughter. I loved her so much. Now, she was studying medicine and in her final year. How time stops for no man.

Each of them had something special about them: the sister, the friend, the lover and the baby of the family. What I was in knots over now was Ismail: how had he wormed his way into this household? I suppose it had come down to his sly ways. Just look at how he has destroyed Tahiya and shattered her vibrant energy. If only I'd been around, she would never have married him at all.

Mama Fawzia was Baba Abdelsalaam's cousin, her eyes submissive and her wide tribal shulukh sloping upwards from the top of her cheek along the edge of her eyes, ending where tears flow. Her lips were thick and greenish, the result of being punctured repeatedly with needles, and then stuffed with pine tar; touted as one of the best cosmetic methods amongst village women. Her hair was long and black, greased with lamb fat mixed with sandalwood, her braids hanging down either side of her face like aerial roots. Her buttocks were enough for a child to comfortably fall asleep on them, her thick legs ending with two small feet stained with henna all year long.

A beautiful woman with a whisper of a voice, kind-hearted, though her smiles were rare.

I now remember leaving this home to join the Military Academy; I had just been looking for the quickest way out after all that had happened, away from Mama Fawzia's glares and Tahiya's outright hatred for me. How could her hot infatuation have turned so cold? She went as far as treating me like a servant, directing humiliating tasks, like laundry and shining shoes, my way. Mama Fawzia would egg her on, and they both had waged war on me. One day, Tahiya told me that Mama Fawzia wanted me to peel, cut and then dry onions for the approaching Ramadan season. It was the worst thing that could have been asked of me; I unreservedly hated preparing onions. My eyes couldn't bear it.

And with that, my life split in two: a secret one where I was a servant to Tahiya and Mama Fawzia, and a second life in the outside world. Most of the time, I would scrutinise people's words and actions to see how much they knew about that fateful night.

I grew to detest Tahiya. I still don't know what she told her mother about me. She naturally must have put all the blame on me, even though *she* was the one who enticed and pursued me. *She* was the one who invited me into her room. We just got carried away. Not all the blame should be put on her though — a real man would own up to as much — but I was something of a coward.

Every door that would have allowed the issue to be aired and absolve everyone — because in the end no one was *really* hurt — was closed. Tahiya was thankfully still a virgin, but it seems I was the only one held culpable. Like any person accused, the more I tried to assert my innocence, the more the accusation stuck to me. Being at the scene of a crime is the worst position anyone can find themselves in.

Now, to be frank, I had been on the verge of committing the crime, so I needed to be somewhat repentant. And so I peeled and cut all the sacks of onions found in the cupboards of Baba Abdelsalaam until my tears dried up.

I knew that they must have been watching me through some hole or the other, cackling away. But someday I was going to be somewhere else, and they'd all miss me. After secondary school, I decided to join the Military Academy and that was that.

Baba came with Jalaa and Nidal to my graduation from the Academy, the glaring absence of Tahiya and Mama Fawzia unmissable. I was disappointed; I had been secretly hoping for the joy and pride enveloping everyone to get things back to how they had been, but those women proved to be truly vindictive.

When we finally returned home from meeting Baba Abdelsalaam, Marco seemed irate about something or other. The entire journey back he had been gritting his teeth, brooding, staring out of the window at the dark roads. Darkness had fallen and Khartoum was wrapped up in subdued night lights, an evening glow settling around the place. Well-dressed people with naturally-styled Afros crossed the roads, whispering to one another. The roads were nearly empty, and notes of music rose and fell whenever we passed by one of the nightclubs.

I stopped in front of the Excelsior on El-Gamhuriya Avenue, which was pulsing with all kinds of foreigners: Turks, Armenians, Greeks, businessmen, adventurers, tourists.

I addressed Marco, who was looking at me inquiringly. 'Let's get something to wet our throats and have a chat.' I stepped in front of him to enter the hotel and headed for the restaurant and bar. The ambience took my breath away: the chairs, the gleaming wooden tables, the symmetrical trimmed bushes, the beautiful pictures of far-off forests, several of vicious crocodiles crouching with their jaws shut, splendid photos of the Nile as it enters the city of Nimule in the farthest southern tip of the country, unusually modest for such a river, appearing in the shape of a swamp wrapped in tall fine grasses crawling round the trunks of the thick trees standing as tall as border guards. I appreciated this place with its serenity, everything in it predictable, the same style as it always had been: the smell, the pictures, the handsome waiter, and even the music were the same. Abba tunes that gave the whole place a cinematic feel, as if John Travolta was going to burst in dancing at any moment, flocked by beautiful girls.

We sat at a table near the entrance — we didn't have any

intention of staying up till dawn. We ordered beer and some appetisers: cheese, olives and some pickled vegetables.

Marco was quiet the entire time. I wasn't sure how to get him to talk. I went with, 'Two long years have passed since the last time I saw my family; I'm an awful son. I'm kicking myself now after seeing how Baba has ended up after I left him all alone to face Ismail. What's worse is, Ismail ended up marrying Tahiya and it seems like he finally destroyed her.'

Eyeing his glass with disdain, as if he wanted to direct it at me but didn't dare, he said, 'Were you a son or a servant?'

His question fell on me like an axe. 'What do you mean?'

'You know what I mean.'

'I was... I was...'

'Why did you run away? Did it have anything to do with you insulting Abdelsalaam's, I mean, your master's honour?'

Without realising it, I stood up and almost punched him in the face, but caught myself just in time. I unclenched my fist. How did he come to know all this? It was wrong, all of it.

While considering me, he added, 'So Ismail was ri...'

At that point, I let out a half-laugh. But I was still as tense as ever. 'So Ismail's the one who shoved all that crap in your head.

'Listen, Ismail hates me, so don't expect him to say a single true thing about me. He had been trying to take my place and manipulated his way into Abdelsalaam's heart and home. But when it comes to business, he's reckless and dull-minded, of limited intelligence, really. That's aside from him having a chip on his shoulder, being lazy and a thief, too. That's why Baba Abdelsalaam wanted to keep him at arm's length. Ismail has only ever been about undermining me, and trying to provoke me by saying that I'm just a servant to his uncle.'

'No, Peter, Ismail's telling the truth. You're just trying to cover things up because you love this family so much. But all the boys who came to the North, whether by force or willingly, ended up as either servants or slaves, and had to change their names as well as their religion. What Arab name are you hiding, Peter?' He laughed cynically, then added, 'Abdullah? And what's more, you then tried to sleep with a girl you called your *sister*. Not only were you hardly a good servant, you were a traitor as well.'

I tried to get him to see some sense. 'So you believe Ismail, who you've only just met, and refuse to even hear me out?'

Marco's exasperated tone shifted to one of anger, his patience exhausted. 'Go on then, tell me the truth. I'm listening. Just admit it already.'

I looked at him squarely. 'There's nothing to confess, it's just a different story altogether. Listen, I don't deny that there are atrocious things that happen to young boys who come from the South to the North: their identities are washed away, whether by their own choice, or deception, or coercion. But what happened with me was different, maybe it was all just pure luck. Baba Abdelsalaam is a different kind of man, not political in the slightest. For him, politicians are people that we have welcomed to ride heavily on our backs, handing them the reins. They have no qualms about exploiting us, both Northerners and Southerners, just so they can get ahead, the nation be damned. No one deserves that sort of treatment.

'So he keeps his distance from politicians and the people who blindly follow them with their heads and backs bowed.

He pays no attention to their irrational estimations of entire groups of people without even bothering to get to know them first.

'Baba is a well-travelled man who has met people of almost every nationality; he's used to differences and not afraid of them. And that's why one day, when there had been a lot of whispers and sneers about our relationship, he said to me, "Listen here, Peter. In my heart, you're my son, and all that matters to me is that you allow yourself to feel what you're feeling. If you're frustrated, let it out. If you're sad, swim in it. Let people say what they want about our relationship. What I want to know, is what you feel deep down for me and my family?"

"You're my father and your family is my family."

"And that's what counts," he said. "Anything else is just resentment and envy. People are selfish, Peter."

'The truth is, Marco, I didn't feel for even a single day that I was a slave in the way Ismail puts it. If we do go down that road of thinking, a slave or servant remains that way till the end of his days, because his master will make sure to keep him in chains to guarantee his obedience. That never happened to me. I had a top-notch education, I wore good quality clothes, ate my meals with my family and read the latest books. Even Baba noticed and said, "I feel that salvation for many is in your hands. Knowledge opens the mind and heart, and frees the soul from acting recklessly, without thought. Your father sacrificed himself for his people, he lived a man and died a man, and here you are following in his footsteps, but in a different way. You've done well, my son."

'I can't deny that in the beginning of our adolescence, both

Tahiya and I were full of lust and nearly made an enormous mistake. We were just kids.' I saw a cynical smile on Marco's lips that he quickly rearranged, but it made me pause. My feelings for him after that split moment had changed somewhat, muddied. 'Do you know what really happens to girls when they are circumcised, Marco? It's the worst thing that can happen to a person.' I lowered my voice, feeling vulnerable. 'Their vaginas are removed.' I waited a bit and swallowed hard to move the lump in my throat. I emptied the contents of my glass into my stomach and continued, a bit calmer. 'When it happened in front of my eyes, I rejected it, but I couldn't do anything about it. It was an unshakeable societal custom that everyone was in on. That day, I definitely felt like an outsider, a stranger. I felt powerless hearing my young sisters screaming the next day as they tried to release a few drops of urine. They took tiny steps, their legs tightly bound together so that the wound wouldn't open. Their lips were dry and their cheeks dull, and their eyes swam with countless questions.

'I couldn't look at them. I ran away and would spend entire days outside the house. Sometimes I would sleep in Baba's store in the souk. That's what stopped me from taking it any further with Tahiya. I didn't want to reopen those wounds for her, or me.

'Again, it's just luck, the luck of us men. We always have a chance to take a step back, even if it means hurting someone else in the process. I don't deny that Tahiya was my first love, but after that day, my feelings of pure brotherly love were realised. But damn it, how did Ismail find out? That wicked man must be holding this over her head. I can now see why she's so broken.'

I banged down on the table so hard that a couple of olives jumped off the appetiser platter, and would have rolled onto the ground if Marco hadn't reached out and caught them at the last moment.

Marco was listening, his expressions in harmony with the torment that was clearly visible on my face.

'I regret that I got carried away with Tahiya, and here she is paying such a high price while I'm living such a full life, with a happy and stable family.'

Trying to pacify me, Marco said, 'It's out of your control, Peter. Making a mistake like that is unforgivable. You leaving was best for everyone.'

'I don't know, I feel like I was a coward. I should have confessed and apologised. Stayed close to my sisters and been there as a support for Baba Abdelsalaam.'

'No one would trust you if you confessed. Don't be hard on yourself. Now you've got the chance to be close to them again. It seems whatever is tying the family together is very strong. I was taken aback by how warmly they welcomed you and how they'd missed you. It seems like everyone has forgotten about what happened, everyone except for Ismail.'

'I need to know how he found out and how he keeps getting away with his shenanigans. I'll make sure to put him in his place. Luckily, I got Jalaa's office address. I'll visit her there and she'll fill me in on what else I've missed.'

'Be careful Peter, Ismail is a really smooth operator — I'm sorry that I was swayed so easily.'

'Don't worry, Marco, any person in your position would have been livid. It's a disgusting version of my story that he told you. We did not cross the final line.

'As for changing my religion and name, I'd be lying if I said Abdelsalaam didn't broach the topic with me because of the pressure around him. But I showed him how unwilling I was, and that very day he gave in and said, "It's not up to me to get you to heaven. I've done other things that will get me there, including raising you into a strong man who can go head first through life without fear. It should be enough for the world that your heart is clean, for that's what is most important, not religion."'

After revealing to Marco the deepest corners of my heart, in addition to the overwhelming welcome I received at Baba Abdelsalaam's house, I felt a peace engulf my depths like the winds of a cool ocean. The wings of my spirit were freed and left me floating, contented. Secrets are as heavy as a wooden chest full of ammunition, and I was certain that tonight I would sleep without anything tugging at my conscience.

9

Separating the puppy from the litter was the approach Ummi adopted when our chests started to swell outwards and hair started to sprout on Peter's face, his voice growing thick. Her hawk-like eyes would watch us; she, the virginity sentinel that never slumbered in a city known for its loose morals, as she'd always say. She would have preferred to raise her daughters in her distant village, trapped by the desert on one side and bordered by the Nile, shielded by lofty palm trees, on the other; where a woman wrapped her head and chest in her khimar, only going outside on two occasions: to leave her father's home for her husband's, and her husband's home for the grave.

It was the nature of her husband's work that pulled her from her village, taking her on a drawn-out journey that felt never-ending. If the village hadn't had the Nile running alongside it, it would have been swallowed up by the sand. The train she took traversed a long route through the wilderness, passing by several poverty-stricken villages on the verge of disappearing, cities in the process of being revived, and stations on sands with intertwining iron tracks like veins on the arms of a man in his prime. In the larger cities, she would display her fruit, grains and handicrafts.

My mother was worried I wouldn't get married before I was twenty; she felt greatly disappointed because her eldest daughter would miss the marriage train. And so every funeral, every wedding and any other social occasion where people gathered, became an opportunity for her to parade my femininity and beauty — which I would call modest, at best. She'd often call out to me saying, 'Jalaa, oil your hair — it's looking coarse'; 'Jalaa, rub the rest of the sourdough on your skin — it's looking rough'; Jalaa, Jalaa, Jalaa. All I wanted was to be left alone to finish the book Peter had smuggled to me.

My mother wasn't happy in the least with Peter being around. She was jealous of the woman who had been too close to her husband, but was no longer around. Her son embodied her essence and even her smell. My father laid down the law however, saying, 'Peter is a son of this household, and whoever doesn't like it, the door's wide open.'

My father kept a close eye on how my mother interacted with Peter. Whenever he spoke with us, he'd always say 'Your brother, Peter' and he'd tell Peter 'Your sisters', and so the seed was planted in our small heads until it bloomed into reality. Peter was a gentle child and an ambitious, intelligent, calm teenager. He'd treat everyone with respect, especially Ummi, which made her hatred for him slowly take a back seat. At one point in time, we all relied on him. That was until he joined the Military Academy. He was then cut off from the house for years, until he surprised us that day when we saw him standing tall at the front door, his eyes welling up, the tears refusing to fall, while Ismail stood blocking the doorway.

Peter was to become the man of the house when my father decided to travel to assess the progress of his trading, a frenetic import and export business, stretching to all corners of the earth. When he was in charge, our house was pure joy: we'd read books, debate the ideas of democracy and communism, the visions of Mandela and Gandhi, and over-analyse all the theories of liberation. We'd visit the museum and spend our days off in the zoo located at the intersection of the White and Blue Niles, feeding the giraffes and elephants with twigs we'd scoop up from the ground, pulling faces at the monkeys and filling their long, slim-fingered palms with pumpkin seeds, and then stare at how they effortlessly shelled them to get to the kernels inside. We'd try to lure the python to slither out to see how thick and long it was, but all we'd get was a glimpse of it curled up inside the stone cave, eyes glistening.

Sometimes we'd go to the cinema to watch cowboy, Egyptian, Indian or Italian films, struck by our favourite stars on the screen, and we had many: Sofia Loren, Brigitte Bardot, gorgeous from every angle. Once at home, it'd turn into a competition between us to dress and style our hair, emulating the women we'd seen on the big screen at the Coliseum.

One day in the car we turned into the Gordon Music Hall, where we came across some whites — some had sun-kissed skin, and others were reddened heading towards fully cooked — from all over the world, dancing to melodious music. The men's sturdy arms around the waists of women and girls wearing miniskirts, or jaksa fi khaat sitta as they were popularly known. That day, one after the other, Peter held us to teach us the slow dance, a tender dance, in a distant part of the hall while we suppressed our mischievous laughs.

When my father was around all these delights disappeared, putting my mother at ease. Sometimes she would send Ismail to watch over us, even Peter, in his absence. Ismail was unbearable, starting conversations that always ended with everyone bickering, and making us return home early. My mother would smile gloatingly and look at Ismail with eyes full of appreciation.

Ismail was and still is someone who enjoys making others' lives difficult, as sly as a fox. He has an uncanny ability to entrap others, willing to wait however long it takes. He carefully observes people, spies on them and learns their secrets to use for his own interest when the opportunity presents itself. And I don't doubt that he exploited this skill of his to join the National Intelligence and Security Service — the mere mention of its name caused others to tremble.

The fact that Ismail had it in for Peter was plain for anyone to see; he resented my father taking a stranger, rather than his blood, his nephew, under his wing. He stirred up turmoil to drive wedges between Peter and us, distorting Peter's image in my father's eyes so that he would throw him out. But all his efforts were fruitless. He only succeeded once Tahiya and Ummi teamed up after Tahiya had lured Peter to her room.

When Peter came to visit me in the office, and then invited me for lunch at Papa Kosta in downtown Khartoum, he told me his side of the story.

'I think Tahiya felt rejected,' I told him. 'She wasn't looking for a brother's love in that moment. Getting revenge was her only way of processing it. We, her sisters, tried to downplay the whole thing and pretend nothing ever happened, but she got Ummi and Ismail involved, which is why everyone gave you the cold shoulder. We never thought you'd just get up and disappear for all that time. We all regret how we treated you, even Ummi and Tahiya. Ummi realised how attached Baba was to you. His mood turned foul and he put himself under a lot of pressure at work because you were the only one he trusted, Peter. Baba started to burn out little by little, fading away. He lost that fighting spirit and gave in to Ismail, who ran everything into the ground.

'Ismail managed to marry Tahiya because of his conniving ways; he told Baba that Tahiya wasn't a virgin any more because of you, Peter and that we had to safeguard the family honour. A stranger shouldn't come to marry Tahiya and disgrace us on her wedding night. All this coerced Baba to marry off Tahiya to his nephew of all people. He was an animal with her. The day after their wedding night, she was admitted to the hospital with severe bleeding — he had ripped her open with a letter opener. Her face was swollen, her body revealing bruises all over. She didn't speak or even cry. She had fully surrendered, ready for death.

'Our eyes accosted her with questions after all that had happened that night, but she blanketed us in silence. Baba, Ummi, and even the whispering doctors, their heads bowed, heartbreak in their eyes. Then, instead of words, things were brought to light by silence: we were sleeping with her in her old room, because some nights she would wake up sweating, rocking in place. One day she told us, "From the start Ismail accused me of being a slut, that I would do anything to have sex, even with a servant, someone like Peter, and that I was just a whore and that he, a real man, had intervened and saved me.

"Ismail felt compelled to leave me vulnerable so people could chew me up, even though I swore to him nothing happened that night with Peter, and that I had lied because I had been mad at Peter at the time. But he took it as gospel truth that couldn't be recanted. He beat me to discipline me, so that I wouldn't dare do something like that again. He rubbed me beneath him forcefully, but he couldn't penetrate me. I thought that would be my saving grace, proof of my innocence and Peter's too, but he didn't hesitate to get his pocket knife and slice me open. He called me the clever whore that had sown herself back up to trick an oblivious husband." Her sobbing grew louder, crying and crying; someone unable to defend herself or at least clear her name.

'She continued once we had calmed her down. "After he thrust the knife in my flesh, I heard a primal scream. It was my own, and it became one with another scream from the depths of my memory, taking me back to that fateful day of so-called 'purification'. An echo bouncing back in the caves of my being. I yelped and screeched and clawed at him, my voice cracking. He smothered my mouth and thrust himself into me, hour after hour. I felt myself trickle out of my body. I noticed the white bedsheet underneath us, a red liquid spilled out onto it like a rain cloud expanding and stretching into the sky, taking on the shape of different creatures as each second passed. My eyes blurred with tears, and I fell away from the world into a peace that I had never felt before.""

After I recalled what Tahiya had shared with us, I cried. Peter's jaw was tightly clenched, but he was unable to change a thing. His feelings of guilt had seemingly increased. He blurted out, 'If Ismail ever touches a hair on her head again, I'll put a bullet through his.'

We each took a few breaths and started to chew our food in silence. The toasty aroma of Papa Kosta's bakery worked its way into our inner parts, freshly baked bread like that of our mothers, overwhelming us with nostalgia, love and safety.

During lunch, Peter asked me about what I'd been up to and what had led to this considerable change. He was taken aback by the woman I had become, from a girl unlucky in appearance, who mostly kept to herself reading books, whose mother was preparing her to be a mother hen herself, to an educated woman, known as an agitator, a member of the Sudanese Women's Union, a lawyer who fought the handwringing kind of cases, such as defending prostitutes when they had been treated unjustly or abused in brothels, where men seeking a good time would queue up.

I laughed modestly and said it was thanks to him because he had encouraged me to read, which revealed what my path could be, freeing me from the shackles of limitation. After immersing myself in books by feminists like Simone de Beauvoir and Germaine Greer, I became another woman, with considerable power, ready to take on the entire world if needed to achieve my dreams and ambitions, and to never hesitate to stand up for vulnerable women wherever they were. I wholeheartedly believed in the right of a woman to make her own decisions and to refuse the shackles slapped on her.

'So you've become a women's rights activist, one of those who declares war against the scales of gendered power.'

I chuckled. 'Exactly.'

Peter smiled, his eyes shining with pride, but he still wanted to confirm something. 'Just how much did Simone de Beauvoir corrupt you, though? Are you one of those who has sworn off marriage and children?'

His knitted brow was evidence enough that he was concerned about my answer.

'Motherhood is part and parcel of our bodies; it's there and not something we can just amputate because we believe in the freedom of choice. Relations between men and women are rarely on equal footing, and are fraught with dualities: strength and weakness, the leader and the led, superiority and inferiority... the economic, social and cognitive authority that men enjoy, that they only have because they had the freedom to experiment and make mistakes. As for us women, we aren't as lucky, so many refuse to enter into the institution of marriage, or when we do get into it, it's a nightmare for someone like me.

'Choosing a life partner is practically impossible, especially in a culture like ours. During one of my times away at a conference abroad, I got rid of the deformity that the mutilation of my genitalia had caused, and went back to the way I had been when my mother brought me into this world. I repaired myself, slapping all those customs in the face, and that itself is considered a challenge to someone who expects fruit baskets to be tightly shut, just so that he can be the first one to enjoy it, however he wants. Like what happened to

Tahiya. Her life became an unbearable hell, and on top of that, we're all expected to bring forth a stream of children, like baby machines. I believe that women have the right to enjoy sex without having to bring the prospect of children into it at all. Just like men allow themselves to let loose. Isn't that so? That the last thing on men's minds in the middle of sex is children?'

With an ambiguous smile playing on the corners of his mouth, Peter said, 'Like the prostitutes that you defend so valiantly. I see them all as exploited, though. It's wrong that they have to sell themselves to fill a financial need. Doesn't that make you feel sick? Then I asked myself, how do you spend all that energy defending those women when your own sister is wasting away under lock and key?'

I looked him squarely in the eye. 'I don't mind what they do one bit — as long as it's their choice. Tahiya chose obedience, to bend over backwards because of her children.'

'The choice itself is a philosophical dilemma,' he countered. 'Are they really in the best position to be making such decisions? To make such a decision fair, the person should have a good amount of understanding and knowledge based on lived experience, to make the best choice for that individual. I generally don't like to undervalue your efforts or discourage you, but there's an exploitation that takes place even if it's wrapped up in the label of freedom of choice. Women's bodies are exposed and exploited in images everywhere: advertisements, magazine covers, you name it. Their beauty is always up for sale. Human dignity is for sale, Jalaa, misleading people under the guise of freedom of choice.

'But my real advice to you, as my younger sister, is don't hold back on your motherly instinct, and let things naturally run their course. "Standing in the way of nature only brings bad things," as Lucy says.'

Then he laughed loudly, averting his beautiful eyes, while all his white teeth were on display, each set neatly, one next to the other.

'Who's Lucy?' I asked playfully.

'A wild and free mother who lives at home with us; she's Marco's wife, the friend that was with me when we came to see you all.'

'Ah yes, he seemed nice.'

'He's the closest friend I've got by far. Lucy throws out these sentences now and again, passing on the wisdom of her mothers back in the village. What she says sometimes actually makes sense, you know? What I mean is, don't limit yourself to the thinking of Beauvoir and Greer, live life naturally and don't fight your desires. Humans are just animals when it comes down to it, they've got desires that can't be fought: like the need for a good friend, love, marriage and having children, they're all instincts.'

Gently refuting his sentence, I said, 'That may be the case for someone who doesn't have much to do, but that's not me.'

He nodded attentively.

'But that didn't stop me from getting into a relationship when I joined the Faculty of Law at the University of Khartoum.' I quickly tossed this out on the table in front of us, which made all his senses stand to attention, keen to know more.

I was flooded with enthusiasm to speak to him about my experience at the University of Khartoum, right from the first day when I found myself treading lightly in front of the main library, the building like the backdrop to some bygone era, its ancient architecture of sandy red brick, made up of arches and domes, with motifs sculpted into the walls. Looking at it all made me feel like I was in front of an ancient house of worship, until I, too, became one of its regular patrons, drawing from its knowledge, culture and philosophy.

'Despite Ummi's objections, which nearly convinced Baba to keep me from continuing my education, I became someone who didn't hesitate to do what she wanted and who would never give up on her dreams — not under any circumstances. Then, one day, I was pleasantly surprised to find a stack of white clothes on my bed, and a good number of sandals along with a bag, a lot of notebooks and pens. It was my father's tacit blessing for me to go to university.

'I was on cloud nine that day, and noisily ran down the stairs to hug Baba and kiss his head. My happiness made him happy. The first day at the University of Khartoum was a real shock, but soon enough I melted into the crowd of Sudanese and European students. I found myself in daily contact with young men, and it was inevitable that my heart would start beating wildly with love.'

Peter was observing me and smiling now and again, nodding for me to go on.

'I came across Hassan Abbas, and I only understand now why I was drawn to him: he's a lot like you.' I laughed a short, brittle laugh and went on. 'He's not as tall as you, more average height, wheat-complexioned, with chiselled shoulders like the edge of a wall. His eyes shone with intelligence, and he had thick moustache handles on either side of his small mouth. His personality was that of a revolutionary, commanding, and

yet warming others up to him with his poetry and singing —
he didn't struggle to light a university hall ablaze with his
speeches.

'From the first day we met, we were inseparable, except
until a few months ago.' I said this with my eyes lowered. I
exhaled slowly.

'He's the son of a train driver from the furthest reaches
North of the country, but his family settled in Atbara, the
Railway City. The son of a fierce unionist leader, a railway
worker. In the union, with the snap of a finger, they're able
to gather more than thirty thousand workers together for a
successful strike and make the central government reconsider
its decisions.'

I thought to myself of how Hassan had been raised in
Atbara, a city in permanent tumult that politicians were loath
to anger. A city for whom the train was its soul, its tracks the
veins tying together all of Sudan, thanks to the hearts of thirty
thousand men or more, whose affiliations all dissolved into the
melting pot that was their occupation. Railway workers who
had come from far and wide across the country to inject life
into all the stations and villages that would barely stand up
against any natural disaster.

I remembered that he'd tell me time after time how his
father would allow him to accompany him on long journeys,
cutting vertically through the country from Halfa in the furthest
point North to Wau in the southwest, and from Port Sudan in
the east to Nyala in the west, passing through Er Roseires. He
immersed himself in all these cities as an adolescent, learning
about their agricultural produce and how to greet them in each
of their languages, his internal rhythm in tune with all the

songs he came across on his travels. And so between him and these cities a relationship as solid as railroad tracks was born; he was always possessed by a deep yearning to visit those places, like the yearning of a train whistle when it draws into a station as another leaves.

I'd be captivated whenever he would hum this song: *Train of longing, hurry and take us to where our loved ones are.*

'He must have inherited his rebellious nature and revolutionary spirit from his father, and his city that refused any injustice. At university, he was a political activist, leading demonstrations and all the disturbances that aroused the ire of the state. I'd never come across someone as brave or as noble as him. But he's not the family kind — the cause is everything for him.

'If the party demands it, he'll never hesitate to drop anything and everything. He's always on the front lines of the resistance. Maybe that's what made me cling to him even more each time he survived.'

'At that time I feared losing him forever; what's strange is that to this day he's still a university student because he keeps missing the final exams — academic qualifications aren't on his list of priorities. There's even a rumour flying around that the party asked him to stay back as a student solely to bring in recruits.

'We ended up having a difficult conversation in front of the examinations hall. Its unique ceiling that looked like the wing of a bird about to take flight is where we often sought shade. He told me he wasn't going inside.

"Why not, Hassan? Please, let's just finish this year together." But he refused. I accused him, and the whole party actually, of being irresponsible. The party would fall apart if

178

every member decided to stay where they were.

"You've forgotten why you came to university to begin with, Hassan. You're addicted to how students always put you on a pedestal. You've forgotten you still have a whole life ahead of you."

"What life are you talking about, Jalaa?"

"Our life together, of course!"

"I'm married to the cause, Jalaa, you know that. I'm never going to be a family man."

"What do you mean?"

"I mean that this is my life, and I don't want any other. You've got to focus on *your* future."

'I felt my eyes watering and entered the examinations hall, feeling like I was suffocating in a poorly ventilated room, and from that day everything changed.

'Despite the not-so-happy ending to that story, if you think about it, I was lucky enough to be reborn in this historic, prestigious university. We spent all our time in that coffee shop for activists, debating everything under the sun: religion, politics, economics, philosophy, whether or not God exists, and as usual Hassan Abbas had been the star of it all, his thoughts on a whole other level. We always had a hand in committees for organising festivals and poetry nights; the last one was a poetry festival for the Palestinian poet Mahmoud Darwish. We stood in the western square like bamboo sticks, that's how crowded it was. Students and intellectuals, journalists and teachers, standing shoulder to shoulder, filled with joy. He held my hand so tenderly, making me glance at him sideways. He was reciting in time with one of the literary department students, the words of a stanza of a Darwish poem:

My watch fell into the grey water
So I didn't make it to your luminous meeting.

'I turned to the side to find myself facing a man I wanted with all my being, and I hoped to spend my entire life with him. My eyes filled with tears again, and this time I cried. Panicked, he asked, "What is it, Jalaa?"

"I love you, Hassan Abbas. You're my everything."

'He hugged me to him and kissed my head, whispering, "You're my goddess."

I cried my eyes out on his chest, sobbing and wailing. Love always hurts.

'The festival finished at midnight. He escorted me to the dormitories, and we stood in front of the door for a long time, our hands intertwined. Uncle Yaqub, the doorman, stood there about to shut the half-open door, calling, "Yallah my girl, hurry up son, let's call it a night."

'I freed my hands from his fingers as if I were a part of him and he a part of me. Even though I'd see him soon, this small goodbye was bittersweet, dragging us down as we floated high on Aladdin's carpet."'

I rested my chin on my chest and Peter patted my shoulders. Then he asked me, 'What happened? Where is he?'

'He's married to the cause like he said he would be, but we meet now and again. I never broach the subject of marriage or a family, but I'll always wait for him. Though the flames of his love have died a little, he'll always be the man I want, but can never have.'

Peter stayed silent. Then he said, 'I appreciate that, Jalaa, but I'm telling you, love can make miracles happen, and this national, political cause tires of men quickly. Sometimes it just spits them out. So stay ready.'

Despite my wet cheeks, I felt lighter. I thanked Peter for listening so attentively; it's difficult for me to be so vulnerable in front of someone else because they all know me as the Iron Lady.

'So, Margaret Thatcher, it's late. Let me take you home and say hi to Baba while I'm about.'

We stopped by Sweet Rosanna, and he bought some of their basta and basbousa. Once back in the jeep, he gifted me the packaged sweet, nutty pastry and the semolina cake by putting it in my lap. On the way home, we reflected on a few things: how I'd start visiting him more so that his children could get to know their aunt; I could build on my relationship with Theresa, and also get a chance to meet the sage Lucy. We agreed to wage war on Ismail and free Tahiya from his clutches — we had to come up with a foolproof plan.

That's what led to us meeting up more often, discussing family matters, my father and his illness — he was seeing some improvement now that Peter was back. As for Ismail, well, he started to really let his devils out when Peter started coming by the house more often — he felt his throne being threatened.

Thankfully, all of Ismail's movements were under everyone's watchful eyes, now that they had moved into a flat on the second floor of the family home. Even his behaviour towards Tahiya changed because he sensed that her 'supposed brother' — as he called him — Peter, would step in.

I explained to Peter how, after he left, Baba brought me

into the fold of his business. He also came to support me in my efforts to get into the University of Khartoum, complete my education and expand my circle of contacts. I was no longer expected to just train to be a housewife and help Mama around the house — I had bigger things to do. It was almost as if I were considered a replacement for Peter, who had simply got up and left, leaving Baba exposed, vulnerable — Baba didn't trust Ismail in the least and had sensed his nephew's envy from the outset. I came to know Baba's business inside out after becoming his lawyer; it was only then that I discovered the document-doctoring Ismail had been up to, exposing his aim to dispossess Baba of his properties piece by piece.

I had my own suspicions from the hint of menace in his words. There was no question that, with a simple flick of the wrist, he could throw me, a political activist, in jail. I was someone who disturbed the nation with 'pointless protests', as he and his cronies called them. He took advantage of being in the national security service and threw his weight around. I would ignore him, but at times his threats sent shivers down my spine. After Peter showed up again, however, we all felt a halo of protection cloaking us. Even Tahiya started showing signs of rebellion and began to stand up to Ismail's arrogance with something of indifference and disregard.

I received a letter from Hassan Abbas; the postage stamp had a camel on it. I went into my room and opened the white envelope, framed by blue and red borders. When I freed the letter from its numerous folds, a distinct scent floated up from the letter. He was there, arms around me, in that very moment. I gave in to his embrace, my eyes closed, the letter against my cheek, so I could inhale it in full. His body was there before me, his thick curly hair, his sideburns that only ended at the tip of his earlobes, his white shirt fitted against his body, chest hair peeking out, and black trousers that flared at the bottom. How could I forget his captivating smile? I stayed like that, allowing myself to bathe in his warmth. Then, I started to read the letter:

My heart and soul,

It was these sorts of beginnings that made me melt in his arms. His letters carried an imprint of his peripatetic nature. Every few months, a letter would arrive from a new territory, a different city or forgotten village where he was teaching. Hassan feared getting caught in the octopus-like clutches of cities. He'd tell me many a story and always sign them with a heart pierced by an arrow.

I don't know what I want from someone who keeps fleeing one place for the next. 'Being in your presence for two years is enough to keep me going. I know you're still with me, and I with you, even if I'm far away,' he would say.

How I wanted for him to meet Peter, wondering how it would play out for two such beings to encounter one another. I wrote him a letter asking that he spend Christmas and New Year's in Khartoum, so he could get to know Peter and we could all spend some time together. I promised that I wouldn't stand in his way when he wanted to go back to serve those on the margins of cities and villages, fighting adolescent illiteracy. The next day, I posted the letter feeling upbeat at the thought of what Peter and Hassan's encounter would be like. I waited for his response with eagerness and anxiety, which only dissipated when I came across him leaning against the frame of the front door to my office, his arms crossed over his chest. A thick, carefully knotted, giraffe tail-hair bracelet adorned his wrist and he was wrapped in a black-and-white striped wool shawl as protection against the bitter December cold. Black and white were his favourite colours. Even when it came to colours, he shied away from neutrality.

He hadn't changed all that much, but his facial features were sharper and his eyes glittered with — was that longing? As he stood on the threshold, he smiled tenderly and my heart fell to my feet. Hassan Abbas? With a childlike wonder, I stared at him, wanting to laugh and cry all at once. I didn't hear my voice as I called out to him, as if I had done so with my eyes alone.

He advanced slowly, his heeled shoes drumming against the black and white tiled floor, as if they were a natural extension of himself. He sat perched on the edge of my desk and stretched out a hand to wipe away my tears of joy. I nestled into his neck without saying a word, and left him to wash over me, to the core of my being.

His overpowering presence left me bubbling with joy; having him here was a well-deserved compensation for the months of self-imposed separation. I filled my spirit and memory with small, intimate details that I would live off till our next meeting, its date unknown; these small moments would be enough.

His passion was for teaching and mine was for human rights. I was fully immersed in the political and in the movements for social change. And so we had agreed that neither of us would get in the way of the other, or restrict ourselves by marriage. We weren't ready to shoulder its responsibilities, but it didn't stop us from getting closer. We chased our dreams and lived out our ambitions parallel to our love and respect for one another, as well as our appreciation for all of each other's achievements. He would say that if our love entered the institution of marriage then I'd become a mindless housewife and he'd become mundane daddy Abbas. Up against the greedy demands to have a family and to keep it safe, our abilities to be critical thinkers and persistent in our dreams would fall by the wayside, simply consumed by the ties of kinship that would inevitably multiply like a mushroom colony.

We'd be camped out in our love like pigeons, so according to him it was better if we stayed the way we were: with him married to the cause, and me to the law.

Sometimes I'd reject such reasoning, saying that we would be stronger together, that we'd support one another. One time, he forcefully shook his head and said, 'Our society is like a coin mint, spitting us all out, one and the same. I can't guarantee that I'll be the same person I am now, if put in a different situation. There's a dark cave called the subconscious, where old personalities are piled up, of which anyone can rise to the surface and take control. What we intellectuals show of ourselves is the personality we allow others to see, but it's fragile, ready to shrink away at the slightest confrontation.' He arched his eyebrows to show he was saying all this partly in jest. 'And how can I be with a woman anyways who reads Simone, and has a dog-eared book by Germaine Greer called *The Female Eunuch*?'

We sighed and postponed the conversation. I saw truth

in Beauvoir and Greer's beliefs, but it didn't stop me from feeling the urge to be a wife or a mother one day.

The December cold was biting, announcing that Christmas, National Day and New Year's were just round the corner: loud celebrations that would only end at daybreak. Yellow lighting faintly illuminates the streets. Artificial Christmas trees of all sizes stand at the entrances of hotels and clubs for the diaspora communities, like the Italian Apollo and St James; the trees are dressed in bells, lights and stockings, some of the ornaments in the shape of Santa Claus with his puffed out cheeks, his face lost in a beard of white clouds. Khartoum's sky is bursting with fireworks shooting upwards from the roof of the Republican Palace, the president's way of wishing his Christian subjects, guests including traders, tourists and businessmen, and the communities from friendly nations the best of the season. Indians, Yemenis, Armenians, Cypriots, Italians and Arabs buoying the atmosphere with their presence and filling Khartoum with joy.

Posters for jazz concerts were stuck to signposts at the start of main roads and bridges, for venues such as halls, hotels and clubs crowded with adoring fans. With his denim jacket and guitar slung over his shoulder, Sharhabil Ahmed was the king of jazz. Members of other bands — the Scorpions, Dem and Lumarica — would accompany him on stage. All of this was a good omen for Hassan and me, that we'd spend the end of the year happily surrounded by fanfare.

On Christmas day, Mama, Nidal and I all got into a taxi to greet family friends and then stopped by Peter's house. The atmosphere was festive, and a large sheep had been slaughtered in honour of his guests, Mama Fawzia in particular. His wife,

Theresa, was warm and generous; Lucy appeared somewhat apprehensive and busied herself with the many children milling around in their best clothes. Vibrant colours, squeals of delight, hands sticky from sweets. They darted off in all different directions, a swarm of butterflies, then boomeranged back to Lucy as if she were tied to them by some invisible thread. I came to learn later that just as the shepherd eases the fear of his lambs, so does the ghost of Lucy's mother, Maria-Edo, for her daughter and grandchildren. Lucy's nugget of wisdom that day was about how, when others envy you or are astonished by you, you're more likely to be a target of harmful magic: which is what usually happens when they see her litter of children.

Whenever a guest arrived, they would be met by twenty sets of curious eyes staring at them: the children's, and those of Lucy and Theresa, women who would have driven Simone de Beauvoir to death from grief if they had ever met.

Marco was cheerful, doling out tearful laughter and punchlines like sweets.

The house was like one hosting a wedding and had a large door with open arms to receive all, which stood next to a solid tree, its branches waving in the wind, and the spacious hosh was crammed with relatives, neighbours and friends. Men in the living room; women flitting between the cooking tent and the shaded areas, chatting on all topics, bubbling with happiness. The smell of grilled meat floats in the air, the children flying in and out like bees, their hands shooting out to grab ice cream cones.

Peter took out some cases of imported wine for the guests, and little by little, everyone started getting drunk. The women kept to their beer cans and fizzy drinks.

Mama and Nidal excused themselves, as they needed to be at home to keep an eye on Baba. I chose to stay under the pretence of helping Theresa tend to the guests who kept streaming in. I was only concerned about one person.

As the day gave in to evening, Peter put on some Zairean music. Everyone danced. Even Lucy joined in with her children; she wiggled her waist, encouraging them to follow her lead. Now and again she'd throw in some village moves. Marco jumped up and wrapped his arms around her, the children now surrounding them; he slowed down her quick village rhythm, and they swayed together as if they were a single entity, while dozens of glittering black eyes slipped in and out of the shadows.

I noticed Hassan Abbas entering apprehensively, crushing out a cigarette butt that was still half-lit. He started to search for me, his eyes darting here and there. I rushed to Peter and we walked together arm in arm to welcome Hassan. Each of us hugged the other as if we were old friends. We sat on a table a bit removed from everything, in the corner, and started chatting. After two glasses, Hassan grew emboldened and started talking to Peter openly. Politics was one of the issues that dominated their conversation, especially the problem of Sudan and how its southern part wasn't granted its independence as an outcome of the Addis Ababa agreement, aggravating the existing discontent. Any time a peace accord was struck between the central government and the rebels, the southern elite were given positions of power and properties, and some even left the South to live in Khartoum itself. Soon enough they forgot what they were fighting for in the first place. Other issues were Arab versus African identity or a blend of the two, and the martial law pressing down on people's chests.

Hassan was visibly relieved when Peter responded, 'Even though I'm an officer in the armed forces, I'm against the army taking control of civilian institutions. This is one of those historical mistakes that will follow us to the grave. The fever of military coups orchestrated by political parties, with which we have inaugurated our way of governance, unfortunately, won't end. It will keep breeding like seaweed. Even the most insignificant soldier can dream of being in the seat of power. The military institution has been infected by the sickness of ideology. Talk of how corruptly the economy is being run has even broken into the simplest of homes. It won't be easy for the military to come back from this. Soldiers used to take an oath, that under any circumstances they would die to protect the lives of others. But these days, the military is too power-hungry to do its actual job and defend the nation, ready to let friends and everyone else perish — as long as soldiers stay in charge, that is. And for such a soldier, farting, let alone pulling the trigger, becomes difficult.'

Hassan's head tipped back as he snorted, while Peter started to shake, suppressing his laughter.

Hassan addressed Peter, saying that he remembered how his father had been arrested several times during riots by the railroad workers, and how he had been tortured on numerous occasions. 'He instilled fear into those at the very top, until they came to view even a citizen's demand for his basic rights — rights that are the ruler's responsibility to give — as a pickaxe that could destroy their throne, and they won't hesitate to point the mouths of their rifles to the citizens' chests to silence them. The people will be shot with the very bullets that have been paid for by taxes and levies imposed on them. Each citizen buying the bullet that he will die by.'

Peter nodded his head in agreement while he poured another glass for Hassan. Hassan gulped his down in one go, his face contorting from the burning sensation snaking down his throat. He then smiled awkwardly, 'I must admit, I was wondering about the nature of the relationship between you and Jalaa, and the rest of her family. When Jalaa talked about you like her brother, I thought it was one of those dysfunctional relationships we hear of, full of hypocrisy, bitterness and guilt, in which certain people in this part of the country try and make up for historical injustices.'

I squirmed. Why was he saying such things? He took advantage of our stunned silence. 'I thought you were like one of those young boys that are brought to serve in the houses of Arabs, and that you had been made into a Muslim and an Arab. I have several friends whom I only later found out had other names; their church and tribal ones had been erased. Like Abbas, Younes and Abdullah, and how they used to be Thomas, Ajak and Mangu. I was stumped that Jalaa kept calling you her brother Peter, and not by any other name. How did you do it? It seems that Abdelsalaam is one of a kind.'

Peter coughed out a muted laugh saying, 'I don't know if it was survival or something else. For me, just the idea of those boys down South migrating by any means possible to the North to avoid being thrown into the war, is what I call survival. Regardless of the distortion of their identities as you say, because of political or social imperatives, my father Abdelsalaam is a different kind of man, who would tell me frankly, when he saw people trying to pressurise me to change my religion, "Listen, Peter, it's not my job to get you into heaven, like all those fools keep saying. I'm not sure I'll get in myself. On this earth, man has to live his own life, and make his own way to heaven. I see that you have a good heart, and even if you did go to church every Sunday, it's enough that we both believe in one God." So he didn't pressurise me in any way, and I think it's my good luck that I survived twice. The first time from being enlisted in the South, and the second time from having to change who I am.

'My father Abdelsalaam didn't leave me to the religious bullies or people railing at me. He stood up to them with a resilience that gave me the chance to live my life, for the most part, quietly. Politics has robbed us of everything, Hassan, and instead of believing in the virtues of our co-existence, we've started to reopen past wounds and rub salt in them. Some have contented themselves with hate-mongering until that's all they do. So much so, they've come to believe they don't have a duty to enact real and desired change.'

'Unfortunately, so many of today's elite just point to the ill of ethnic and religious diversity, as if that's the real issue. I've been to every inch of this nation, and Peter, everyone is suffering.'

'Yes, that's what I mean,' Peter responded. 'I've also been to several areas and stayed long enough to make me see things in a different light. Having to change one's religion or name becomes insignificant compared to a village where the children are running behind a train to pick up scraps just to get by, or where one dies from a scorpion or snake bite, simply because no one could access an antidote in time.

'For me, the question of identity is no longer tied to party or religion, but instead, it's about having the opportunity to play my full role as a citizen in the political, military and cultural spheres — all in the hope of contributing to pulling the nation out of the crises it's suffering. Yes, I'm from the South, but I should be able to express my opinion on what's going on in the North, in the east and the west. Yes, I'm from the South, but it doesn't mean I don't care or want a better life for the rest of the nation. And the flip side of that is whatever is going on in the South should be everyone's concern, a problem for Sudan as a whole, not some distant rural cousin that we try to avoid. We belong to the nation as a whole, not just one part of it.'

Hassan replied, 'Issues like political participation for all, social justice, racism, religious discrimination, lack of belonging, people not finding themselves represented accurately in the media, or at all for that matter — these are all interlinked and can't, really shouldn't, be separated. When we treat the country as parcels of land, the way we isolate a donkey's anus when treating it, we hone in only on a specific area without considering the causes that have poisoned the bloodstream of the animal. So I took it upon myself, as my prime mission, to work in the darkest of places, to make a difference.'

Peter nodded in agreement.

When the discussion reached this point, I asked Hassan to dance with me to the bouncy rhythm of Leo Sayer's 'How Much Love', a song that invigorated every cell of my body. I felt like this song represented my mixed feelings: love and stability versus fear and the unknown. We swayed side to side together in time to a beat neither too slow nor too fast. He wrapped his arm around my waist, and with his other hand clasped mine to his chest, by his heart. We danced as if we were alone in this world.

He whispered in my ear with a voice that found its way to my insides like beams of light. 'Merry Christmas and Happy Independence Day.'

That sentence was all it took for my walls to come crumbling down, and for me to surrender to the flow of love that was washing over me.

It was a jam-packed week, during which the usual arrangements for Independence Day took place: the trees were decorated with lights, the lower thirds of their trunks were painted with white lime, and the sidewalks were painted black and white. The streets were clean and flowing with a celebratory atmosphere, musical notes were in the air, bodies crowding in the city, local rhythms and those from all over the world pulsating: old and new. Everyone was walking on air in one way or the other.

We ended the year by attending a once-in-a-lifetime kind of party, which William Andre's Jazz band brought to life. I remember how Hassan would call him the Brown Gazelle, because he was just as famous as a loping basketball player in Sudanese sports circles; he was a man of many talents. At the party, he sang a new song, *Ya Qalbi Kifaya Mozah*, which made everyone rush to the dance floor. After that, we stepped together, Hassan and I, into the new year.

I then found Peter and myself bidding Hassan farewell at the train station bustling with people shuttling in and out. I don't know how I still hadn't grown used to saying goodbye to him. Every time, I felt as if something jagged was cutting through me. Peter also was trying to mask his pain at this parting. Hassan removed his sabiba giraffe bracelet and tied it to me; he then squeezed Peter's hand warmly and got onto the train. Several months later, my father died, and Hassan quickly rushed back to console me, after which his letters stopped. During the chaos of '76, which went by many names, but that a lot of us called the Mercenary Happenings, I was worried for him, but I never lost hope that he would one day surprise me, with his arms crossed over his chest, leaning against the doorframe. I felt abandoned, but I had a reservoir of memories that I could live off for the rest of my life.

10

In 1976, the year of chaos, all hell broke loose. Depending on who you were speaking to, the events of that year had a different name. What these labels achieved was the division of all into three camps: supporters, opponents and those who were just plain confused. We had never been more bewildered as a nation; our land slipped into more and more violence. On the streets, questions, regrets and bodies lay out in the open. Could I really be the only one who felt this all so keenly? What left me vulnerable was that I didn't fall into any of the three camps: neither a supporter nor an opponent, and of course, I wasn't confused. Despite not knowing where I stood, I still hadn't abandoned my duty as an armed forces officer to counter the foreign attack that had struck the nation — foreign according to the first-hand information that had been supplied to us.

Several times the phone rang. Ringing and ringing in my private study, better known among the household as the Control Room. Why was it ringing continuously without pause? It was Friday, our day off, and barely dawn. The ringing made me extract myself from Theresa's embrace and stride over to the office to answer the phone. It was the top command ordering me to come urgently to headquarters, using the backroads; I should take great care to arrive safely.

I began to curse under my breath; it must be another coup. When will these people igniting coups stop coming out of the woodwork, spawning like algae? Every Tom, Dick and Harry wanted to take the reins and kick the sides of the others to spur them on — a blatant insult to the army and civilians alike. What use is it for the lowliest soldier to rule the country when he doesn't hesitate to put his life at risk? He becomes president, and then what? He's killed and made into a national hero. What have we gained? I abhor men who bring battle to the bosom of cities, as civilians should be spared at all costs — especially women and children. I know saying such things could get me swiftly court-martialled; we are living under military rule, after all.

Ignoring Theresa's anxious questions, I quickly got dressed and strapped my gun in, after ensuring the chamber was loaded. I knocked lightly on Marco's door and opened it; I didn't want to wake up his little ones squeezed into every available space on and below the beds. He leapt up, sidestepping the small limbs flung out across the floor; small feet and hands, like branches of a tree after a hurricane.

'What is it, Peter?' he asked, his eyes wide.

I tried to mask my worry. 'They've called me down to

headquarters. I don't know why exactly.' I entrusted everyone to his care and made sure no one would leave under any circumstances, unless life outside appeared to have gone back to normal. I handed him a slip of paper with Jalaa's phone number, so he could check on them while I was away. I didn't elaborate any further and squeezed his shoulder briefly, 'I'll call you when I get the chance.' He escorted me to the door as if paying his final respects. I only came back to the house three nights later, when I found everyone on the verge of holding my funeral.

I gunned the engine of the jeep, and its unnecessarily loud choking noise made everything seem that much worse in the eerie quiet of night. Once on my way, I spotted some nightclub regulars loitering around on the streets; I almost snapped at them to go on home, but decided better of it, taking a deep breath instead. Sometimes being struck by a catastrophe is less painful than anticipating one. It was going to happen all the same.

I spoke to myself the whole way to try and calm down. My anxiety was getting the better of me the closer I got to the headquarters. It felt like it was on a different continent altogether — when did it become so far away? The roads grew completely deserted where I was now; on I drove into the bristling night.

As for civilians, the people who usually made merry by moonlight, or the regular cinemagoers — they and their houses were fast asleep in the dark. The dogs weren't howling just yet, a good omen; they were yet to pick up the scent of disaster.

I arrived just as a meeting was about to begin. Gunfire rang out from different directions in the city; my heart dropped and chaos ensued amongst us. We barely managed to compose ourselves enough to draw up a quick plan of attack on the enemy that still hadn't shown their faces. Who were they? Where had they come from? From our extensive experience with the occasional coups by ambitious soldiers, we thought we knew how best to engage with them.

The army swooped down on the city and the enemy did the same. I suppose we were enemies from the perspective of the ones who'd attacked the city at dawn. Battles took place at the entrances to the city, the broadcasting house and at the entry and exit points of the bridges that tied together three cities in Khartoum state — Khartoum itself, Khartoum Bahri, and Omdurman — like the joints of a human skeleton. Our enemy was more organised than us, gaining control of such strategic locations with exceptional speed.

We clashed with the attackers without learning anything new about them, and had only bits and pieces of unverified information at hand. Were they even Sudanese? Vicious fighting ensued in the middle of the city for so many hours I lost count. The enemy began to retreat and the armed forces took back control of the strategic locations, but then things grew exceptionally complex once the attackers sought refuge in residential neighbourhoods. Compound walls became their protection and alleyways their hideouts. In our crosshairs, everyone was fair game. The silence was deafening, as if the people were yet to wake, but they were in fact paralysed by fear. Even the dogs and roosters swallowed their barks and crows. At midday, reinforcements arrived from nearby cities and quickly launched into the haphazard fighting. We were clearly falling apart because there wasn't one central chain of command issuing orders or assigning missions. As agreed, everyone just started striking the nearest target, out of anger, humiliation and fear.

With each hour that passed, the situation grew more dire. Damn them for being spineless and hiding in residential areas. They thought this would make us hesitate to shoot them, but it didn't. In those moments, I remembered my immediate and larger family. Theresa and the girls; Lucy, Marco and their children; Jalaa and her sisters, and my mother Fawzia. How I hoped they were all staying indoors.

The warfare continued the entire day, especially around the airport, the broadcasting house, the headquarters and surrounding neighbourhoods. It was the same place where Baba Abdelsalaam's house was. My mouth went dry. I could almost hear his voice amidst the rattle of gunfire, 'The girls, Peter, your sisters.'

A fury exploded within me and I ordered my soldiers to strike with an iron fist. We weren't men if we abandoned our nation while we were still alive, while it was being brutalised by whoever this was. My soldiers made their way out, spurred on, courageous. Were we in a war? I didn't know, there wasn't time to ask such questions. Of course, it was a war. In a country like ours, any two soldiers can spark a war when one trains his rifle, full of dozens of bullets, on his compatriot.

Chaos prevailed, the barrels of rifles pointed at chests. Death was strutting around in the streets in the form of stray bullets, hunting down citizens inside their homes, because there was no clear target; it was as if we were fighting our own shadows, our own ghosts. Were they Eritreans? Ethiopians? Sudanese?

Shadows quickly fell, and the city was drowned in darkness. No one lit any lanterns, the streets were pitch-black. Houses were pulsing with whispers, and no one inside had the nerve to even let a candle flame flicker. Everything and anything was done to camouflage life from death, which was whistling in every corner; bullets crisscrossed the sky like the most treacherous of fireworks. Darkness during wartime was a chance to re-strategise and attempt to deceive the enemy. It was also a chance to close the eyelids of the lifeless whose pupils were protruding into the void.

I accompanied my soldiers to the large hospital to deposit the dead in the morgue and tend to the wounded. The hospital was being pulled in all different directions, blood splattered on the walls and keening echoing down the corridors. A woman had lost her child, and a pair of sons were grieving for their father after he had exited the bathroom and a bullet lodged right between his eyes. Another mother had lost her daughter, and a third woman was injured in the operation room. My soldiers and I steadied ourselves against the wall, exhausted. I caught sight of Hayat, my younger sister, sewing up a gaping wound in a soldier's shoulder. Shaking myself awake, I strode towards her. Without even greeting her, I launched into a barrage of questions. 'Why are you here? How did you get here? You should be at home!'

'I'm dealing with a patient,' she said coldly. 'Please wait outside.'

I slowly backed away, never taking my eyes off her.

Her brown skin was luminous, as if there were sunrays under her skin. Her posture was upright and rigid like a well-trained soldier's, her face beautiful, setting those in pain at ease. Her cropped hair perfectly matched the delicate contours of her face. Her tapered fingertips flitted over the open wound that she willed to get better. Suddenly a surge of pride took the place of my big-brother fears.

I returned to my soldiers, encouraging the injured ones and helping others carry their comrades' bodies to the morgue. Through the haze of exhaustion, I heard a voice like gurgling water. 'Sorry I was so curt with you Peter; it's my job.'

I turned and smiled at her, though now was hardly the time to do so with everything going on. I nodded my head slowly and then patted her shoulder, getting close enough for my nostrils to fill with the scent of antiseptic. 'You're doing a good job,' I whispered.

With a kind look that eased the day's miserable suffering, she said, 'I couldn't have stayed at home when so many people need help.'

Panic struck me again and I said gruffly, 'You could get yourself killed.' She let me know she wasn't a child anymore.

'Yes, yes, Dr Hayat!'

She stifled a laugh that nearly leapt from her eyes.

I said decisively, 'Let's sort this out.' I added, showing her my index and middle finger stuck to each other, 'Together. Get back to work.'

In her white coat spattered with blood, she returned with confident steps to her patients, who were piled up as far as the eye could see. Fatigue was evident in her posture, but she was propelled by an extraordinary energy, reminding me of a hearth burning with large glowing embers.

The president's speech the following day was inspiring, promising. He described us as brave protectors of the nation. Each of us felt his powerful speech was directed at us specifically, which made the burdensome sorrow of the previous day dissipate.

We started to cleanse the city of them, of their ghosts and ours. Everyone was the enemy, even those Eritreans and Ethiopians who had been living among us for so many years. We attacked, arrested and chased all suspects. After the attackers started to withdraw and infiltrate homes, we led merciless raids into all the households of suspects. The easiest thing was to shoot at the slightest hesitation we felt. The killings were haphazard, any soldier could see that. On the third day, it seemed that we finally had the reins of the situation in hand, and some of our colleagues even celebrated the victory by shooting bullets into the sky, causing more people to panic.

The smell of gunpowder hung heavy in the air, cars burning everywhere I turned. Fires here, fires there. Citizens yowling for the injured lying on the roads or their beloveds killed in the crossfire. I heard the continuous rat-a-tat-tat from every direction, army trucks screeching as they tried to brake, skidding across the asphalt. These sounds inhabited the corridors of my ears for several weeks; my muscles ached and my head was cloudy from the lack of sleep. Once things calmed down a little, only then did we become aware of our condition: eyes sunken into our skulls from fighting off sleep, our khaki clothes stuck to our bodies, moist with sweat and blood. Disoriented minds filled with ghosts, and the sounds of relentless battle.

Despite our relief at finally quashing the coup, the atmosphere was gloomy. The source of melancholy could easily have been the tender souls still hovering on the outskirts of the city.

We banded together once more and put in place a plan to safeguard the city: continuous inspections to crack down on the hideouts of any mercenaries. Eventually, I managed to break away to go home and get some rest. Marco, Theresa, everyone embraced me, crying like orphans. I apologised, explaining that I hadn't been able to reach them as the phone lines had been cut. Once the connection came back, I turned the dial to check on Jalaa and the family, not failing to mention that Dr Hayat was fine. I spoke with Mama Fawzia after she snatched the phone from Jalaa. She kept saying Hayat's name, and I reassured her all was well, that Hayat was under my direct protection. I also made sure to tell Mama Fawzia that Hayat was saving many lives. The warmth of her smile travelled through the line, and she thanked me in the form of a prayer that all mothers are good at giving.

After a warm shower, I slipped into a deep slumber without nightmares or dreams, sleeping like the dead.

In the first days, I slept with a clear conscience, the sleep of someone who had carried out his duty to his nation and his people with courage. Then, the mourning tents started to appear in my way wherever I went, the dark fabric structures popping up here and there. Where and when had all these people died? Victims that no one mentioned; had all of these people been killed accidentally?

The soldiers continued to burst into all the houses by force, searching for mercenaries in a city-wide clean-up campaign. Every citizen was a suspect, and the men were questioned to determine if they were Sudanese or otherwise, as their similar-looking features caused confusion. Some citizens volunteered information about houses in their neighbourhoods. Ethiopians live in that house; bachelors live there. This made the soldiers focus on those homes with newfound ferocity, front doors caving in under their heavy soles.

In such frenzied times, the worst characteristics of people bubble to the surface: cowardice and hypocrisy. Betrayal of your countrymen under the guise of patriotism. How else were they able to furtively extend their fingers to their neighbours' houses to be searched? In other dictionaries, it may have been defined as cooperating with the authorities, but I saw it as a vile way of settling old grudges between citizens by exploiting the soldiers on duty.

The atmosphere was laden with the smell of rotting corpses.

How would we be able to differentiate between the enemy and those on our side? We all belong to one land, one continent, with no sea separating us. I felt lightheaded. So much loss of life. My sleep from then on was nightmares and ghosts.

I dropped by to visit Baba Abdelsalaam's home and found the walls riddled with holes. Jalaa pulled out the empty shells that had fallen through the windows and circular air vents, shells that had flown through the city sky like meteorites.

Everyone was in a state of semi-shock, because from upstairs, Jalaa had noticed a number of Majrus trucks passing by below, transporting bodies and amputated limbs, piled up like animal skins, to unknown destinations. A white sheet with blood soaking through in several places covered them, but she saw what was underneath when the wind lifted it.

She stroked the giraffe hair bracelet that circled her left

wrist; Hassan Abbas' bracelet, which he had placed on her at the train station. When she noticed me staring at her, her tears started to flow freely. We then sat in a corner and she shared what was running through her mind. 'Do you think Hassan's safe? What's happening to our country? These massacres have to stop.'

'Thankfully Hassan is outside of the city.' As for the massacres, I was about to admit that even innocent people have been killed unintentionally, but I held my tongue at the last minute so as not to scare her further. I had to hold on to the belief, as it goes in the army, that collateral damage is inevitable, but that didn't stop a cloud of grief from settling on my heart.

Amidst her stream of tears she said, 'I don't know, I could swear I saw his face on one of those bodies down there.'

I shook my head violently. 'I doubt it. I'm sure you'll get a letter in a few days that'll put your mind at rest. And anyway, you were the one who was in the line of fire, not him.'

She smiled faintly, and it seemed that I hadn't managed to put her at ease completely. I didn't know how deep the gulf within her was, but from where I was, it seemed enormous. A heaviness that made a woman as bold and fearless as Jalaa, seem weak and pale. Sorrow over a lover she had no news of, sorrow over a nation where none of us knew the direction it was headed.

When I made my way towards the gate, I was surprised to see Ismail sitting in the courtyard. While plucking a guava from one of the branches, he cuttingly asked, 'How did you know an attack was going to happen, eh? Marco told us your message, "Be careful", before we even heard a single gunshot.'

I responded to his question with my eyes flashing a warning. 'Mind your own business, Ismail.'

But his question simply stirred the hornet's nest already within me.

Hassan Abbas was a nice young man, ambitious, sharp, with original ideas. I hoped with my entire being that he was safe. Jalaa didn't deserve to lose someone like him, and neither did I, even though I was just a new friend, nor did the adolescents who depended on him to make a difference in their lives. Luckily I had managed to slip my phone number into his pocket when the train was leaving for the western part of the country, where he would begin his project to eradicate illiteracy. *I truly hope he hadn't secretly come back here during those bloody days to surprise Jalaa. I should really pray that he'll turn up unharmed.*

I'll make sure that everyone keeps an ear out for the phone ringing; he could call at any moment. Oh God, don't take him from us. My alarm soared to new heights — how many innocent people had we lost during our stumbling in and out of neighbourhoods? Ultimately our operation was successful, but we didn't have enough time to verify identities before we attacked. We just shot on sight.

Headlines were dominated by tragic news items: the failed grisly coup attempts, the number of martyrs who were soldiers, officers and citizens; eighty martyred. It seemed like a pretty modest estimate when I saw the Majrus trucks piled high with corpses. They were the enemy, the number of their dead didn't really concern us, they were simply martyrs to the other side. They were nothing more than traitors, rogues, agents; this lessened the feelings of guilt that occur when you kill a person, even if they are the enemy.

But the news of the murder of the crooner and well-known basketball player — William Andre — by a hail of bullets, was a shock to everyone. The streets were bubbling with anger, and questions buzzing around the nature of the inspections and clean-up campaigns, during which so many citizens had been humiliated and even killed in some cases. The heartbreak over the loss of the Brown Gazelle was palpable. He radiated in everyone's memory for leading Sudan to first place in the Arab Basketball Championship just a few months before, boosting the nation's morale and spreading joy. How could a country's hero die such a gruesome death?

I shouldn't get bogged down with all of this. Just like any good soldier or officer, I need to celebrate the defeat of the other side; it's a war, and there's bound to be collateral damage.

During those days defending our country, life had stopped still, the nights growing darker and bleaker. People would quickly return from work before sunset because of the curfew. Any kind of cheer had melted, musical notes stripped away, replaced by caves of silence. Any kind of light or the slightest movement on the road was considered target practice for snipers. People existed in darkness and silence. Rumours hovered in the air like the smell of decaying bodies; rumours that were readily believed. Citizens went into hiding — would they be accused next? Shot down by a stray bullet? It was hard not to think about the fate of their missing loved ones, hoping for the best, but knowing they had probably been abducted for interrogation or worse.

From the way they welcomed me, it was as if I had been

released from the jaws of death. The children clung to my legs; Marco embraced me, his eyes red; Lucy started to spin in the hosh, her hands raised to the sky thanking God in her language. Theresa couldn't even get up from where she was, completely sapped after not sleeping for three straight days, hoping for the phone to ring, or for a knock at the door. How I pitied her. It's difficult to yoke yourself to someone who could be killed at any moment, but it seems overall the household dealt with my absence with patience and the wisdom of elders.

Harrowing days to say the least, in which we could only get around by crawling. Food was hurriedly thrown together. Lucy collapsed several times because she was afraid for her children; she couldn't run away with them anywhere. She wished she could swallow them whole and keep them safe in her womb once more. What made things worse, as Marco shared with me in whispered tones, was that her mother's spirit had disappeared. Lucy explained to him that the spirits that had ascended in peace couldn't stay in the same place as spirits violently removed from the realm of the living. I agree that we can't all co-exist with those spirits in turmoil, hovering around us and blocking any possible pathways back to our natural selves. No one returns to the way he was before war.

Worry and the desire to shut myself away in my study returned. I read books and scribbled some words on scraps of paper. I drew up maps to ambush those attacking our nation; perhaps we would be able to gain control of them in a short period of time with the fewest possible losses. I also waited expectantly for the phone to ring with Hassan's voice at the end of the line, allowing me to give the good news to Jalaa, who was being eaten alive by anxiety.

When his absence stretched on for several months, his letters nowhere to be seen, I was worried sick. To the point where I'd evade Jalaa, who had become emaciated, her light now dimmed. Her heart held a handful of memories that she fed on. Hassan Abbas was her energy, even if from afar, and at least she had always known that he was working hard, making the woman who loved him proud. Not one day did she grumble; rather, she just sat at the threshold, waiting, hoping that he would saunter in, as he always had.

I reached out to my friends and colleagues in the west of the country, in search of him. Some of them knew him as Hassan Abbas the teacher, and promised to look for him. I was concerned because Hassan had given me the impression that he belonged to one of the opposition parties, and it had come to light that these parties were behind the failed coup attempts known as 'The Revolution of Path Correction'. Their efforts culminated in the formation of a national front to resist the corrupt, dictatorial regime and overthrow it by force.

After this became common knowledge, numerous people were arrested, tortured and put on trial. Swift executions of the coup's perpetrators were carried out. A picture came into my mind of what could have happened to Hassan Abbas. Though I sincerely hoped that he was alive, somewhere. I knew Jalaa herself had reached the same conclusion about his demise, because she was someone aware of current affairs and was close to the power centres of several political parties, but whenever we met, we'd feign ignorance, perhaps trying to push out the darkest of thoughts.

I turned over every rock, hunting for some thread, any thread, to lead us to him. I leaned on my friends in the national security service and we started surreptitiously searching all the prison cells, but it was no use. Jalaa carried herself like a widow day after day, waiting for news that would confirm what she already knew — that he was gone.

She even set her battle with Ismail to one side, despite how he was trying to sink his claws into her father's inheritance and take possession of some of the family's property using Baba's signature. Every time he brought the forged papers, she would easily expose them.

Ismail was a genuine troublemaker, and so we never expected he'd be the one to find Hassan. His work as an operative of the National Intelligence and Security Service was instrumental. I'm almost certain he knew that we were searching for him, and I would go as far as to say that he personally oversaw Hassan's torture, as a way of getting back at Jalaa.

Jalaa called me, telling me to come back to the house quickly. I was there within the hour. Ismail came in, strutting in a way I disliked. Jalaa cautioned me to restrain myself as much as possible.

Ismail sat down and crossed one leg over the other, sticking the soles of his shoes in my face. He revealed that Hassan Abbas had been arrested immediately after it all kicked off and had been transferred from prison to prison because he refused to confess.

I made to say something, but Jalaa threw me a glance, as mothers do, that made me stop short. Ismail went on, but it seemed that Hassan was either a tough nut to crack or no more than a suspect, his reticence suggesting that either he really wasn't involved or that he was covering up for his leader no matter the cost. Ismail shared that Hassan was in bad shape, his ribs had been broken, and he had suffered even more after refusing to eat or drink, dying a thousand times each day.

Jalaa wiped away thick tears that rolled slowly down her cheeks. 'Of course, I could help you get him released,' he added smugly. 'Since its plain to see that he means something to Jalaa. I can assure you all that in a few hours he'll be back here with you. His name is now on the travel ban list, but I could also get him out of the country if desired.'

Her chin trembling, Jalaa said, 'Please, Ismail. Do it.'

I resented that we needed Ismail's help, and I was also convinced that he was only telling us half the story.

That evening, a vehicle arrived with Hassan Abbas inside. He was leaning on Ismail's shoulder, his torturer, as we learnt later on. We all rushed to support Hassan, who was hanging on by a thread: spitting blood, his skin marked with burns, fingernails pulled out. Hayat ordered us to get him to the hospital. She sat up front with me, with Hassan curled up in the back, his head in Jalaa's lap. Through the mirror I watched them. He was looking up at her with eyes reflecting horror upon horror, and she never took her eyes off him, afraid he would disappear once more. She stroked the thick hair on his head, probably thinking of all the torture he had endured over the past months. Her tears started to silently flow. She grabbed his hand; his fingers were covered with sores. She kissed it gently. The idea that love is motherhood in its purest form crossed my mind. I placed my hand on my chest in gratitude. But soon enough I was grinding my teeth in anger instead. We all fell silent, each of us listening to the roar within.

Once admitted to the hospital, Hassan fell into a coma

that lasted a number of days. Hayat personally kept an eye on him and Jalaa didn't leave his bedside. Pink solutions were his food and his treatment; his body was wrapped in bandages in several places.

During this period, I joined forces with Ismail for the first time; for Hassan's sake. The issuing of new identification papers under a false name was one of the most difficult things to achieve, but it was done. When Hassan had recovered somewhat, we placed the passport in his hands. He tried to protest, saying that it had never crossed his mind to leave Sudan, but we reassured him that it was just a temporary measure until things calmed down. He reluctantly agreed and we all accompanied him to the airport, with Ismail as our escort. Ismail, who showed us that he had at least one good bone hidden in his body somewhere. Hassan travelled to the Gulf, bidding farewell to a country he loved every inch of, to his dream of change, to seeing the seed of literacy that he had planted in the minds of youth bloom. He said farewell to his nation under a different name, fearing the very country he loved would attack him further, finishing him off, as well as his dreams and ambitions.

A surge of energy returned to Jalaa. She didn't cry or show any alarm at the prospect of not seeing him again, as long as he was alive somewhere — but would he really be living? So he could be strengthened, she didn't show any weakness; so he could be encouraged, she remained calm; so he could withstand what was to come, she was steadfast. He was at the gate of the final goodbye, the gate to somewhere more welcoming of movement than the restricted prison cells of Sudan. They shook hands as comrades in battle would. 'See you soon.'

None of us knew though when this 'soon' would be, but we said goodbye sensing we'd be reunited before long.

Hassan slowly tilted his head downwards, thanking us without saying a word. Seemingly, a volcano simmered inside. His eyes were shining wet; he was fighting so that he wouldn't break down.

Once we saw the wheels swallowed up into the body of the Sudan Airways plane, we breathed a sigh of relief. Jalaa made her way to the airport exit as if there wasn't anyone else in the world to be concerned about — everyone who mattered had left in the plane that had taken off just a little while before.

Once home, we thanked Ismail, and I was on the verge of apologising to him for the way I had treated him when Mama Fawzia shared that she had beseeched him to look for Hassan because her daughter was slowly wasting away before her eyes, with nothing she did making any difference. So she had broached the subject with Ismail, ready to give him whatever he wanted, all for her daughter's life. The price ended up being a sprawling property of Abdelsalaam's overlooking the Nile, worth millions of pounds.

Jalaa and I were livid. Mama Fawzia interjected, 'What does a piece of property mean compared to the life of a young, good man such as Hassan? And I was so sure that Jalaa would die any day now. All of these properties will come back to my grandchildren anyway. Knowing that Tahiya's children will get them made the bitter pill easier to swallow.'

She was right. Out of respect for this woman that I called Mama, I lowered my gaze to the tiles. Jalaa hugged her mother so tightly, but she still couldn't hide her concern, 'What if he gets married to someone else, and has children with her?'

Mama refused to say anything, stubbornly squinting her eyes into the distance. I felt Baba Abdelsalaam's spirit cocooning Mama Fawzia, imbuing her with additional authority.

In less than a month, Jalaa's fears were confirmed. Ismail married a student plucked from secondary school; she'd laugh naively, not being able to take part in any conversations, as everything was over her head. She was a child; even her high heels swallowed up her little feet. He made her live in his new property.

This girl made Ismail neglect Tahiya and her children. Whenever he did come by, he'd be in and out. What was odd was that none of us actually seemed to mind in the least, except for Mama Fawzia. As for Tahiya, she felt a newfound freedom, coming back to life at last.

I didn't like to trust Ismail in the least, but I'd never forget how he helped us locate Hassan and fly him out of the country. Even if he did extract an arm and a leg from the family, he could have blown the whistle on us at any moment. I hate myself for needing to turn to him for help, but as it is, I'll consider it one of those opportunities you need to give certain people, to show them they can do better, that they can be good, making others around them happy with less effort than it takes to scheme.

Everything that happened worked in Tahiya's favour. Ismail felt a sense of self-worth, having done the right thing, even though it would be seen as wrong in the eyes of the government and his employer. He apologised to Tahiya for treating her so badly during their marriage, and said that he'd be a new man from then on. Tahiya was satisfied with these changes in his personality, and her own sense of self that had been buried since that dark wedding night resurfaced. She started to keep in contact with all of us and one evening even winked at me while serving us tea. My stomach fluttered and I burnt my lips on a big mouthful of piping-hot tea that snaked down my throat like molten lead. I laughed at myself afterwards for thinking it was anything more than innocent flirting.

About a year later, we received letters from Hassan sharing how much he missed the nation, but saying that he was well, working and trying to piece together a fortune, all to marry the love of his life.

I never was scared for a moment about taking part in smuggling Hassan out of the country, even though it was a crime against the state, an ultimate betrayal. I was ready though, to weather the consequences; whatever they might be.

11

I was worried that over the years I had become more and more like one of the Ghala. Those strangers who visit our village from time to time: policemen, soldiers, priests, even doctors. All dressed differently to us, in their own special way. How could I not be one of the Ghala when everyone around me was? Peter, in his fearsome uniform, the metal stars glinting in the light. Theresa, the definition of elegance, her skin as soft as a newborn's, with her ability to wrap that long piece of fabric so perfectly around the folds of her body. Something that I still can't get quite right, however I try. Once I managed to do it, the material cut my loping strides short, and the next thing I knew I was on the ground, my face caked in dust. This prompted me to wind the fabric around my palm in the shape of a bird's nest with a hole in the middle. I then placed this aagherai atop my head to protect my fuzz from the weight of the objects I carried.

It reminded me of the ones we'd make back home, from rags, sticks and soft grasses, which we then used when transporting items such as jugs of river water, freshly chopped firewood, crops plucked from the field and abandoned mangoes that had fallen when a storm blew through the village. Even here in the city, I still carried goods bought from the souk in the same way: vegetables, flour, dishes. Theresa would always laugh at me all the way home.

I tried so hard to develop the knack for wrapping a long piece of fabric around my body and for it to end casually thrown over my shoulder, as Theresa and her neighbours did so expertly, but soon enough it would slip off and end up in a heap on the floor. So instead, I started to tie it in the Kurbaba or Lawo style, the way my grandmothers did back in the village — I'd cover my left side completely, then pass the fabric under my armpit, and end with a tight knot on my right shoulder, in the shape of a flower. Pleats from the knotted flower fell across my body, and my right arm would be out in the fresh air.

Marco, too, had become a Ghala in all senses of the word. For as long as I can remember, whenever he'd come back from boarding school during his short holidays in the village, dressed up in a fitted, short-sleeved white shirt, all the schoolgirls would crowd around, trying to edge their bodies as close to his as they could. Now, he's become some big-shot employee in that hotel, and I can barely recognise him when he's all dressed up. During the day, he's a stranger to me. It's only at night, in bed, when he wraps his arms around me, that he's back to the Marco that I know and love.

My children, now they're a different story altogether. They were brought into this world by the Ghala and started to talk like them, using their odd gestures. When I speak to them in my language, they respond in Arabic, even enjoying the food of the Ghala. When I feed them asida or other foods I make without any spices, they try to swallow it quickly as if I'm feeding them stones. Some of them even spit it out once they're out of sight and toss it under their beds, only for a swarm of busy ants to guide me to it the following day. Or they pretend that they're full. I go on and on about how delicious asida is, how it will fatten their necks, make their arms strong, and their legs as solid as a wrestler's, but no one seems interested in thick necks or wrestling. What a bunch of softies they are; their bottoms are sure to get a beating when they go back to the village.

My clothes, my jewellery, my language and Marco's arms in the dark are what make me feel safe. Some people look at me suspiciously; maybe they consider someone like me from the South as Ghala, the scary kind. Who cares? I'd always been afraid of them until I realised there was nothing to be scared of — they're people just like me. The colour of their delicate skin and how their hair flows down to their shoulders — this doesn't make them ghouls, which is how I used to see them. Now it's their turn to be uneasy, until they finally realise I'm not here to gobble up their young.

I've been able to get a loose grip on their language, snatches of it really. A language that still manages to knock me off balance, making me fall silent in certain situations, while my insides are boiling with words. I say some of these words with difficulty and even so, in those moments, my efforts end in silence. But at least I've started to understand everyone, and most of the time I can say what I want without being forced into wordlessness, or to finish what I wanted to say in my own language, or using my hands. All thanks to those girls with whom I used to play clay dolls under the tree. I have been speaking my own language with Marco and my children.

When it comes to their way of cooking, I've become quite good at all kinds of dishes that Theresa has taught me, which use onions, oil and other spices, but I still feel a neverending hunger burning in my stomach. Vegetables boiled in water with just a touch of salt is what I crave. I gulp it all down while the leaves are still alive. Only after scooping serving after serving of the firm, steaming hot asida on a plate, and chewing large mouthfuls of it till I start to sweat, do I actually feel full.

The hunger in my stomach wasn't the only hunger that I complained of — my eyes were hungry to see the village, with its forests and heads of grain. My ears hungry to hear cows mooing and goats bleating in the grasslands, leaves rustling in the trees, drums beating, thunder rolling, and neighbours calling out through reed fences. My heart hungry for my family; my soul hungry to touch the grave of my mother and those of my siblings; my back hungry to carry newborns and rock them; my hands hungry to harvest fruit and plough the soil; my feet hungry to cross the distance from the village to the river; the fuzz on my head hungry to carry water and firewood; I have been hungry since the moment I set foot in this country.

Having to flee my village and leave its sun behind, which rose from the same place every day and retired every evening behind the mountains and the forest, was the worst thing that ever happened to me. I left behind a destiny of blessings: rain, food, farm animals, a home and my family. That was the worst thing that ever happened to me until, of course, the war came.

Going back to the village was always on my mind, and the sooner the better. Whenever I fought with Theresa, even though it was for silly reasons most of the time, I saw it as a chance to leave this place behind. To go back South aboard that old boat on the Nile. For two, no three years, I never once opened my steel trunk, in the hope I'd be returning soon enough anyway. It would be too painful to look inside. Only after I fully understood that I wouldn't be going back did I hit rock bottom, and allow myself to swim in despair. I started to use some of what was inside my steel trunk, including some sheets embroidered with colourful threads. I gave some bedspreads I had woven with my own two hands to Theresa. As for my jewellery, some beaded and others made of animal teeth and hooves, they sat at the bottom of my trunk, untouched.

After having children, I snapped the strings of some of the necklaces and bracelets, and reused the beads to make smaller necklaces and bracelets that I would tie around the waists and wrists of the little ones. As they grew older, the tighter the string of suksuk, the healthier they were; the looser it became, the more panicked I grew. Beautiful ornaments, but also a tried and true method from my home to keep track of their health.

What remained locked up in the trunk was the jewellery used for dancing during different seasons, left lying flat like the tanned hide we wore during the days of ceremonial mourning when someone died. The hide languished away, waiting for a funeral that never came. This city was strange, no death nor graves at home. They preferred to keep death far away; maybe they tossed their dead out in the wilderness for buzzards and hyenas to tear apart the flesh. How heartless!

It's been ten years I have been away from my village, the same age as my daughter Maria, whom we like to call Edo, named after her grandmother, who hovers around me like a thick, transparent cloud of air. I could only *feel* her presence, whereas I think my babies could *see* her more clearly. She'd play with them while I was busy with something else, like washing their tiny clothes covered in dust and poop. They'd be beating the air with their hands and small legs, babbling and smiling, their wide black eyes following silhouettes floating in the air. I got the sense this was more than a child entertaining themselves with angels, as people say — the bond with this other being felt too strong. Maria-Edo was there, the children's grandmother, sitting on the edge of the bed, stopping my children — or what she probably saw as her own children reincarnated — from rolling off and hitting the floor. And it was more than that — she'd keep them from getting seriously hurt, protecting them from a sharp piece of glass or changing their direction if they came too close to a pot bubbling on the stove.

How can I put into words what Theresa means to me? My sister, my teacher, sometimes another mother, a mother to me and my children, who grew to be Ghala. She was more in tune with them once they had grown up a little, and spoke in a different language to me, with different gestures, especially once they started going to school. Theresa would absorb my explosive temper and console me through the troubles I'd experience with each season. In the autumn, I'd be physically overcome by a need to go back to the village; in winter, this need would seep into my bones and I'd sink, anxiety-ridden, as if waiting for a calamity to strike. We cried, laughed and raised our children together. We still divided our chores, and there was more to be done at home once the children had grown older, as they then required different care and attention. I'd lean towards rapping them on the head with my fingers curled like a leper's hand, my fist as hard as firewood. Or I'd pinch the flesh on their tummies and spank their behinds — that was the only way I knew to discipline them, but Theresa would rebuke me and stop me from doing so. She reasoned that they'd be more likely to beat others in future, and all that knocking of their heads would inevitably affect their reasoning skills. Something else that prevented me from beating my now older children was my mother's ghost, which would run wild in our home, torturing me and taking revenge on me for her grandchildren in countless ways, all of them painful. She was the cause of many small accidents for me: burning my fingers when removing a pot from the stove, stubbing my toes on a door, things sliding out of my hands multiple times a day or stepping barefoot on a hot ember that would suddenly appear out of nowhere.

I stopped beating my children in one fell swoop and instead would give them a hard stare, like a bull ready to butt heads — just like Theresa would do — leaving our children trembling and aware they had done something wrong.

My children were now eight in all: three boys and five girls. The last two years have been a drought, though. I've not brought any children into the world. I'd cry in Marco's lap saying, 'Someone has bewitched us!' He'd laugh quietly till tears would run out of his eyes, and in those moments I'd feel that he too must be upset, and laughing was just his way of dealing with it.

I know why I was struck with infertility — it was a time where we would hear gunfire everywhere, and see bullets whizzing back and forth like shooting stars. I say this as dread settles over me; I remember when the war started in my village and women's wombs closed up, how for several seasons not a single cry of a newborn could be heard. Mama Ilaygha would say that the war petrified the babies into hiding right in the depths of their mothers, their ears listening attentively for when the conflict would end. And I believe her.

The fear that held me hostage that day wasn't for myself, but rather for my loved ones, that they might be hurt. If I were alone, I could await my fate with the courage of a she-goat who finds herself in the jaws of a crocodile. She who faces death with dignity, not making herself some kind of easily chewed prey. But it occurred to me that things could get worse, and that we'd be forced to flee this city — what would we do? I have so many children, at least three who need someone to carry them, while the others need someone to lead them by the hand — it would be an extremely difficult situation. Which is exactly why so many women in my village refused to flee, afraid their children would die or get lost along the way. Their little yet piercing screams would alert the enemy to our hiding places. Those on the run never want women who have newborns on their backs, so a woman is forced to run away on her own, or be far away enough that people can't tell her children off.

The fear I feel takes me back to that forest, to the moment that mother was killed with her baby still in her arms, him crying alone in the darkness. The enormous trees had leaned over him like beasts, their leaves peering at him, until I went to him almost hypnotised. His mother had taken him with her in the hope of crossing into drier expanses of land, only dotted with a few trees, in the North of the country.

I faint every time the sound of gunfire increases, every time my ears pick up on those being hunted in the alleys next to Theresa and Peter's house. When the soldiers started to storm houses and raid them, their rifles waving, I'd tremble so hard that my teeth would chatter, and I'd go limp. What if they decided to kill us? Marco warned me that my behaviour made others suspect we were hiding someone. The soldiers would step it up once inside the house, turning more and more things over until Theresa addressed them and informed them that this was the home of their fellow soldier, Peter Solomon. They would then apologise, kindly, their steps retreating to where they came from.

It was difficult for me to get a handle on my panic attacks. My fear stemmed from the thought that I would lose one of them, and also for another reason, which I would whisper knelt on the confessional pew to the father in church.

I told him, my voice choked with emotion, tears streaming down my face, 'One day, at dawn, I covered for a soldier who attacked the city. I found him hiding in the branches of our thick tree, but I didn't scream or tell anyone where he was hiding. Yes, father, I know I have sinned, I have made a mistake, but I also feel relieved about it at the same time because how can I, father, be the cause of someone's death, even if they are our enemy?' In that moment, that soldier wasn't an enemy, he was just an injured, scared man.

'I feel that I have sinned but I feel at the same time that I made the right kind of mistake, as long as nobody was killed.'

The father made the sign of the cross in the air and said that

God had forgiven me. I thanked the father, my face beaming.

On that night I'll never forget, when the sounds of gunshots filled the air and the city was thrust into darkness, when we had to crawl to relieve our bowels so that no bullet would pierce us between the eyes, my stomach felt extremely unsettled. Whenever there was a shootout, my stomach would tighten and I'd soon feel the undeniable need to push out whatever was in there. Our open-air latrine was in the hosh, in one of the corners of the compound, right next to the street outside, shielded by the branches of the tree overhead.

I crawled that night towards it, the shadow of the tree somehow longer in the darkness. When I got close to the toilet, I slowly stood upright after ensuring I was safe for the time being from any stray bullets. I thought I heard someone breathing hard, trying to stifle a cry of pain, and before I could confirm where the sound was coming from, a sticky and warm lump fell right on the crown of my head, like the blessed saliva of my grandmothers, thickened with their tobacco.

I stared into the darkness, my eyes wandering slowly from branch to branch. I was finding it hard to breathe, my throat dry as if I had swallowed a handful of flour. There was a body stretched out along the branch, a black mass without any features, just the eyes, open eerily wide, begging me. My heart was a beating drum, only to then feel like it was being pulled apart by flames of fire. Our eyes locked in the darkness, fear meeting fear, despair greeting despair, last hopes upon last hopes. We spoke without opening our mouths. I broke the silence, 'Don't kill me, I've got children and I want more.'

And I think he said, 'Don't scream and I won't have to.'

I walked with my back as straight as possible, trying to

keep my balance, so that I wouldn't spill his clot of blood on the ground. I straightened my neck as well. Might as well be balancing a pitcher of water from the river.

I entered the toilet and emptied my stomach of its sloppy insides like a sick cow — when did I eat all this? I washed my head in the dark to get the sticky mass of blood out, some of which dripped down my face with the water into my mouth; it was salty, like tears. My stomach rebelled again and I squatted once more, emptying my bowels. It came to me that we were breathing together like one being, he up there in the branches, fearful I'd give his hiding spot away, and me down below squatting on my haunches, shaking, afraid of him making any sudden movements. Our lungs became one, inhaling and exhaling together, breathing filled with the false hope that one of us wouldn't betray the other. My armpits grew damp with sweat. I thought of how he must be in pain and bleeding. A bullet, or perhaps multiple bullets, had torn through him — what if he shot me here on the toilet? I started to pray; I never had prayed very much, but if there ever was a time to do it, it was then. God simply had to intervene and get me out of this mess. As if it were a cold Christmas Eve, through my chattering teeth I prayed, heart pounding, while dropping some explosions of my own into the soil. I poured out all my pleas to God, and my intestines, for what I hoped would be the last time. I stood up with difficulty, teetering like an old man. I took two steps and felt the earth sloping downwards and full of holes, even though it had been level just before. Making any progress in one direction was a difficult task. How I wished this was all just a nightmare.

I took heart and didn't look at him again. We had made

our promise, and that was enough. Neither of us should hurt the other, one more look could cause the other to lose resolve. If he really was a man, and I believed him to be so — he was fighting in the war, after all — he wouldn't shoot me with my back turned. A shiver ran down my spine. I, Lucy, was going to stand by my word, the mother and real woman that I am. It's more than enough that I hadn't screamed yet, my courage was something not any ordinary woman could match. I slipped past his silhouette, trying to dodge any more blood. I forgot to crawl. Stray bullets weren't a concern anymore, now that there was a gun aimed at my back. Trembling, I entered our room, my breathing short, my mouth dry and gummy. I didn't say a word to anyone and almost passed out. What if he came after me and my children? What would I tell Marco? That I had made a deal with a soldier in our tree?

For several days, I avoided looking up into the branches of the tree. I was just waiting for someone to discover him up there. My teeth chattered with every raid, and when the soldiers came sniffing, I kept my eyes on the ground. Luckily, no one found anyone up in the tree. Was he dead? Then his rotting body would give him away. I did not need to get more involved with this than I already was. Let nature run its course. Rot doesn't know how to hide, and nothing smells worse than a rotting human body, the stench drilling into your nostrils like an awl.

And for several more days, there was no heaviness in the air and not a single drop of blood fell to the ground. When I finally dared to take a peek up at what was in the branches, there wasn't anyone there. He had disappeared, leaving behind a broken branch, whose leaves were starting to brown and dry up, little by little.

Reaching up, I pulled off the loose part of the branch and threw it into the fire with the rest of the dry leaves to burn alongside the rubbish; getting rid of the evidence was key. I felt a strange sense of gratitude to the runaway man who left us in peace without making me taste the pain of burying my children. I was on a mission to restore motherhood to my own mother, who lost so many of hers, to replace those she buried, until her soul could rest in peace. None of my children were just any child; they were each one of my mother's children brought back to life. Every new birth meant that I had dug up their graves, one after the other, bringing out a child, crawling and gurgling. My mission was to cut open each of these small graves that my mother dug, which filled her grass and weed-covered yard, and make the child breathe again. Motherhood was my mission and having children was God-ordained once my mother settled her matter with Him up above. I think she was still here to make sure God made good on what He had told her; she never trusted anyone a day in her life. She was also probably here to take care of the children and satisfy her hunger for motherhood.

Some people see me as obsessed with being pregnant, while others grumble that Marco is forcing me to keep having children because he's an only child, but they don't understand or even know about the mission my mother has entrusted to me. Even now, I can feel her nails digging into the flesh of my belly button, making sure I do as she says. Right before she died, she said, 'May you bring forth enough children to fill the entire Earth. Let there be so many you'll be shooing them away like flies. May you live to be a mother and that alone, and die from the ruckus they'll raise.'

She now roams among us to supervise us personally. Marco also needed to start a large family after his family home was nearly blocked off with a thorny branch — an indisputable sign of the end of a family line. Come to think of it, he also had a mission, as both of us are only children and the last surviving members of our families. Some might see us as strange. But as a survivor of multiple potentially deadly incidents, it's a different matter for me — I hold sacred the continuation of life despite its calamities. To me, life itself is the God that we imagine sitting on a throne in the sky, while He lives in each of us, tying us together with hidden threads. Each of us could be the reason for someone else's life or death, like my story with that man in the tree. Or my story with the tree that now covers the entire courtyard with its shade, and a good part of the street, too. Its branches extend all the way to kiss the roof itself whenever the breeze blows.

Whoever thought that such a tree just needed love, some milk and a name, just like any child? The more I sought shade under Anim, the more I felt it was about to call me 'Mama'. It also endured discipline at the end of my broomstick, when it shed its dry yellowed leaves, scattering them all over the courtyard that I cleaned early every morning. I would sweep the space at night as well, but Anim wasn't put off.

We dug a large circular trench around his fat trunk. The children threw his dried leaves in there and sprayed the trunk with some water, leaving the leaves to moisten and rot, for the tree to absorb them once more. They were greatly entertained by this task; 'Anim eats his poo!' they called it.

Theresa was a skilled woman: she seemed to know

everything, like our village's soothsayer. I told her I didn't realise that getting an education was similar to the soothsayer's pumpkin full of clean water, a pumpkin studied thoroughly to anticipate future weather conditions, calamities, people's health, or if a stray cow would come back to its owner.

She had laughed. 'The soothsayer knows things in her spirit, Lucy, whereas I know things in my mind.' She went on to tell of how we each have a pumpkin inside of ourselves, through which we can anticipate things. We just have to fill it with water. I didn't get much of what she was saying, just like with the soothsayer back home, or like when my mother would share one of her slippery pieces of wisdom.

Theresa told me she had been educated at one of the schools our children attend, and did a lot of travelling with her husband around the country because of his position. She mixed with different people, making her experience of life wide and deep, and that was the foundation of everything for her.

Yes, she had travelled a lot, making her into a Ghala quicker. When you mix with all kinds of people, they each leave an imprint on you, and that is exactly what has happened to me. I'm not the same Lucy as I was when I fled the village. I've become Lucy the mother, Lucy who behaves like Theresa, Lucy who speaks like the neighbours, Lucy who wears clothes like Jalaa. I no longer insist on doing things the way my mothers did in the village. My fear is gone. I learnt to do things differently and it was still correct, still worked. Even so, a dark cloud was always with me: I kept thinking that the curse of death my mother's children fell to would hunt me and my children down. But in Theresa's opinion, 'Some curses never leave where they started, like fish in the sea — in a different environment, they lose their power.' She smiled and only then did I realise she was poking fun at me, and so I find myself rocking anxiously in my seat ever since.

The older my children grew and the more numerous they became, the greater my fears of losing them grew. Shaking my head, I tried to chase away those shadows. Whenever I stopped to take in their beauty and their liveliness, and just how clever they were, I couldn't shake the thought of losing them. Then I had the idea that we should go back to the village during the school holidays, so they could receive the blessings of their grandmothers and we could finally break this curse. I suggested to Marco that we should go, that the children had to visit their grandmother's grave, those of their uncles and aunts, and restore harmony with their hometown. At first, Marco refused, but when he realised my opinion wasn't changing, he finally gave in. It was only a couple of months, after all. We bought gift after gift at the souk and travelled South once more. Though this time it was in a plane. While between earth and sky, I threw up, my stomach somersaulting until the plane landed safely.

It was a tremendous welcome, which was to be expected as we hadn't only returned from the North, but from the edge of existence, as everyone thought we had been killed along with the other truck passengers attacked in the forest.

Livestock was slaughtered, and their intestines were then wrapped round their dead bodies. These bodies were then thrown outside to protect the children from evil spirits. Maria-Edo's grave was partly dug up and a handful of dirt was scooped out from near her head and mixed with water, then sprinkled on the heads of her grandchildren, as if Maria-

Edo their grandmother was spitting her blessed saliva on their heads. The kujur of the village was brought to protect the young ones from snakes and vermin. A black goat was slaughtered, its stomach slit open next to the river so that none of the children would be abducted by the water-dwellers.

I removed the thorny branches from my mother's door and gave it new life by coating it with clay from the river and decorating it with red and grey bricks. Quickly, my children melted into the village as if they had always been there, and in the couple of months we were there, they started to speak the language of my home with ease. Finally at rest, I felt reassured that a person never can lose who they truly are.

The village had changed — it felt more chaotic. The streets were tiny and winding, and the front yards had shrunk; even my mother's grave, which had been in the shape of a massive cross, appeared small to me now. But it was still strong and smooth. The women were embarrassed, and they no longer used her grave to spread out sprouting maize intended for brewing beer, or to dry vegetables. Lovers and young ones contented themselves with sitting on top of it at night and talking away under the moonlight.

My mothers and fathers had grown old, their heads full of grey hair. The children were now young adults. Everything seemed to have changed somewhat. People had let go of their distant farms; the fear of the war was still very much present. Rumours were flying that the war was coming once more. How had the war lived on here while peace breathed freely in other places in Sudan? I felt heat flushing through my body. My dear village. My people. It was nearly ten years ago that we fled the outbreak of war; mistrust and misgivings steamed the air.

Now, it feels like we are right back where we started — why?

Marco confirmed from the news that a southern officer had rebelled against the central government, calling for a single homeland in which the opportunity for growth among the city dwellers and those in the countryside would be equal. My thoughts ran wild, but I still couldn't picture my village becoming like Khartoum. He said it was different to the previous rebellions in which the independence of southern Sudan had been the aim. The officer claimed that this time would be different, that his vision was inclusive, stressing justice, equality and participation by all Sudanese in all parts of government. I don't know why I felt this officer, who was trying to save others, was actually Peter. We quickly returned to Khartoum, as we were afraid for our children. We returned, and I was no longer homesick.

I felt a child moving in my depths. What joy! The trip to my mother's grave had been rewarded. During the time my womb had been shut my mother disappeared, but she reappeared when I gave birth eventually to this child; she played with it, and protected it from falling down.

Motherhood came rushing back to me. Like cats do, I would lick my children's eyes to get them to open after a long sleep; I'd suck their little noses when their airways were too blocked up by a build-up of mucus. I'd dunk my children in warm water to strengthen their bones and then massage them with sesame oil. My milk began to flow again, too much for the baby, but Anim was still there with his thick roots to suck it all up.

As for Marco, he became completely absorbed with his job once his responsibilities at home, our expenses, and the number of our school-going children increased. What made things worse was the high prices and lack of goods in the market. Even hotel customers, the English, Armenians, Cypriots, didn't stay so long anymore. Marco said it was all because of the president, who had started to attack the citizens with laws that made the country unbearable: flogging drunkards, cutting off the hands of thieves, stoning adulterers. Bars were shut along with brothels and nightclubs. I heard him telling Peter once, when they were chatting into the night, drinking imported wine he had bought from a police officer, that since the president had poured all the wine into the Nile, the country had started to teeter back and forth, and that it was only a matter of time before it tripped over itself.

As usual, Peter didn't laugh when Marco cracked such jokes — instead, he was lost in thought.

A few days later, his sister Jalaa burst into the house, and the three of them moved swiftly to the Control Room. Jalaa, Peter, and Marco. Shortly after they came out, their steps hurried. Peter and Jalaa got into a taxi, and it was only much, much later that we saw Jalaa again. Afterwards, Marco explained to me that he had joined the new revolutionary movement. One day, some plain-clothes officers came carrying revolvers. They stormed into the house and kicked down any locked doors. They ransacked the Control Room, tearing apart books, destroying the pictures, and scattering everything everywhere. They took with them any piece of paper or book that they found, the walkie-talkie, the phone, and the small radio with the antennae pointing up towards the ceiling. They took Marco with them, beating him as they went. They dragged him by the collar and threw him into their car. I screamed, yelling after them, shaking the cane that I had hit that dog over the head with. Theresa tried to let them know that Marco was a guest of theirs, but it was no use. Marco scolded me in our own language: that we should be calm and not interfere.

He reappeared a few days later, his nails pulled out, his eye black, bruises all over his body. They had tortured him to get Peter's location, but for the first time, he didn't know where his dear friend was, or so we thought.

The next time this happened, we weren't the same. When they came, Theresa stood with her arms crossed, her eyes throwing spears. Meanwhile, I cursed their mother's arses in my own language, praying that lightning would strike them and burn them to the ground. How they'd made our own hearts burn by taking away the head of our home. I gathered the children around me, and for the first time, I wasn't scared and didn't tremble. I looked directly at the soldiers and tore them apart with a fiery glare, sparks of anger flying.

We were riled up and ready to confront them, but Marco shot us a sharp look to stand down. Theresa's sorrow over Peter's absence — he could have been dead for all we knew — and how she curled up inside herself was just about more than I could bear.

I comforted her, but soon enough I ended up joining her in crying and cursing. Peter wasn't only my husband's friend, he was a father to us all. I was only in direct contact with him on a few occasions, and still couldn't look him straight in the eye; even the sun couldn't look at Peter directly. And yet, he showered us all with a fatherly tenderness that he poured out openly. He'd never sleep when one of us was in pain, and if one of the children was sick, he'd pace up and down the hospital corridors, and supervise their treatment himself. At home, he always kept his distance, not touching anything, but still near as ever, stuck to our skin like a warm ointment. When Theresa and I went into labour, he'd sweat profusely as if he was having cramps too, and would continue in that manner until he heard the cries of the newborn. He would then fall asleep on his chair like a worn-out child.

I can't forget the surprises he'd bring: small trinkets or tasty fish for dinner. I can't forget how welcoming he was of us in his home. Every day I pray to God that he's safe wherever he is, that He will ease Theresa's pain and our worry until we meet again. Deep down I believe he's okay, but that doesn't stop us from our daily dose of crying.

Marco changed a lot. Had he had a heart transplant? He no longer laughed or joked around with us; he'd gently push away the children when they tried to drag him out to play. The wall of sorrow he'd built was harsh and cold.

He preferred silence, and to not get into the details of what had happened, just repeating 'I don't know.' This went on for some years, and during that time the house was under surveillance, and they didn't hesitate to storm in, but for what? They would just rush into the Control Room and tear it apart all over again. Theresa would spend days tidying up everything, putting it back to where it had been — Peter had valued organisation and discipline — what if he had showed up?

One day, I went with her into the room. I felt like dropping to my knees and drawing the sign of the cross as I would at the threshold of a church. The room oozed authority and secrets. It was faintly lit, with many things piled up on top of each other: pictures, papers, books and other things I didn't know the names of.

Theresa picked up a picture of Peter in a gilded frame. It was a portrait of him in his imposing uniform and military hat with the visor sticking out, on his face a look that pierces walls. She started to talk to the picture, 'Where are you? What am I supposed to do without you? Why didn't you prepare me for your disappearing from my life like this? Please, say something. Your children need you. I'm fed up with the lies. When are you coming back from this "long journey?" Please talk to me, Peter.' She broke down sobbing. I squatted down by her feet and wept silently alongside her. When Marco saw how desperate Theresa was to know any sort of information about her husband, the dam finally broke. But he warned us not to tell anyone anything. He spoke to us in our language and preferred to share the details in the kitchen. Though our language wasn't the same as Theresa's, she had lived with Peter long enough to understand what Marco was saying. He was as cautious as a mouse.

'Theresa, your husband is a hero, and right now, he's safe somewhere in our forests. He didn't intend to leave the way he did, but someone informed on him. Thankfully Jalaa was one step ahead, smuggling him out. There was no other way. He either would have faced execution by firing squad because he was a "traitor", or leave everything behind. Know that he has been preparing for this eventuality for years. He had always wanted to play a part in easing the injustices weighing our people down, but wasn't sure about how to change things. Now he's doing something about it.

'We've got to be patient and persevere. The gap that

he's left behind, no one can fill. You're everyone's mother now. You've got to be strong, like a hero's wife. Look at the children, they're depending on you.'

Theresa listened, tracks of tears staining her cheeks. Marco cried too, until his body started to shake. But I could tell that, deep down, he felt relieved — the secret was finally out.

The next morning when I woke up, Theresa was dressed up more than usual. She stood in the middle of the children in their school uniform. Marco smiled for the first time since Peter's disappearance. 'Where to?'

'I've always dreamed of being a teacher, I'm going to apply. I'm going to teach.'

'Why? What are you missing here at home, Theresa?'

'It's not about the money, or maybe not just about money. I have ambitions and dreams, too, and want to do something worthwhile.'

His face relaxed. 'Okay, I can understand where this is coming from. This is the Theresa I know and love.'

Theresa quickly found a job as a teacher in our children's school, and this made them stand even taller. She underwent a dramatic transformation, starting to take an interest in the news, reading newspapers and listening closely to the radio. She started to take part in the discussions that Marco and Jalaa would have; Jalaa had come by quite often to check how her brother's family was doing. They'd talk in hushed tones about a country that was down in the gutter: inflation biting everyone; the war that had broken out once more in the South. Theresa now rarely went into Peter's Control Room.

I didn't really feel the country going to the dogs or the

rise in prices while I was at home, protected in the house and surrounded by my children. But when I heard that the war had broken out in the South again, I felt a pain in my chest. My village. I started to listen closely to their conversations, my nails digging into my palms. What about my people? I would listen while carrying out my chores, which had become a mountain for me to climb every day. I'd do all the housework alone, although Theresa would help out with some tasks now and again in the evening. I'd cook for everyone, clean the house, mind the children. Come to think of it, I wasn't really alone, as my mother was roaming around, taking an interest in my children, rocking them to sleep, fluttering above them at night.

12

The winter of '84 was bitter. Everything within me, and without, felt bleak; I'm not sure if it was just me who felt that way or everyone else did, too.

The dry winds would create dusty swirls beneath one's feet, scattering yellowing leaves, old newspapers and plastic bags. People walked with their heads bowed, inflation weighing heavily on their shoulders. Products were scarce and greedy merchants started to monopolise everything, profiteering with prices that only suited them in these seasons of want.

The year before, the president of the nation had declared sharia law and brought it down on everyone's heads like holy tablets that ought to be obeyed. The public witnessed this sudden and complete transformation of the president into a fanatical religious leader, a sheikh really, commanding what was 'right' and forbidding all kinds of 'evil'. Now, holier than holy, he was inspired to seize all imported wines from warehouses, shops and bars. Next came the smashing of these bottles on the asphalt road next to the Nile — Nile Street, as it was known.

The spray from the spirits flew in every direction, and the heady fumes escaping from the glass bottles and cans protested; anything from hissing to violent explosions could be heard. The wine streamed, red, watery and shimmering, creating small tributaries that flowed towards the Nile.

The president's military uniform grew wet. Splintered wood. Shards of glass. Fearsome is how he looked clambering up the mound of wooden crates filled with whisky and sherry bottles and empty beer cans as he cleansed the city and nation of filth and impurity. Higher-ups in the army and the police helped him carry out the act. With each crate smashed, another would appear, ushered in by a junior soldier. Everyone within a short distance appeared to be intoxicated, the air saturated with alcohol. Whispers on the grapevine, corroborated by opinion columns in newspapers, shared how junior police officers had stolen some of the surviving crates, still intact, squirrelling them away in abandoned houses, stealing sips where they could. They had then returned to the battlefield to pour out more foreign wines, chanting 'Allahu Akbar' and victorious cheers of 'Sharia! Sharia law till death!' alongside the shattered glass and wood.

This buoyed the president's spirits even further: he broke more bottles, a manic grin plastered on his face the whole time, a sense of satisfaction visibly coursing through him. God had forgiven his sins and he saw his path to the promised land of Paradise. A land that he could now enter peacefully, to be immortalised alongside the righteous and the martyrs.

This delusion of a promised heaven infected nearly everyone. It was as if the nation had entered into a new era of religiosity, one that gave their souls wings, allowing them to soar high above others, resulting in their dissociation from reality itself. Such fanatics were filled with a rare courage that allowed them to describe others as infidels, blasphemers and heretics; guilty of treachery, treason and rebellion.

Drunkenness and sex outside of marriage were met with lashes. Brothels shut, prostitutes thrown out and hands of petty thieves cut off. Prisons and detention centres overflowed with dissidents and those disloyal to the regime: tortured, abused, killed. More coup attempts were instigated by other military officers who believed they could be more merciful and wiser than the current president. They sacrificed their lives to free the people, but the ending was always the same: death by firing squad, their bodies swallowed up by unknown graves in the wilderness.

A new insurgency broke out in the South of the country, calling for the end of marginalisation and the spread of development opportunities equally throughout the nation; that the South should practice self-governance; that Sharia law should be abolished; and that the cultural and religious diversity of the country should be rightfully recognised.

The regime met all these demands with violence, and labelled these insurgents as enemies of Islam and the nation, infidels, Israeli agents.

Political and social life suffocated under the regime's heavy hand, hatred spilling into everyone's psyches. Tribal and religious affiliations were dredged up, accompanied by a public sense of injustice. The economy was in a shambles and the standard of living dropped considerably. Heavy clouds of frustration and helplessness continued to darken the nation's skies.

Nothing eased the violence that was brought on by the anger and frustrations filling the streets, the farms, the universities, the houses and even the forests. Activists mysteriously disappeared, as did labour and student union heads.

Protests became a daily feature. Whenever one subsided, another more significant one would sprout, bearing further offshoots. Whenever a strike was extinguished, more strikes that crippled the sinews of the regime would catch fire. Teachers on strike, judges, railway workers, transport vehicle drivers, students, labourers and employees. These strikes filled the prisons with more inmates than they could handle; individuals reportedly slept standing up. Citizens were abducted and imprisoned in secret locations. The anger of the people was a raging torrent; the fear of the regime ballooning day after day. Even though most of the regime's opponents were in jail — artists, poets, journalists — it resorted to more brutality to reassure itself.

In these circumstances, I received two messages. The first in an exquisite white envelope, grey soft lines intertwining with each other like air currents in the cold winter, a postal stamp on it pulsing with life: a tree surrounded by a stream flowing from the river. Then, in an elegant script that I knew all too well:

To Jalaa Abdelsalaam
May this find her well,
Khartoum, Sudan

I loosened the letter with trembling hands. A cologne wafted out that rent the fortresses of my soul. My temples were clicking as if they each had a heart of their own, beating wildly.

To the Queen of My Heart,

Missing you is too high a cost, and so I'm coming home.
The nation needs me.
We'll meet soon.

Your man,
Hassan Abbas.

Ten years of forced separation. I cried bitterly, kissing the letter until I took pity on myself.

A month-and-a-half later, I got the second message via a visitor. There was a light tapping on my office's wooden door. 'Come in,' I said, without raising my head from the papers fanned out before me. Cases that were hung in court a week after lawyers had gone on strike, protesting the government's intervention in the judiciary's decisions, and the government's attempts to manipulate some of the cases prosecuting corruption, dragging out the entire process, hoping no sentences would ever be handed down.

Before me stood a slim young man. He could have been

a Nile herder, so tall that I thought his head might be lopped off by the ceiling fan. Teeth white as milk, his skin dark. And smooth. He stretched out his hand to shake mine; even his palm was dark — like someone heavily addicted to smoking. The blue circles on his spotted shirt were filled in with white. His trousers white, of a seemingly rich material. His almost golden hair must have been dyed with the usual cow urine in the pastures of the distant South. His even lighter-coloured moustache gave his youth away. Eyes shining defiantly, like someone who had just one-upped an opponent. I thought at first he must be working for someone, an informant, but he didn't look like the other young men I regularly spotted in public.

'I'm Majak.' After a short pause, he added, 'Janabo Feter sends his greetings.' It was the first time I heard Peter's name being pronounced like that, with an F. Undoubtedly a Southerner, as I had suspected.

I cocked my head and blinked rapidly. I drew closer and hugged him as if he were Peter. He kept his arms stiffly by his sides, his bones close to the surface of his skin. My eyes grew moist and my head started to swim. 'Alhamdulillah, alhamdulillah.'

He stood rigid, a pillar in the middle of a building. Visibly taken aback by my effusiveness, he remained silent. I swiftly took two steps back and wiped my cheeks, trying to regain authority over the situation, my footing unsteady.

I readjusted the fabric draped on my head. I gestured for him to have a seat. He sat down calmly. 'I'm sorry if I…'

I swatted the air, interrupting him, 'No, no. It's all my fault. I just can't believe it, you see.'

I glanced furtively at the door and the window. 'How is he?'

'Well. He says he's well. You need to help his wife and children get out of the country. To Egypt. He'll join them there. He says that he's been missing this whole time so that no one could be accused of anything he's been involved in. You will know everything at the right time. As for now, the mission is to get them out as soon as possible.'

'Right away,' I said without considering all the risks involved, as if hypnotised. The young man made his way across my office, his body slinking like a panther, and disappeared into thin air.

The memory of that one horrible day dropped before me like a heavy curtain suddenly unfurled.

A year before, the day in question had been passing at a snail's pace — just like any other ordinary day. I was sitting at the typewriter, hammering out a statement on behalf of the Women's Union, to make the general public aware of what was happening in our country: from inflation to the shortage of fuel, medication and even bread. All this while, the regime was preoccupied with Islamising the nation, without even taking into account the existing diversity of what it means to be Sudanese. They were oblivious to how dangerous what they were doing was; it could tear apart the fabric of society and we'd have another civil war on our hands. The demands of the South were fair, and they should have every right just like any other citizen in this country. And so, we the Women's Union were adding our voice to that of every other union and party calling for the restoration of freedoms and the release of political prisoners.

It was in the regime's best interest to heed the voice of reason; it ought to leave the stage otherwise. When I reached this thought, I felt a shadow hovering behind me. I turned to find Tahiya in my room, her face swollen with bruises and her lip bleeding.

'Bastard!'

I strode out of my room and heard her collapse onto my bed, weeping. I went down the stairs, taking two at a time. I found him slipping out the back door to the garden, almost colliding with the lion fountain.

I retraced my steps and tried the number I had for Peter. I couldn't turn the telephone dial quickly enough. My fingers kept slipping.

'Yes?' a deep voice answered.

I screamed down the line, 'He's beaten her again, Peter! He really did a number on her this time!'

I heard the phone being slammed down. In less than half an hour, Peter was with us. While we seethed, lobbing out insult after insult, he stood silently, clenching and unclenching his teeth.

He waited downstairs until past midnight for Ismail to return. Tahiya's husband approached the front door, catlike, and poked his head round the door to make sure the coast was clear. But Peter caught him and tightened his grip round Ismail's neck, pinning him against the wall as one would a wooden piece of art. 'I told you once, I told you a thousand times. Keep your grubby hands to yourself. You've had enough chances, you filthy animal. Time's up.'

He then let Ismail's body drop to the ground and took out a revolver from his belt. Once he had cocked it, he pointed the barrel of the gun at Ismail's head. We all screamed and begged Peter to let him live. But he was hell-bent. Ismail pleaded with Peter and, with his eyes, appealed to us to keep screaming. But it was no use. Peter was now kicking him, the gun still pointed directly at his head. None of us were able to calm him down until my mother entered the kitchen. 'Peter, leave him be.'

Ummi's voice brought him back to his senses. He slowly lowered the gun. 'Why do you torture her, Ismail? What for? I'm going to tell you something that you should never forget. Nothing ever happened between us. Get that through your thick skull. She's my sister. Out of respect for the man who took me in and made me the man I am today, she'll always be my sister. Either you treat her with respect or divorce her. Be a man for once, Ismail. Be a man and just divorce her.' He pointed his gun at him once more. 'Do it.'

Ismail divorced Tahiya there and then. Peter then opened the front door. 'Get out!' he roared.

Ismail raced out, his trousers wet, his life flashing before his eyes.

Peter then collapsed at Ummi's feet, begging for her forgiveness. He kissed Tahiya's head because she had borne the brunt of their teenage encounter, one that painted her a fallen woman in Ismail's eyes.

After that, Peter went back home. A couple of days later a friend of mine who worked for the National Intelligence and Security Service came over to my office. He shared that Ismail had been badmouthing Peter and reported him to the authorities as having contacts with the rebels down South, giving them insider information. He claimed Peter smuggled out some dissidents with false identities, such as the likes of

Hassan Abbas. They had found Peter's phone number among the papers and pamphlets that they had confiscated from Hassan. Ismail also accused Peter of having close ties with those who carried out the failed coups; he obviously must be the mastermind behind it all, or at the very least part of it.

'I've come because I know you and your family well, Jalaa. Ismail's always been the type to get revenge, a troublemaker to say the least. You've got to warn Peter. He needs to get out of the country in the next twenty-four hours.'

I had a client waiting outside, a livestock dealer complaining about how another dealer hadn't provided the right number of cattle. His eyes widened when I came out and locked the office door. He tried to get a word in. 'Follow me,' I commanded.

I darted down the hallway, blood pumping in my ears. The flapping of his jalabiya behind me, the slapping sound, made me more on edge. I hailed a taxi and told him to tell me more about the case. He began grumbling about the other dealer. That's all I heard. I was too distracted, a drum beating inside my chest. *Peter. When will we reach his house?* An idea came to me. I told the man that I'd take his case on. He twirled his dangling moustache thoughtfully. 'How much do you charge?'

Without hesitation, I stated, 'I want you to take someone with you out of the country, tomorrow. If you go via Gallabat to the east of the country, that will be the quickest. Those are my charges. And consider your case settled, and the money that's owed to you in your pocket already.'

He stared out of the window for a moment, then turned and smiled at me, satisfied.

We reached Peter's house that afternoon. The heat was

suffocating even though the sun was well on its way to sunset. I asked the cattle dealer to stand outside.

I strode into the house, panting. Where was he? Theresa coldly pointed to the Control Room. I knocked and he let me in. I was only there a matter of minutes. He cracked open the door and called out for Marco. The next thing I knew we were leaving. Peter stood in the middle of his home, tongue-tied. He gave everyone a cursory, obscure look, but stared intently into Marco's eyes. Marco looked back at him just as intensely, without any tears or movement at all, as if to say, 'Go. They are safe with me.' And then we left.

Once seated in another taxi, we went to the livestock market. The dealer had a truck with nearly three hundred sheep crammed together, only their heads visible. He squeezed Peter among them, and he vanished into their woolly tufts. The truck's engine sputtered to life and it trundled ahead, leaving the sun behind.

When I made it back to my office a few days later, I found out that Peter's house had been raided and his family attacked. They had arrested Marco and tortured him. I have been detained and tortured a couple of times, but they never got anything out of me.

I waited an entire year for some sort of signal from Peter, even though the trader reassured me that the 'goods' had been transported afterwards in a small car towards Ethiopia.

The day to travel arrived. It was funereal in the airport. Lucy hugged Theresa's girls while Theresa wept. She entrusted her home and possessions to Lucy, and sternly reminded her not to beat her children. Marco stood with his hands inside his pockets, shoulders rounded, staring hard at the ground. It was time to get going. At the check-in counter, I was surprised to find my name on the no-fly list. I had really wanted to escort Theresa and her children safely to Peter. I pounded my fist on the counter. During my tirade, a slim young man with hair tinged like embers on the verge of catching fire showed up at the counter beside us. He presented his credentials and quickly slipped behind the barrier. Once on the other side, he winked at me. He pulled a small suitcase behind him, wearing white trousers with that same spotted shirt, as if it were a secret signal just for me. I finally surrendered and bade Theresa and her children farewell.

My heart breaking, I waved to them and flashed him a knowing look. I'd be waiting for another message from him.

Infuriated and humiliated all at once, I left the airport. I sat on the steps with my suitcase next to me, in my hand my passport that forbade me from travelling. Without even realising it, my insides poured out, and I dissolved into a weeping spell. Such moments of farewell left me fragile. I hid my face with my trembling hands.

I felt a shadow thicken the air around me. Someone sat down next to me, and put an arm around me without saying a word. His cologne crept up my nostrils. Lacoste. The same smell that had wafted up from the letter I had received from the Gulf. Its sender had told me that he was on the way. It was him. Hassan Abbas. Always keeping his promises. Forts within me came crashing down, and my spirit felt free to wander and hope in an endless love.

I leaned against the shoulder of my love, my dear friend, tears still falling. An odd mingling of sorrow and joy, between bidding farewell to loved ones and welcoming my beloved.

Between worry over him getting mixed up in confronting the bloodthirsty regime and happiness at the possibility of being together again, of walking together towards the country we always dreamed of. A sure promise of near salvation from dictatorial rule.

My weeping grew louder, as if I were blaming him for being away for so long, for being deprived of him. At the same time, I blamed him for taking the reckless step of coming back and putting himself in danger. He never let me go and still hadn't said a word. He allowed me to shed all that I had been holding inside. My weeping turned to silence, and I stretched out my arm around his lower back, clinging to him. I didn't lift my head from his shoulder, as if I were an additional limb of his. His chin remained resting on my hair, and now and again he'd rub his cheek on my head as if he were wiping away tears. He softly placed his trembling lips on my forehead, kissing me soundlessly.

We finally ventured to face each other. Grey hairs had taken over his head, but his hair was no less thick. The same black, thick-rimmed glasses. It was him, my beloved. He clasped my hand. 'Marry me?'

I hesitated. 'Do you think I'll be able to have your children?'

With his usual poetic flair, he countered, 'All the children of this soil are ours.'

I nodded in affirmation.

How I had dreamt of him, how I had yearned to feel his child kicking within me, how I had wished to take our child to my breast. How I had envied Lucy! She was a full-fledged mother while I kept my motherhood tucked away, deploying the writings of Simone De Beauvoir as a flimsy excuse. Motherhood was a call of Mother Nature's that was difficult to answer.

We returned home and informed Ummi, who ululated feebly, beaten down by illness in old age.

It was a simple wedding: a few colleagues, my sisters and their families, Marco, Lucy and their children, who filled the house with life and commotion.

As the days went by, Hassan grew absorbed by his duties to the party, coming home late from their secret meetings. He supervised the committees that edited and published flyers to increase political awareness among the public, while also overseeing the team that wrote slogans of protest on the city walls, not least the direct 'Get out on the street, we're no longer asleep.' He and his colleagues took advantage of the general mood of discontent that had spread due to rampant corruption and scarcity of goods. People wasted away in lines all day long, only to go home with ten loaves of flatbread that were noticeably smaller than usual.

I was also busy with women's organisations and attempted to unify all of our voices to support the revolution that was bubbling on the horizon. We'd be stronger against the regime as one body.

My intimate nights with Hassan were punctuated by deep talks about politics and our country's fate. To lengthen their time in power, the regime kept creating smokescreens: opening the doors for dialogue with all opposition parties, reassuring citizens that the economic situation was improving, calling rebels for peace talks. All of this worked in favour of the revolution though, as it further exacerbated the levels of public frustration; the youth-led opposition spilled out into the streets with flyers and posters in neverending protest.

Hassan also told me of how he engaged Peter after Peter had come as part of the delegation from the Sudanese People's Liberation Movement to discuss the possibility of forming a coalition or pact between all the parties to support the peaceful revolution of the youth from across the country. All had gathered in hope of supplying the leaders with a shared vision to free the nation from its cyclical wars and economic turmoil.

I listened to all he was saying, holding my breath. Hassan confessed his fears to Peter that this new movement, the SPLM, would inevitably become tribal and regional. That it would fray the fabric of society and become a way for every side to advocate for their own rights on their own terms, excluding other Sudanese. Hassan emphasised how his compatriots in the movement had to be cautious about falling into such patterns of identity and regional affiliation.

Peter responded with his usual calmness, 'This movement calls for justice for Sudanese from any walk of life. You know better than anyone, Hassan, that for me, the issue of belonging to Sudan as a whole is at the forefront of my mind. I'm not just a son of the South, I'm a son of this entire country's soil. In my eyes, the issue of identity is innately tied to one's ability to participate in the social, political and even military affairs of the nation. To have the right to protest for better rights, to have a role in the government, to further the development of society without being seen as part of some foreign conspiracy. A nation isn't just defined cartographically; rather, it's about a citizen's rights and obligations.

'We would never want our nation to make any citizen

feel like an outsider, and vitiate their self-worth every day in different ways. What we're aiming for is to expand participation so that any one of us can see ourselves reflected in the mirror of the nation. It's a nation for everyone, not just the few who monopolise everything, ignoring the groaning of others with evident arrogance. If I hadn't found my perceptions and vision reflected in this movement, I wouldn't have joined — it represents me and my different upbringing. If we don't look at our history with a critical eye, and admit the wrongdoings that have occurred, we won't budge as Sudanese from the chaotic spiral of secession, coups and armed rebellions. We don't want a repeat of the last thirty years. The central government only understands the language of force. Every individual has his demands and so the wise thing to do would be for the nation to open its heart and mind to listen to the people. The regime's stubbornness helps no one; neither does throwing accusations of the public being infidels and defectors whenever citizens speak their minds and live out their lives. Using religion to enforce the peace and as a weapon is poisonous because the protests are real, the frustrations are real, the revolution is very much real. All this distortion of people's intentions will end soon enough, and the public will discover that these accusations were simply a pack of lies.'

'What you're saying makes sense, Peter. You've put me at ease. I'm fully aligned in forcing the nation to throw off this religious smock; it's better off being naked!'

Peter had laughed loudly, and added, 'It's just like our leader says: that the nation neither goes to church nor the mosque; it's a group of institutions that should be preoccupied with people's rights and obligations in light of a national

constitution where citizenship is the foundation of belonging
— not religion or race.'

13

After Mama Theresa and her children left, the way that Mama Lucy moved and spoke was like she was at a funeral. She almost didn't make it. All of a sudden she couldn't do this, and she couldn't do that, even though she had more than enough experience running the household and taking care of us. The only thing she actually couldn't do was help us with our homework. Books for her were a place where lines of ants crowded the pages. I don't think she ever got the point that these 'ants' were a gateway to another life, another world, one full of different sounds, colours, and smells — all on those pages of paper.

She even channelled her despair into a song:

> *Theresa,*
> *You were one of my own, my sister.*
> *I told you my secrets.*

Theresa,
You were one of my own, my sister.
Let's play again.

I call out, but your voice
Shuts me out,
Far, far away,
A stray star in the night sky

You climbed atop that enormous eagle
He flew away with you
You made a home
in the heart of someone else.

Whenever she began crooning this song, we knew our entire day was going to be a gloomy one. The house was empty of her dear friend and sister, Mama Theresa, but we filled it up, making use of every space available. Five teenagers, eight pretty much grown children, one child leaning on bedposts just starting to walk, and two babies stuck to her, never leaving her breasts, always staring at the rest of the siblings with their unblinking eyes. The boy was named Peter and his twin, Theresa. Although Mama Lucy would call the girl Ghaniyo, a pet way of saying 'my sister', and she would call the boy Ongerey, meaning brave one.

We spread out throughout the house like air, a large family by anyone's standards. The sadness we felt over losing our extended family only lasted for a day, after which a feeling of celebration took over as we distributed their belongings among us. We took over their spaces in the house, getting to stretch ourselves out fully on the beds and in Mama's Lucy's heart. A fresh change from being packed on top of one another like sardines.

The only thing my mother didn't know about me was that I would also feel my grandmother's presence. She'd fill my dreams with her whispers and peer down at me through Anim's branches. One day, I dreamt of us swimming together in a pool of water clear like a mirror. Suddenly the water turned warm, sticky and red. My arms and legs grew heavy and I felt something pulling me towards the bottom, something like living grasses that had tentacles to suck me up and paralyse me. I was slowly drowning. I don't know how she managed to climb ashore. She looked at me and laughed, not concerned about getting me out of the pool of blood. Betraying me and saving herself.

I sank deeper, the blood suppressing my breathing. My voice was trapped in my throat and my chest felt as if it would burst. I woke up screaming and gasping for air. Mama Lucy was standing over me, shaking me violently, the twins clinging to her as usual. She no longer had to hold them up anymore; they'd each latch onto her so tightly that they wouldn't fall to the ground. They clawed at her breasts and clothes the way a baby monkey does the fur coat of its mother.

I felt wet. I touched my thigh and my fingers came back smeared with blood. Mama Lucy's face lit up as if hearing good news. She hugged me fiercely and then removed the bedsheets to wash them. In a voice that sailed throughout the household she said, 'Maria-Edo, my darling, you are now a woman! And soon to be a mother!'

My twin siblings looked on blankly. I caught my father's shadow slipping out of the gate. I stared at my mother, my eyes begging her to lower her voice. My eyes darted around the room. I felt my cheeks grow hot and wished the earth would open up and swallow me. 'Don't be embarrassed, dearest. It's the most natural thing. If we were in our village, I would have planted a flag on the roof of our home to announce your birth as a woman, and I would have filled up a good number of barrels with beer. We would have celebrated you in such a way that even you'd be surprised.'

At times like these, I missed Mama Theresa. She would have seen this all differently. Mama Lucy just treated me like a wild animal in heat. In Mama Lucy's eyes, I was just going to be a new version of her, obediently bowing down to the curse of motherhood spoken into being by my grandmother, stuck between earth and sky, peeping through a hole, watching the graves of her loved ones come to life once more.

DEDALUS CELEBRATING WOMEN'S LITERATURE
2018 — 2028

Dedalus began celebrating the centenary in 2018 of women getting the vote in the UK by a programme of women's fiction. In 1918, Parliament passed an act granting the vote to women over the age of thirty who were householders, the wives of householders, occupiers of property with an annual rent of £5, and graduates of British universities. About 8.4 million women gained the vote. It was a big step forward but It was not until the Equal Franchise Act of 1928 that women over twenty-one were able to vote and women finally achieved the same voting rights as men. This act increased the number of women eligible to vote to fifteen million. Dedalus' aim is to publish six titles each year, most of which will be translations from other European languages, for the next ten years as we commemorate this important milestone.

Titles published so far:

The Prepper Room by Karen Duve
Take Six: Six Portuguese Women Writers edited by Margaret Jull Costa
Slav Sisters: The Dedalus Book of Russian Women's Literature edited by Natasha Perova
Baltic Belles: The Dedalus Book of Estonian Women's Literature edited by Elle-Mari Talivee

Forthcoming titles will include:

Take Six: Six Catalan Women Writers edited by Peter Bush
Take Six: Six Latvian Women Writers edited by Jayde Will
Take Six: Six Irish Women Writers edited by Breen Ó Conchubhair
Take Six: Six Estonian Women Writers edited by Elle-Mari Talivee
The Dedalus Book of Knitting: Blue Yarn by Karin Erlandsson
The Victor by Karin Erlandsson

For more information contact Dedalus at:
info@dedalusbooks.com

Recommended Reading

If you have enjoyed Stella Gaitano's *Edo's Souls* you should enjoy the other books in the Dedalus Africa list:

The Word Tree by Teolinda Gersão
Our Musseque by José Luandino Viera
The Desert and the Drum by Mbarek Ould Beyrouk
The Madwoman of Serrano by Dina Salústio
Catalogue of a Private Life by Najwa Bin Shatwan
Co-wives, Co-widows by Adrienne Yabouza
The Ultimate Tragedy by Abdulai Silá

Forthcoming in 2024:

Tchanaze by Carlos Paradona Rufino Roque

For further information about Dedalus' titles please visit our website: www.dedalusbooks.com
or email: info@dedalusbooks.com
or write to Dedalus Limited, 24-26 St Judith's Lane, Sawtry, Cambs, PE28 5XE for a catalogue.

Co-wives, Co-widows by **Adrienne Yabouza**

'At 49, Lidou is in his prime, a prosperous builder of houses in the Central African Republic and the proud husband of two beautiful wives, Ndongo Passy and Grekpoubou. The only cloud on his horizon is the recent onset of impotence, for which he persuades a pharmacist friend to get him some pills. The day after his first dose, Lidou has a heart attack and drops dead, which gives his opportunistic cousin Zouaboua the chance to accuse the two newly-widowed women of poisoning Lidou, so that he can snatch his cousin's property out from under their noses. If they're going to keep what's rightfully theirs, Ndongo Passy and Grekpoubou must fight with all their might against a backdrop of corruption in which bribery oils the wheels of society, eroding decency and loyalty. It's a weighty topic in many ways, but Adrienne Yabouza writes so lightly and colourfully that this is a delight to read.'

Alastair Mabbott in *The Herald*

'…the arrival in English of this new voice is worth celebrating.'
Tadzio Koelb in *The Times Literary Supplement*

£8.99   ISBN   978 1 912868 77 3   128p   B. Format

The Desert and the Drum by **Mbarek Ould Beyrouk**

'*The Desert and the Drum* is a nicely turned novel of the clashes of tradition and modernity — not so much versus each other but the clashes within each. The constricted tribal ways are challenged by modernity but the faults that prove so damaging here are inherent to it: Rayhana is battered and broken by the demands of traditions, "the other world" of modernity is something of a release valve, yet also doesn't offer true escape. Beyond how it treats these themes, much of the appeal of *The Desert and the Drum* is in the presentation of local color, Beyrouk presenting contemporary Mauritania, on its smallest and most isolated scale as well as on the bustling modern-metropolitan one, very nicely through Rayhana and her experiences. So much she experiences is almost beyond words — such as the machinery the foreigners bring for their mining expedition and what they are doing to the land — but that goes just as much for her emotional experiences across her various stations, and her wide-eyed fumbling efforts to express all this that is new and unknown to her (and, often, her tribe) make for an impressive narrative.'

M.A.Orthofer in *The Complete Review*

£9.99 ISBN 978 1 910213 79 7 170p B. Format

The Madwoman of Serrano by Dina Salústio

'From the powers of the madwoman and the midwives to various events that take place in Serrano, Salústio uses magic realism wisely and sparingly. Above all, Salústio tells a wonderfully inventive story, mixing in magic realism, creative story-telling, the strange behaviour of a group of people in a remote village, family saga, city vs country, women's issue, sex and, inevitably, tragedy.' John Alvey in *The Modern Novel*

'Realism and myth crash together in a strange and jagged interaction that sees the modern, urban world of microwaves, therapy sessions and business deals grate against ancient rites, hearsay and magic. A death certificate shows that a man has been poisoned by strange thoughts; apparently infertile women go to the city for "pharmaceuticals" that turn out not to be quite what they seem; and the mysterious madwoman of the title makes predictions that play out on city streets, as well as in the rural dreamscape of the village.'
Ann Morgan *Book of the Month* in *A Year of Reading the World*

£9.99   ISBN 978 1 910213 98 8   224p   B. Format

The Word Tree by Teolinda Gersão

Margaret Jull Costa's translation was awarded The Calouste Gulbenkian Portuguese Translation Prize for 2012.

'Set in colonial Mozambique, Teolinda Gersão's bildungsroman follows Gita, a young girl forced to pit her love of country and family against her mother's bitter prejudices. Portuguese immigrant Amélia's resentments pervade the novel, providing a compelling antagonist to Gita. This personal narrative of control, and subsequent neglect, has wider significance. Mozambique is a country on the cusp of war, eager to gain independence. Home truths are told through memorable imagery, such as the quizumba, the hyena whose body splits because it wants to travel every path. Mother and daughter, black and white, old and new worlds – the narrative perspective shifts effortlessly, returning each time to a fundamental question: why should anyone think they are worth more than anyone else?'   Sarah Gilmartin in *The Irish Times*

'This is the only one of Teolinda Gersão's 12 novels available in English, and it has just been chosen as the best novel translated from Portuguese in the last three years. You can see why: it's as acute about childhood as it is about adults, and the writing is as sensuous as it is sad. Amélia has left Portugal for pre-independence Mozambique, escaping her family and a failed relationship. She answered a newspaper advert from a man who "seeks a decent young woman aged 25 max". He promised her beaches with pale sand. She got a lonely life as a dressmaker instead. The section of the novel dedicated to her is the most moving in the book, a series of pin-sharp revelations of envy and isolation. She wants to join the elite, perfume she can't afford. In the sizzling African heat, she dreams of owning fur coats to give the world she left behind a slap in the face. As a portrait of a desperate colonial it's worthy of V.S. Naipaul. But Gersão does youthful exuberance as well as she does middle-aged desolation. Amélia's daughter Gita experiences things, as children do, in a sensory cascade. "Yes, everything in the yard danced," she says, "the leaves, the earth, the spots of sunlight, the branches, the trees, the shadows." Hers is an open-hearted, child's-eye view, of the kind that sees pain as clearly as pleasure. "Go away and never come back," Gita says to her mother. Amélia's resentment is the worm in the apple. Gersão's skill is to make the apple sweet and the worm sympathetic.'

Simon Willis *in The Intelligent Life Magazine*

'Salazar's forty-year dictatorship in Portugal and that country's colonial wars in Africa cast their long shadow over Teolinda Gersão's *The Word Tree*. This is the first of Gersão's novels to be translated into English. As the Mozambican Laureano reflects, "the men crossing the sea from Lisbon didn't want that absurd war either". Laureano's wife Amelia had come to the country from Portugal in search of a better life, but mentally never leaves her homeland, whereas her daughter Gita loves the country and grows up to resent the colonial presence. There are lush descriptions of the country, while the racial order is starkly spelt out: Amelia "clings to the belief that fair-skinned people are the very top of the racial hierarchy, and that dark-skinned Portuguese people are almost at the bottom, just above the Indians and the blacks".'

Adrian Tahourdin in *The Times Literary Supplement*

£9.99 ISBN 978 1 903517 88 8 204p B. Format

Catalogue of a Private Life by **Najwa Bin Shatwan**

'*Catalogue of a Private Life* compiles eight stories that illuminate the effects of civil war on Libyan society. The stories, originally published in Arabic in 2018, often touch on the absurd while examining the brittle lines between betrayal and loyalty, cruelty and tenderness.'

The National

'Shatwan writes beautifully. Her style is pared down to bare essentials. No flowery excess. I found it fascinating that the spareness of the language actually made the stories otherworldly and captivating. The stories read like parables with extra layers of surrealist strangeness and political critique. This quality makes the stories alluring, brings a touch of magic that pulls the reader into a world where animals have a mind of their own and objects have intentions. Underneath this stylistic ingenuity is a powerful critique of how war normalizes violence and desensitizes a culture to destruction.'

Ainehi Edoro in *Brittle Papers*

'In a world that is unpredictable, Shatwan graces readers with eight ordinary stories with extraordinary insight.'

Arab News

£7.99   ISBN 978 1 912868 72 8   96p   B. Format